THE HEADS OF SERGEANT BAPTISTE: THE COMPLETE ADVENTURES OF THIBAUT CORDAY AND THE FOREIGN LEGION, VOLUME 4

The Heads of Sergeant Baptiste

The Complete Adventures of Thibaut Corday and the

Foreign Legion

Volume 4

By

Theodore Roscoe

Boston · 2012

EDITED AND DESIGNED BY

Matthew Moring

PUBLISHING HISTORY

"The Heads of Sergeant Baptiste" originally appeared in the May 28, 1938 issue of *Argosy* (Volume 282, Number 1). Copyright © 1938 by The Frank A. Munsey Company. Copyright renewed © 1965 and assigned to Argosy Communications, Inc. All Rights Reserved.

"Snake-Head" originally appeared in the January 7, 1939 issue of *Argosy* (Volume 287, Number 3). Copyright © 1939 by The Frank A. Munsey Company. Copyright renewed © 1966 and assigned to Argosy Communications, Inc. All Rights Reserved.

"The Wonderful Lamp of Thibaut Corday" originally appeared in the April 29, 1939 issue of *Argosy* (Volume 290, Number 1). Copyright © 1939 by The Frank A. Munsey Company. Copyright renewed © 1966 and assigned to Argosy Communications, Inc. All Rights Reserved.

"Corday and the Seven League Boots" originally appeared in the June 24, 1939 issue of *Argosy* (Volume 291, Number 3). Copyright © 1939 by The Frank A. Munsey Company. Copyright renewed © 1966 and assigned to Argosy Communications, Inc. All Rights Reserved.

Published by arrangement with Argosy Communications, Inc.

THANKS TO

Joel Frieman, Walker Martin, Audrey Parente, Gerd Pircher, Rick Ollerman & John Wagner

Printed in the United States of America.

TABLE OF CONTENTS

THE HEADS OF SERGEANT BAPTISTE

CORDAY PUT the cake box on the café table, and smiled at the young British consular agent, who eyed it hungrily.

We had been waiting for the old Foreign Legion veteran to come along; telling the new American Express chap about him while we waited. After what we'd been telling, I think the man from the American Express was surprised to see the old Legion veteran come into the café with a cake box.

The British consular agent chuckled. "We forgot to tell you old Thibaut Corday, here, is a cake-eater. What? Goes after French pastry like a kid goes after ice cream. Sad day when that beard of his isn't full of pastry crumbs."

The old French soldier sat down a little stiffly. He nodded at the American who was a stranger to Algiers. "I like pastries, that is the truth. My good friends, here, tease me about it. They think because I was a soldier of the Legion it is odd I should like little cakes.

"Alors"—the old Frenchman waved his hand indigantly—"did you ever see a Tommy Atkins without his tea? A Yankee Marine without his chewing gum and chocolate bar? Pastry, then, is a French institution. The art of pastry-baking a national achievement, the high accomplishment of a proud people!"

The chap from the American Express looked disappointed. Here in Algiers—the city veiled in that sense of mystery that comes with North-African dusk—the newcomer had hardly expected to hear of French pastry.

"But perhaps you are surprised a Legionnaire should be a connoisseur of such delicacies," Old Thibaut Corday suggested. "You wonder how cake could have anything to do with the Legion."

He struck a fly from the cake box at his elbow. "Then I may be able

to surprise you some more, *monsieur.* There is a story concerning the art of baking and the Legion that I have never told my Anglo-Saxon friends. A story that has to do with pastries and another kind of baking. You have heard of pastry-bakers, then, but did you ever hear of head-bakers?"

"*Head*-bakers?" The American stared.

Old Thibaut Corday picked a crumb from his beard and ate it grimly. "And I do not mean the chief cook in a bakery shop. But you recall—is it in the *Legend of Sleepy Hollow*—about the body without a head that chased a man? Then did you ever hear of the heads without a body that chased a man?"

The American Express chap didn't look disappointed now. He was staring at Old Thibaut Corday as if he thought him mad; and certainly the old soldier-of-fortune's eyes, like his words, were hardly normal.

"So you imagined no connection between witchcraft, say, and chocolate eclairs? You did not know the baking of pastry is a similar art to the baking of human heads? French pastries are sweet? But the frosting that ices a cake may also ice the human spine. And there was one time in the Legion, when the thought of baked goods turned my blood to vanilla and my cinnamon beard to frost. I will tell you about it, *monsieur,* and knowing you for a newcomer to our coterie, I have brought this box of cake for my illustration. First I will tell you the story, and then you will see the illustration."

Lady-fingers and Legionnaires! Murders and cocoanut macaroons. Buttercrust *brioche* and baked human heads! Old Thibaut Corday took a bag of *petit-fours* from his pocket, and ate them while he talked. Never had he told us such a story, and never was there such an illustration....

CHAPTER I.

IT STARTED (Old Thibaut Corday licked a finger and began) in Sidi-bel-Abbes, which is the general headquarters of the Legion in Africa, and the place where everything in the Legion always starts.

Sidi-bel-Abbes is not far from Algiers, and it is worth running over there to see. There are the barracks of *Le Premier Régiment Étrangère.* It is there the raw recruits of the Legion are whipped into the marching dummies that will be sent out to die for France in Madagascar, Mauretania, Tunis or Tonkin. Look about, and you will see the typical garrison-town. The canteens crowded with soldiers; the park benches crowded with Legionnaires and their girls—it has not changed much since I was there, except for the faces of the Legionnaires and the girls. And the little pastry shop in the Lane of the Blue-Eyed Camel. The little pastry shop in the Lane of the Blue-Eyed Camel is not there. The little pastry cook who ran it does not live there any more.

We called her Sugar—although that was not her name—and she was a nice girl. She was brown-eyed and friendly and trim with a way of wrinkling her nose when she smiled that made you want to put an arm around her. She must have been about seventeen when she came to Sidi from Marseilles with her aunt who set up shop. That forbidding aunt with her queenly bosom and black mustache—you know the type.

It was rumored that she was not Sugar's aunt at all, and perhaps her father was somewhere in the Legion. It was also rumored that there might have been a touch of molasses in Sugar somewhere a few generations back—dark eyes, golden skin perhaps a shade darker than beach-tan, a certain graceful freedom of movement—eh?—but you know the talk of officers' wives.

Brown sugar or white, that girl was the sweetest thing to look at in Sidi. If the officers' wives didn't visit her pastry shop, the men did. She was no garrison sparrow like the other girls around Sidi.

Non, her aunt saw to that. To church every Sunday she would go with her Testament and parasol, Auntie following like a guard. When that old griffon died, the girl ran the pastry shop by herself. She did not sell the shop and run up to Paris and go wild with her aunt's savings, that girl. She was brisk and capable and she went right on minding her business and running the little pastry shop in the Lane of the Blue-Eyed Camel and baking French pastry.

And what French pastry! *Ah, mon Dieu!* It is not everyone can bake French pastry, you comprehend. The art of such baking demands talent. That little girl in the Lane of the Blue-Eyed Camel had more than talent; she had genius. To this day the memory of her eclairs makes my mouth water.

That girl had a natural gift for icings and flaky crusts, but her genius did not stop with the frosting-bowl and the oven. An artist at baking, she was an artist at art, besides.

You know the wedding and birthday cakes one sees in the windows of ordinary bakers—those pagodas of goo and icing; cathedrals of frosted dough. Compared to that sort of thing, the girl's cakes should have gone on exhibition in the Louvre.

She could take two raisins for eyes and a row of mints for teeth and make a gingerbread man that looked human. She could cut little camels out of fruitcake that were wonderful pieces of carving. I recall a Bethlehem scene done with Christmas biscuits and a statue of Joan of Arc in angel food that would have won prizes in any art gallery.

With a genius like that she should have gone to Paris and opened a studio instead of staying in a North African garrison town, selling penny cakes to soldiers who did not appreciate them.

But she wanted to remain in Sidi-bel-Abbes because her aunt was buried there.

Like all great artists, that girl worked only for the joy of the achievement; she did not know her pastries were masterpieces; she had another ambition. She wanted to get married! *Oui,* she wanted to go on baking her little cakes, and she wanted a husband. Did you ever before hear of a girl around a garrison town who wanted a husband?

But did you ever hear of a Foreign Legionnaire who wanted to marry?

WELL, there was Yankee Bill the Elephant. I do not think he meant any harm. The shop made a nice place to sit with its smells of vanilla and spices and maple creams, and he would while away an evening licking the frosting spoons and spinning yarns. That big, bluff giant from Texas! It was he who gave her the nickname of Sugar. I suppose he had pinched a thousand dimpled cheeks and told their blushing owners they were the only girls in his life.

But try to domesticate a rover like that, a great untamed mastadon who has trumpeted through a thousand boudoirs and trampled over a jungle of darker littorals—a wild elephant. Marriage? In the year he went calling on Sugar it probably never occurred to him. I can imagine the panicky spread of his ears at the word, the fright in his eyes. Loved her?—*certainement!*—but how could he explain? She was a nice girl, too, do you see? He would see it, too, for all his roughness; an elephant like that appreciates that kind of girl. And an elephant like that is the type to grab his hat and flee; too dumb and worried to ever go back and tell a girl why.

There there was Christianity Jensen the Dane. Doubtless he saw she was lonely; went there only to sympathize. She was not a hard girl to sympathize with, and if she wanted a shoulder to weep on, why that little Legionnaire from Denmark was the kindest man in the world. Quiet-spoken, gentle, always playing with the Arab kids in the street—one could see how the little pastry artist might lose her heart to such a man. One could also see her face on an evening when, alarmed by some romantic hint let fall, Christianity realized things had gone too far and had to blurt the confession that he had liquidated his grandmothers with arsenic in Copenhagen.

Then there was the Englishman from London—they were talking of furniture when he suddenly remembered he already had a wife.

Kress the Hungarian, handsome, gallant, but a gambler—she was sewing her wedding dress when the bad news came, and they never caught the Arab who stabbed him during a domino game in the bazaar. Then Blücher the Prussian—he even bought a marriage license!—it was the quick-witted bureau agent who recognized him as an escaped inmate of a Berlin asylum, dangerous because he seldom appeared insane.

Why is it, *messieurs?* Why is it always some girl like that little pastry baker, attractive, capable, hungry for affection—why is it always some clean-eyed, warm-hearted girl like that who must see her dreams turn to dust and have her heart shattered one time after another?

Non, it is always some woman like that false-haired, truthless eyed dancer at the Absinthe Café—that painted Yvonne!—it is always some woman like that who can catch a husband. That Yvonne was a snake, and she had had five husbands in five years at Sidi-bel-Abbes. In five years the little pastry baker had only had scoundrels who left her waiting at the altar.

It is not my proudest memory that I was among those dogs. *Oui,* I made love to Sugar, too. *Le bon Dieu* knows I did not expect her to take me seriously and the moment I found out she was serious, I retreated. *Non,* Legionnaires are not the marrying type, unless it came to some snake like that dancer in the Absinthe Café.

It was the officers' wives who called Sugar "the sweetheart of the regiment." Perhaps that is why she kept trying. If she was disappointed by the young lieutenant from Saint Cyr, the Bavarian, who deserted and was shot, the tall Russian who turned out a drug-addict—if one after another her romances went by like the years, she did not quit hoping. But what is the advertisement about "never a bride"? Our outfit was five years in Sidi, then five in Madagascar, then back to Sidi again. Sugar was still there, waiting.

But that year of our return, she became engaged to Sergeant Baptiste.

IT must have been the desperation from ten years of disappointments. Or it may be that love is truly blind. But anyone could see this Baptiste was a scoundrel—a bigger blackguard than all the rest of us put together.

He was a Belgian from Antwerp, and he had come to the Legion to save his neck after a nasty business in the Belgian army. How the girl could have thought him handsome with that close-cropped yellow head, the eyes too near together, missing front teeth, brutish jaw and nose bent sideways toward his left ear! How she could have believed his lies about the scar some woman had carved over his right eyebrow; the tales of heroism in battle; the windbag blowings and boastings! How she could have believed his promise to marry her!

But then he did give her such a promise; he did give her a ring. What if he borrowed fifty francs from her to buy the ring—and bought it for three in the bazaar! What if he continued to borrow more francs—and spend them on wine, cards and dominoes! That he courted her for money and free meals, that was something she did not believe! We told her about it, we who liked her and were her friends. We told her that Belgian non-com was a brute and a *blagueur!* She stormed at us in his defense, that girl. She was not going to let us undermine her faith in this last chance—we who had undermined her faith in us.

Faith? That the girl could have had any left in men after ten years in a Legion town, that shows you the sort of girl she was. She had faith in love, you comprehend; and because she believed in love, she believed in that Belgian gorilla who had said he would marry her. You should have seen the way she strolled with him on the boulevard. The pride with which she sat beside him at the band concerts and garrison church. *Ma foi!* it began to look as if that Belgian brigand actually meant his pledge. One heard talk of a ceremony and a priest.

When the day was set, we Legion dogs could hardly believe our ears. For the outfit which had been in Madagascar had been ordered to Senegal, and a shift to Senegal would have proved an excellent excuse for Baptiste to escape marriage. *Alors,* the wedding was announced for the morning of our departure, and the little pastry cook was to come to Senegal with us as the non-com's bride.

There was something pathetic in the list of guests invited to the wedding feast. The wedding feast was to be held in Sugar's pastry shop the night before our company's departure. Sugar was giving the party, and she invited the guests.

Yankee Bill the Elephant. Christianity Jensen. Robbins, the Englishman. The young lieutenant from Saint Cyr. All of us were there;

all the ragtag and bobtail who had one way or another failed the girl, gathered together to wish her a matrimonial *bon voyage* at last. It was a little gesture of grace, *messieurs.*

I went, like the others. And never will I forget that wedding feast!

WE wished her luck, *messieurs.* We toasted her happiness, and we even toasted the guest of honor, not present as yet, but represented as presiding over the middle of the table. And there the girl's genius, her great artistry had reached its peak.

But I could go to a thousand art galleries and never see the equal of that bust of Sergeant Baptiste! The head and shoulders of that Legion non-com, modeled life-size in cake and painted with different flavors of icing. The raisins in the candlelight became eyes. A dab of lemon froth for close-clipped hair, visible where the cap was tilted. The bent nose, the grin, the scar—all tricks of vanilla and caramel and fondant, molded into a face with human expression. I do not know how the girl did it, but even the bulldog thrust, the confident carriage of the man's head was there.

Alors, I think I know how, after all. For all the artistry of the girl went into that cake, all her love for the baking of French pastry, all her love for that Belgian clapperclaw. And that was another thing about that piece of sculpture in cake—it was Baptiste for certain, but Baptiste as seen through the girl's eyes. Not our sergeant as we knew him, but rakish, devil-may-care, brave; the man she would domesticate by marriage; the hero-husband of her dreams.

And Sugar? At her end of the table she was radiant; radiant as only such a girl could be when, after years of disappointment, she sees her dreams about to come true. And if her eyes gave a worried glance at the empty chair at table's head—*chut!*—it was only ten o'clock.

At eleven she asked the lieutenant if it were possible Baptiste could have been delayed on duty, and the lieutenant said that was so.

Then her frown did not come even at twelve when a messenger who had been dispatched to the barracks reported Baptiste nowhere on duty—but of course some important business must have held him elsewhere.

Only at one o'clock did she grow a little pale, *messieurs.* A little too cheerful in her talk. Laughing a little too loudly.

The rest of us pretended not to notice, but we could not help noticing. A contagion of fidgets went around the dinner table.

Secretly we began to curse Baptiste. The *commandant* had given us all-night leave, but tomorrow would be a hard day, and we needed some sleep. But no man would have thought of leaving Sugar's wedding feast.

Would Baptiste never come? *Sacré Dieu!* it was half past one.

It was Robbins, the Englishman, who started telling about Senegal. In some respectable past the Englishman had traveled, and he described the West African coast, the jungle to which we were going, the natives.

Had Sugar ever heard about the Senegalese trick of curing human heads? A craft practiced by the witch doctors. They would cut off a white man's head and shrink it to the size of a fist, well preserved. It was wonderful how they did it. The skull bones were removed, and the head shrunk by some secret process of baking. The head did not lose its shape, either. When shrunk to fist-size, it was hung up over the witch doctor's door as a decoration. Very taboo. Robbins had seen such heads no bigger than oranges—one was a woman's with red hair.

Ah, oui, alors, all very interesting, and meantime where was Sergeant Baptiste? The clock-hands on the wall were semaphoring at two.

"HE borrowed forty francs," the girl spoke out in sudden distraction. "Late yesterday afternoon he borrowed it to buy himself a new cummerbund for the wedding. Do you suppose he has met some harm? Been robbed?" Tears came to her eyes, appealing around the table. Then she forced a smile. "What a fool I am; he will be here, of course. More wine, *messieurs?* And about the little heads, *mon ami.* Go on."

"Eh? Oh—the heads—!" That stammering Englishman was a fool. "Well, those African witch doctors practice all sorts of magic. I don't know, some people say it's true. Suppose the witch doctor wants the head of a particular enemy. He goes out and makes a little dummy out of clay or wood, and then he cuts off the dummy's head and sits back and waits for the real one to come in. Like this head you've made of cake—say you were a witch doctor, you'd cut it off, then sit back and wait for Baptiste's—"

Somebody kicked him under the table, and then, seeing the horror on the girl's whitened face, the idiot babbled hastily: "Superstitious nonsense, of course. I mean to say, they're nothing like this one made out of French pastry. How did you do it, Sugar? I was a sculptor before I joined the Legion, and I know art when I see it. The likeness is wonderful!"

"So wonderful I would like to bash it in the eye," Yankee Bill the

Elephant whispered to me, glaring at the cake.

The little pastry artist did not hear that, fortunately. She was staring at the English Legionnaire. "Those witch doctors who bake the shrunken heads"—voice frightened—"they will be near the outpost where the regiment is going?"

"But our company is being sent down there to wipe them out," Jensen the Dane offered cheerfully. "As for this head made of pastry," he squinted at the cake in mid-table to change the subject, "you should have been a sculptress, Sugar. Close one eye and look at it, and it is almost as if Baptiste were there—"

Then Baptiste *was* there—at least, his voice was in the room; the man, himself, being somewhere out in the street. I will remember forever the girl's face as she ran to the doorway with his name like a song on her lips. Her face as it altered when she looked out; she threw hand to forehead, staggered back. We were in the doorway behind her, you can believe, and we were staggered, too. And we weren't the only ones staggering!

That sergeant was staggering. Red-eyed and staggering. Weaving his way up the Lane of the Blue-Eyed Camel under the street lamps, and bellowing as he came. The little pastry cook called out to him, and do you know what that Belgian did? He went by the door without so much as looking at her. *Non,* he did not so much as glance at the girl who had waited half the night for him to come to their wedding party. Like a great bawling ape he passed the doorstep, cap on back of head, uniform slovenly. And the reason he did not look at Sugar—there was another girl on his arm!

Oui, there was a woman clinging to the elbow of that swine, and I do not have to tell you who it was. Yvonne! All powdered and painted like a circus parade, hat of floppy ostrich plumes and flounces sweeping the dust—a calliope matching the Belgian's bellow with a soprano that scratched your ears. They were singing the *Marseillaise,* I remember, and it was one time our national anthem made me sick. What happened on top of that made me sicker.

"Baptiste!" The little pastry artist's cry was heart-breaking. "Sergeant Baptiste! Wait! What has happened?"

He stopped and turned, that great dog, glaring as if he had never seen her before. Blinking his red-lidded eyes. The dancing woman wheeled to leer with him, and they made a pretty couple, I can tell you.

"Why, it's Sugar!" he bellowed. "Sugar and some of the boys!"

"Yes, it is Sugar," the girl in the doorway spoke hardly above a whisper. "And what are you doing with this other woman, Baptiste?"

HE did not answer directly. He was staring through the window of the pastry shop. Staring at the table with the almost-melted candles, the emptied wine bottles, the sculptured wedding cake. For a minute he blinked as if he were seeing double. Then slowly, villainishly, a light of comprehension dawned on his ugly face. The pigged eyes twinkled. A snort came through the bent nose and all the broken teeth showed. And the man began to laugh. He shouted and haw-haw-hawed. Bent convulsed, and pointed at the cake beyond the window. It was funny. Very funny.

"Look, it's me!" he was squalling. "Me! Baptiste! A piece of cake! Ha ha ha!" He stamped his hobnails on the cobbles. "Do you see how rich it is? I was here although I forgot to come! I forgot—!"

"Forgot?"

It was the other woman who answered that. In the voice of a fishmonger. Pointing. "I would prefer you choose some other man for your gingerbread after this! What are you doing with that stupid cake, there, made to look like my husband—!"

"Husband!"

But you cannot imagine that sergeant roaring with laughter. "I forgot all about it! By Saint Philip of Benguela, I forgot! Ha ha ha! Ah, ha ha ha! I stopped for a moment at the Absinthe Café, and now I've married Yvonne instead!"

If I live to be a million I will recall the girl's face as it whitened then. Have you ever seen shock, *messieurs?* She did not faint. I thought she was going to, for she swayed back once, but then she was standing like a rock. Then she moved backward into the room, slowly, without seeming to breathe, as a marble statue might have moved, experimenting with brittle limbs.

The Legionnaires behind her opened a path to let her through—I was too stunned to move, on my own part—and I don't know where she got the pastry knife. But there was a curved little blade shining suddenly in her fist—the room like a charade in stone, and that ugly married couple glaring in through the window.

Hate? Never have I seen such hate as I saw on the face of that girl. "Men!" She spat the word, and it sprayed through the silence like vitriol. "Liars and cheats! All men! Promises are nothing to you! Women—good women—are only for you to trample underfoot. But you are sorry for me, eh?"

Her eyes traveled around that group of stunned wedding-party guests, and I tell you the look in them raised my hair. "You are sorry for little Sugar, is that so? I see the compassion on your faces, you dogs who have all cheated me of happiness. But now I am going to cheat you all of yours. Save your pity for yourselves. I will have your happiness now! As for that vile thing out in the street, I will have his head!"

Word of honor, the way she said that coated my heart with ice. I wish you could have seen her then, moving like a sleep-walker, knife upraised, her eyes like emeralds with hatred, her complexion in the candlelight turned bronze. Do you know what I was thinking? All at once I was remembering the stories of the local gossips, and thinking that girl looked African, a savage priestess with her knife uplifted in the air.

"A while ago we were speaking of heads!" Her voice had changed, too; became toneless, foreign. "We were speaking of heads, little shrunken heads, and how the witch doctors cut off the head of a dummy to assure themselves the real one. May the witchcraft apply to all of you within hearing! But I want the head of Sergeant Baptiste!"

So you thought this was going to be a love story, did you? Or a story, perhaps, about pastry baking? Well, perhaps it is about pastry baking, for with those last words, the girl drove that cake-knife down smashing on the cocoanut-frosting cap of that pastry bust in mid-table, crushing the gingerbread skull into a million crumbs. The knife flashed again, and the cake head jumped from the chocolate shoulders and rolled across the cloth. She was slashing it to pieces when we got out of there.

On our way to take the troop ship to Senegal, we were marching out of Sidi-bel-Abbes at dawn. Our route took us down the Lane of the Blue-Eyed Camel.

The little pastry shop was roaring like a red-hot oven. Axe-men were trying to smash through the heavy shutters and thick front door that were locked on the inside; the shop was a blazing inferno.

"Sugar!"

Dieu! How we yelled her name when the crowd told us the girl must have locked herself in. How we screamed it again when we broke ranks and rushed around the building just as a fireman chopped open the back door.

I am glad I wasn't in Sergeant Baptiste's shoes that morning, I can tell you. He was there to see that blackened figure in bed under blankets of flame, that charred outline of a face upturned to the fiery ceiling. Even a jackal must have a conscience, and I wouldn't have wanted that suicide on mine.

And I am glad I wasn't in his shoes on the morning two months later when we were on our way to the interior of Senegal, and found his body lying in the bushes without a head!

CHAPTER II.

NOW WE are coming to the part of this story that has to do with witchcraft. French pastry is left behind us, and the baked goods from now on are of a different kind. Be warned, then, that French pastry is more digestible. You wish me to continue? Be prepared!

Observe, then, the map of Africa which in outline so much resembles the profile of a skull facing East. There is Sidi-bel-Abbes at the top of the cranium like a fly-speck; and there is Senegal, like a smear of green decay on the outlined brain. Oui, that country is like gangrene at the brain-base of this profiled skull—the place where the continent is crazy from the heat—the place where Africa is maddest.

There are plants that eat animals and fish that climb trees. Black rivers going nowhere through baobab forests, and jungles like oceans of spinach cooking in the sun. It was a hell of a place to find the headless body of Sergeant Baptiste.

We were on our way to Fort Défi when it happened. A week's march inland from the coast where our troop ship had dumped us, and twenty days on the trail left to go. *Alors,* we were already in the sort of jungle that makes Legionnaires hug their campfires at night, but Sergeant Baptiste had not hugged the campfires with us.

He had acquired a habit of walking off by himself around the sentry posts in the dark, talking to himself because no man in the outfit would talk to him. We hated that scum, and he knew it. We blamed him for Sugar's suicide, and just because he had left his bride in Sidi did not mean we had forgotten his marriage to that dancer.

So even our colonel would have nothing to do with the cur; but that morning a sentry found him without his head was something else again. Grouped around that Belgian's body, we stared at the jungle and fingered our collars. Where had the man's head gone?...

For the last five days we had seen nothing but vines and tangled trees. There was something missing that morning besides Sergeant Baptiste's head. And our colonel's laconic, "Headhunters!" did not supply the answer.

It satisfied the colonel, and we spent the day thrashing the jungle for tracks, but there were some of us in that company who could not shrug off the sergeant's head with the word, "headhunters." It did not explain how a man could lose his noggin in Senegal two months after a heartbroken pastry cook had whacked off its effigy in cake. Our comrades knew the story of how Baptiste had jilted Sugar, but they did not know about that wedding-cake business. We party guests had kept that climax to ourselves.

Yankee Bill, Christianity Jensen and Robbins, the young lieutenant from Saint Cyr and I—it was funny how we drifted around the same campfire that night as if by common consent. Funny, too, how pale we were.

"The cur had it coming to him," was Yankee Bill's blunt comment. "Everybody says so. He murdered Sugar as sure as if he'd killed her with his own dirty hands."

"But how?" Christianity Jensen muttered, staring at the jungle beyond the fire. "That is what I want to know. How?"

"Why, in the dark, you jackrabbit," Yankee Bill pointed out the dense blackness under the trees. "Some skull-robber crept up on the Belgian and copped his cocoanut, how else?" He chuckled amiably. "You don't think Corday, here, did it just because he said last week he'd like to knock off the sergeant's head?"

"I said I would like to knock it off, not *cut* it off," I reminded him savagely. "Every one of us here said he hated that Belgian to the core. *Sapristi!* I would feel better if I had done it, for that matter."

"So would I," the young lieutenant from Saint Cyr agreed. It was hardly his place to fraternize with the men, but he had stopped by our fire to light a cigarette, and he spoke low under his breath, staring at the jungle, fear-eyed. "It is certain these Senegalese butchers did it, but that it should happen as it did—!"

Yankee Bill shrugged matter-of-factly. "The non-com was prowling along the sentry lines, wasn't he? Alone. In this thick dark—"

"Exactly. There were sentries out there. Others out there in the darkness." It was Robbins who voiced the eerie question—the query I, myself, had wanted to ask. "There were others out there for the headhunters to pick on. Why did they pick Baptiste—?"

There was no mistaking the Englishman's implication; he was staring off through the night with eyes as big as butterplates, Sweating so that his face steamed.

Even that thick-skinned Yankee got it then. "Holy cow! You don't think because Sugar—because she cut that piece of cake—"

"That pastry shop was a thousand miles from this place. Somehow these headhunters knew." The Englishman's eyeballs swelled. "They got Baptiste's head, didn't they? If that girl wanted our heads, too—"

There it was, *messieurs,* a terrible possibility in the Briton's choked-off implication—for the girl had wanted our heads, too; had called us also to account for her years of blighted romance; had expressed the wish that the curse invoked on that faithless Baptiste might apply to us, betrayers also.

AND the fact remained. Two months had gone by. We were deep in the jungles of Senegal, a thousand miles from Sidi. But Baptiste had lost his head. And after that—if witchcraft could make that sergeant lose his head, it could do the same for us.

Perhaps, telling it now, it sounds like a ridiculous matter for speculation. But deep in that Senegal jungle it did not sound ridiculous. I am not superstitious, even though I do always cross my fingers at sight of a hearse; I am a Hugenot, and I have read Voltaire. But Voltaire is no good in the middle of an African jungle.

Well, there were five of us who had our thin coats of civilization peeled off that night. Five Romeos who went to our blankets shivering. I could not get to sleep, for all our colonel's doubling the guard, and it was not the mosquitoes that kept me awake, either.

What kept me awake was a mental picture of Sugar beheading Baptiste's pastry image in far-off Sidi—then the picture of that Belgian's body, headless in the local underbrush.

It did not help that for the next three days our colonel drove us through that jungle like a finetooth comb, and no trace of any headhunters was found. That colonel was mad because Baptiste had lost his head—not because the sergeant had lost his life, you understand; nobody shed any tears about that!—but the War Department had sent us down there to wipe out headhunting, and here this non-com had had his skull robbed before we had even reached our outpost.

"Find that head!" was the colonel's order. "Search every cannibal in the neighborhood, and the one with Baptiste's head is a kill for the firing squad."

Naturally. Except there were not any cannibals in the neighborhood. Our Legion company scouted the morass of jungle, and those devils who had made off with Baptiste's head had not bothered to leave tracks behind them. If the jungle knew where they'd gone, it would not tell. Under Hell's own sun, not a leaf was moving. There were no headhunters in sight. There was nothing but jungle. One stopped to listen; one heard no sound.

But then have you ever heard a silence so quiet you began to hear things? That Senegal jungle was like that. A whisper as of feet somewhere off in the underbrush. Something breathing in a thicket at one's elbow. Only the steaming of a rotten orchid, perhaps, or the soundless tearing of a spiderweb across one's face, but I began to imagine head-thieves creeping up on me from behind every bush, and once I could have sworn a crouched figure was watching me through some vines. *Dieu!* Our last night in that spot I stood guard duty over the sergeant's grave, and a million ghosts were rustling through the dark around me,

Alors, three days after it was reported missing, the colonel gave up looking for Baptiste's head. That morning our column resumed the march.

I could have whistled from relief as we started up the jungle trail in the dawn-glare, in spite of the fact I had stood guard duty half the night, that it was the devil of a trail, that the colonel drove us like a slaver to make up for time, and that in the Foreign Legion one marches without breakfast.

Having pointed out that, may I make another observation? That leaving a sergeant behind you in the jungle is one thing, but leaving his head behind may be another.

Not understood? Regard! At noon of that day's advance our column halted by the trail for lunch. Now at best a Legionnaire's rations are not quite up to a dinner at Delmonico's—hardtack, *singe,* a bit of chocolate—but the fare I discovered in my knapsack that noon would have given anyone permanent acidosis. I was hungry when I grabbed inside my knapsack, too; for the first time since Baptiste's fatality I had recovered a little of my appetite.

But when had I packed inside my knapsack a dried-up cabbage?—which was what the thing felt like, on my honor, when my fingers, rummaging for biscuit, first encountered it there.

Can you see me fumbling in surprise, tugging the thing out to see what it was? Can you see it in my hand staring up at me, then—inedible, leathery, ghoul-eyed? By Saint Anthony's Holy Fire! I opened my mouth, but it was not to take a bite, I can tell you. I had lost my appetite again, *messieurs,* but I had found the head of Sergeant Baptiste!

CHAPTER III.

CONCEIVE YOUR own sensations if you were to open your lunch box in a picnic grove some Friday and find a human head among the jelly sandwiches. Multiply by ten, and you have a dim idea of mine.

Talk about dropping a hot cake! And even so, before I could pop that dreadful prize back into my grab-bag, it seemed to have been in my hand for seventy-five years.

That head in my frozen fingers looked at me, and I looked at the head. It was a trifle smaller than it had been in life—ptomaine complexion and cheeks gone leathery—but there was no mistaking the eyebrow scar, the punch-bent nose, the missing front teeth. The eyes shone up at me like fish scales, and there was a sunny glint to the soft blonde hair. To say the less of it, it came to me with a shock that the head had been baked! In some oven. To a brown, *messieurs!*

Well, seventy-five years went by as I clutched that thing, and if it was seventy-five seconds in reality, that did not explain for the gray hairs afterwards in my beard.

And seventy-five seconds or years, that is not enough time to figure what to do with a lost head just found in your knapsack. Call the colonel? But heads in Legionnaire's knapsacks are against the rules; he would want to know how it got there. Pass it around? My companions would relish it no more than I did. *Sacré Dieu!* It was too late to return it to its owner, and with an article like that who would want to play finders-keepers?

My confusion ended on a thought that turned the sweat-beads to snowflakes on my forehead. Suppose someone besides Yankee Bill had remembered my wish to "knock off" this beastly noggin! Suppose some Legionnaire in the company had murdered the Belgian, copped his head and stowed it in my kit to throw suspicion on me? That didn't explain why it looked baked, but I had no time for wondering about that.

I had only time to get that thing back into my haversack before one of my companions spied it. Lucky my brother Legionnaires were occupied with their own mess kits. Jensen the Dane was nearest, with his back to me about four feet away. *Dieu!* I dropped that item back into my knapsack just as he turned to speak to me, and when his eyes were on me I was buckling up the flap.

"What? Have you gulped your garbage already? Myself, I am not the gourmet I used to be. Perhaps," he jested wanly, "I have ruined my stomach on French pastry."

I told him I was not hungry, either; and, Aunt of the Devil! before I could stop him, he moved over and sat down on my knapsack. "Me, I haven't been hungry since that sergeant lost his dome," he growled, munching a biscuit. "I wish that fool Britisher had never put all that witchcraft stuff in my mind. I—what are you sweating for?"

"It's hot."

"You look blue. I do not blame you. I wish we were out of this, and we have only arrived. Have you noticed the silence? Standing guard the other night, I felt as if all the specters of Tophet were around me."

"Would you mind hauling your carcass off my knapsack?" I croaked. "And I could do without this chatter about specters."

The comedian looked at his biscuit. "Well, I do not know about your conscience, Corday. I—I once told that girl in Sidi I would marry her. I hope she did not hold that against me. After what happened to Baptiste, I—I don't mind confessing I've been worried about my head—"

"And I am not interested in the confessions of a roué!" I told him thickly. "Go away. I want to be alone!" Never in my life had I wanted so much to have a moment by myself, but try to be alone in the French Foreign Legion!

Do you think I had a chance to get rid of that head? Not that noon, I didn't! I started a sneak for the bushes, and the corporal hailed me back to inspect my rifle. I dodged behind a tree, and there was the colonel reading a map. Every way I turned I was under some watchful eye.

ALORS, I had two heads, marching through the jungle that afternoon. My own and Sergeant Baptiste's! And I would not be able to tell you which was in the worst condition. Certainly my own brains were cooked. I tried to figure a way to sneak that thing out of my kit, and every time I thought of it my senses would swim like fish in a globe.

For a mental hazard I give you that—marching through African jungle with your sergeant's head in your knapsack. I could feel the thing bulging against my shoulder-blades, too, nudging me to remind me it was there.

Oui, that burden on my shoulders weighed at least ten tons, and the pressure wasn't lightened by the idea that one of my companions might have put it there. Mounting guard the night before, I had left my knapsack near a campfire, I remembered. Could the head have been slipped in then; the fire's heat given it a baking? But, sacred stove! what Legionnaire would have played such a trick? And if no Legionnaire played it, what then?

That night we camped on the edge of a swamp, and I housecleaned my knapsack at first opportunity, make no mistake about that! I couldn't sleep with that piece of baggage on the ground beside me. Any minute the colonel, prompted by the workings of some fiendish plot, might demand an inspection.

I was sharing a pup-tent with Yankee Bill, and I thanked *le bon Dieu* that the big American was on guard duty that night. Working in pitch darkness, I took that dreadful thing out of my knapsack, wrapped it up in a couple of big plantain leaves I had hoarded for the purpose, and waited for the camp to go to sleep. The jungle close around—the fires burning low—black-shadowed tents and the heavy breathing of exhausted men—peering from my canvas dog-house, I scouted the encampment for other signs of insomnia.

If spying eyes were on me, I could not detect them. A ghost moon floated over the jungle-tops that night, and the swamp was a graveyard of skeletal trees, their wet black limbs adrift in cobwebs of fog. Specters? That swamp was the meeting place of all the specters that ever walked! If you think I wanted to go sloshing into that haunted morass with a head under my arm, you are wrong.

But I had to get rid of that thing, you comprehend. At the risk of a sentry's bullet or some lurking, unnameable hoodoo. Crawling like a crocodile, I got past the sentry-lines; slithered off into that witch's-roost of fogged trees, green moonlight and bilious water, and deposited the head of Sergeant Baptiste in a pond.

That evil pool—a murky splash—but it hardly bears the telling of! Enough to say of that package that it floated a little way before it sank, and just as it sank the leaf-wrappings broke open like the petals of a water lily, revealing that terrible blossom. I had a last look from those dried-up, shining eyes. Then it gave a sort of glug and sank slowly out of sight, after which there were a lot of bubbles as if the wretched thing were breathing on the bottom.

AND then—if you will permit me a paradox—that head was more in evidence, after sinking out of sight than it had been before. I had slithered a good distance into that swamp, and all the way back to camp it was there. Yellow-haired and leathery it loomed in the moon-mist. Its reflection grinned up from the stagnant pools.

Imagination is funny, is it not? Take the following morning on the march. Shouldering arms and forward is not so easy after a sleepless night, you might think.

My mind was going like a squirrel-cage when we broke camp near that swamp, and as our column trudged off in the suffocating sunrise I was having a brainstorm of ideas. One of the ideas was that there was again a lump in my knapsack. A lump exactly in the place where that foul sergeant's head had been.

Tonnerre! Was I going crazy? Certainly there was no lump today in my knapsack. It was my imagination— A lump? Bah! Still—there was something there. An unfamiliar, uncomfortable bulge. Round and heavy in my kit. Nudging me in the shoulder-blades.

"Camel!" Yankee Bill growled out behind me. "It is hard enough marching this trail without stepping on someone's heels every five minutes. Must you stop every third step and hitch at that pack?"

"Keep away from me!"

Gloomily he reproached me. "Well, you don't have to take my head off for asking." Then, as I wheeled, infuriated by this ill-chosen phrase, he came abreast of me and fell in step, frowning. "What is the matter with you, anyway? You been bucking like a bronco ever since we hit the trail. One would think you were packing a hive of bees."

"Forget it," I gave him. "My canteen is gnawing me; I stowed it in my knapsack without thinking. Fall in behind me where you belong."

"Your canteen," he grunted, "isn't in your pack, you jackass. You left it back in that camp this morning, and I'm carrying it for you. I never knew you to forget your equipment before."

I didn't thank him for handing me my *bidon.* More than ever I was conscious of a lump in the pack on my shoulder—an irritation foreign to the weight of military baggage I had ordinarily carried a thousand times without noticing, up until yesterday afternoon.

"And you look sick," the American squinted, solicitous. "You could trip on the circles under your eyes. Say—"

"Perhaps you think you are the colonel holding inspection!"

"Do you have to be so touchy? Say, what's going on in this Legion outfit, anyhow? Last night it was Robbins, doing guard duty with me, and babbling he heard ghosts out there in that swamp. I asked him if he still thought Baptiste could've lost his nut on account of Sugar, and he couldn't answer for his teeth rattling. Then that kid lieutenant from Saint Cyr, I bumped into him prowling around like a sleep-walker. Said he couldn't turn in, and got me off behind a tent, and began to snivel. 'I was engaged to Sugar, too,' he told me. 'My father wrote me from Paris and made me break it off. Promise never to tell anybody.'"

The big Yankee shook his head at me. "I promised, see? and I'll never tell, either. Only it sounds like everybody's going crackpot. Just because these skull-robbers snipped Baptiste's noggin after poor Sugar chopped up a piece of cake—"

That animal! His hide was too thick to feel the atmosphere of that jungle. *Non,* he was going to let no witchcraft rubbish scare him. He fell behind muttering; and not three nights later I was to see him shivering over the campfire with his face the color of lard, afraid to look behind him, and going to sleep with his head under the blankets, too. Eh? But that was afterward. After we had gone miles deeper into Senegal. After I had felt that spine-chilling lump a second time in my haversack, and peeped inside to see what it was about.

For the lump persisted that morning, you understand. Grew on my consciousness with every mile. Annoyed me at first with the persistence of a mosquito-bite; then set me to wondering, imagining, fidgeting into a nervous itch that had me frantic in my mind. "Ignore it!" I cursed to myself; and the very act of ignoring it established its reality. "There is nothing in your knapsack!" I repeated over and over. *Voilà!* The more I said that, the more I could feel something there.

All right, in the Legion one marches fifty minutes and rests ten. When the orders came to fall out that morning, I did not flop beside the trail and nurse my toes as did the others. I was off behind a convenient bush, prying into my kit and cursing myself for an imaginative fool. Do you know what I was imagining? I had thrust my hand under the haversack flap, and I was imagining I could feel a head of hair!

I got my hand out of that haversack, I can tell you. Then I made the mistake of looking in. The lump, I learned, was not my French imagination. By the forty monks of La Trappe, it was not! One glance was enough. A corporal shouted at me to fall back into line, and fall was the word for it, *messieurs. Dieu!* That I could hold myself upright at all.

Once again there was in my knapsack the head of Sergeant Baptiste!

NOW I see by your faces that you are saying to yourselves, "Old Thibaut Corday is a liar!" You are not? I am honored by your belief. But we are coming to a series of events in this tale of heartbreak and baked goods, a jabberwock of impossibilities you will not believe. Blood of Bonaparte! I did not believe them, myself, when they happened. I thought some little tongue in my mind was lying; my senses were deceiving me. *Oui,* as I knew they must be deceiving me when I found that dried head in my haversack, fish-eyed, bent-nosed, still cordial, the morning after I had drowned it in a swamp.

Once more it was weighting my shoulders as our Legion column resumed the march, and the question of how it had come there the first time was nothing compared to the puzzle of its second appearance. I knew someone must have followed me into the swamp and dredged up the thing, then beat me back to that camp and returned it to my kit. Whoever was playing that game of Hide-the-Head with me must have some reason up his sleeve, and it was a game I did not like to play in that silent jungle of Senegal.

Like it or not, I found myself playing it again. Sweating icicles as I marched across that hothouse Senegal wilderness. Trying to keep my face straight with that awful bogie on my shoulders. Desperately hunting a chance to chuck it while the *commandant* ordered the column on a dog-trot and the quick-eyed non-coms gave me no opportunity.

By the end of that second day with Baptiste's head on my shoulders, my knees were weaker than water. When we halted to make camp that evening I was too sick to do anything but sit on my knapsack and shake, and I told the inquisitive colonel I had the fever. I tell you, the good Father Christmas, knowing his bag of gifts had turned into a sack of children's bones, could not have been half as shatter-nerved as I was.

That night I threw the head over a cliff. We were bivouacked handily on the rim of a gulch which was like a great trench gashed out of the map of Africa—a vast jungle canyon filled with eerieness and moonlight, and a river smoking far at the bottom like the waterway of Arab legends that goes to hell.

I flung the head of Sergeant Baptiste into that chasm, and I lay a long time on my belly, peering over, to watch it fall.

Can you see it as I saw it, going down to the size of a speck, a moonbeam? But a little way down, the wind tore off the leaves I had wrapped it in, and the dwindling face looked up at me. It may have been in my mind, I admit, but the grin seemed to change to a grimace as it fell. The dead, staring eyes had the same shine of fear they had had that night in Sidi looking through the pastry shop window. About halfway down, the mouth came open as if hollering.

"Va-t'-en!" I cursed it all the way down, and when it vanished in the river with a tiny splash, I was so weak I had to lie there for twenty minutes before I could crawl back into camp.

To sleep? Ha ha! When I closed my eyes I would see that little pastry shop in Sidi-bel-Abbes; Sugar, transformed from love to hatred, slashing off that Belgian's head in cake. When I opened my eyes I would see the moon-striped wall of the jungle, the emptiness over the gulch, that hollering head going down. Twice I crawled back to that canyon-rim and looked over to make sure, and a dozen times before morning I opened my kit to be certain the head wasn't there.

"The villain who tried to saddle me with that evil specimen will have a hard time fishing it out of that canyon," I said to myself. "And if I ever get my hands on that practical joker I will decapitate him like the Guillotine."

Certainly Baptiste's wicked noggin was not in my knapsack the morning after I threw it into that gulch. I looked to see. There was no lump nudging my shoulder-blades on that day's march, turning my legs to jelly.

Baptiste's murderer had wanted to kill two birds with one stone. Evidently. Only who could this enemy be, trying to load me down with criminal evidence? Now I had rid myself of that incriminating evidence, I racked my nerve-strung brains on the problem of who had put it there.

Try thinking out a puzzle like that under a flaming African sun. Marching through a jungle of unseen headhunters in a heat of one hundred degrees. There were about forty Legionnaires in that detachment who could have wanted to assassinate Baptiste, but which of them had wanted to assassinate me?

IT gave me something to think about, and I spent another sleepless night. I was not the only one in camp with insomnia, it appeared. Sometime during the night our young Saint Cyr lieutenant went by. I saw him scurry past my tent, cat-footed as a burglar, but then he stopped to refuel one of the fires, and in the upglow of the blaze his face looked clammy as an oyster. He must have knelt there for half an hour, stoking and poking up the embers, coughing in the smoke, white-faced. Then—queer for a Legion officer—he faded like a shadow at the approach of a sentry.

And some while after that I heard Jensen the Dane let out a nightmare caterwaul in the neighboring tent. But I had too many worries of my own to make significance of that, or the fact that in morning line-up, Robbins the Englishman looked as blue in the gills as if he had spent the night in a morgue, and Yankee Bill, the following night, was pale as lard and slept with his head wrapped up in blankets.

Those fools, what did they have to worry about? Their consciences, and talk of witchcraft. But I—?

On the third day after I had flung Baptiste's head over a cliff, with that lump no longer in my haversack, I was feeling better. *Oui,* I knew I had put a stop to the tricks of that unknown taxidermist who tried to load me up with his specimens; I would be in the fires of hell before I saw Baptiste's grin again.

And that was where I was wrong, *messieurs.* Unless the fires of hell are those jungle-smothered lowlands at the mouth of that vast Senegal canyon. For three days our trail had balanced along the rim of that abyss, and then it climbed down through a patch of thorns to the place where that canyon river swept off across a steaming African valley. That is the place where I saw Baptiste's grin again. And not in the river where it might have been, either. In a spot where it could not possibly have been, yet where it was. For a third time, you comprehend. I am talking about the head of Sergeant Baptiste. It was in my knapsack!

MY nerves had not recovered from the first two times as yet, and the third time was at night, after I had been on a routine *corvée* at gathering firewood, and had left my pack unguarded in my tent. I found it when I opened my kit for tobacco, and the shock it gave me that time was about a million volts worse than before.

Yankee Bill was off on firewood detail, or he would have noticed something was wrong. I was vaguely aware of it when I crawled into our dog-house, but I blamed the American's laundry never suspecting my own. That head had been wrapped up in my cummerbund like an Edam cheese—in my cummerbund where I hid my tobacco supply. Figure my feelings, then, when I took that bundle out of my baggage, anticipating my favorite cut plug!

I was holding that thing in my hand before I recognized it, too. It was smaller than it had been before—smaller, or I would never have unwrapped it—and it was about the color of tobacco, and I made the mistake of turning it to the light to see what it was.

Never will I forget the look of that thing which I thought I had thrown down a chasm. Never! Evil from the start, this time it was terrible. Shrunken. Ant-chewed. Losing its hair. Without eyes. But the grin had returned to the bent-nosed Belgian face, and there in my hand, despite shrinkage and insects, it looked ready to give me a laugh.

Shall we talk about something more pleasant, my friends? My knapsack was never an ice box, you understand....

The colonel, then—let us speak of that kindly man. With apple cheeks and mustaches like white carrier-pigeons nestling on his upper lip, and known throughout the regiment as "Papa." Again the subject is ill chosen; it was Papa who stalked, sniffing, up to the tent where I sat petrified over Baptiste's head that night. *Oui,* and for throwing something into my haversack instead of saluting, he gave me seven days guard duty and the suggestion I bathe my feet in chloride of lime.

"And if that is a goat in your tent, get it out of there!" he roared. "For the last few days I have been noticing you, Corday!"

He glared, purple-faced.

Noticing me? My word! It bleached me white as a desert bone.

Because I did not stand to attention, then, our Papa added seven more days of guard duty and a tongue-lashing that echoed through the jungle like the roars of a lion. After he was gone, I shook for twenty-five minutes. Suppose he had ordered an inspection of my equipment then!

I lost no time in getting rid of Baptiste's head that night, I can tell you. I was sick of that thing, very sick! Some scavenger had found it in the river that swooped out of the canyon, and that little game of framing me was going on.

Well, this time I had to put an end to it. I had to get rid of that ripe human cabbage before some other busybody came along. Any minute Yankee Bill might return with wood for our campfire. The campfire! I damned myself nine times for not having thought of it before.

Cursing my raveled wits, I tucked the sergeant's noodle under my tunic, and sneaked up on the nearest fire. Most of the men were in their tents, or off in the jungle on wood detail. Watching my chance, I stoked that campfire as no Legion fire had ever been stoked before. I tell you, I piled enough wood on that beastly head to have cremated the Devil, and I crouched there like a priest of Baal to watch it burn.

What is that song about smoke gets in your eyes? To this day the memory of the smoke that got in my eyes that night makes them water and sting. The head of that Belgian heartbreaker went up with a puff that singed my lashes. For a minute it glowed in the flames the way that little pastry cook's profile had glowed in the fires of her suicide. I poked it madly with a stick, to the very heart of that small inferno. Then someone was coming, just in time I scuttled back into my tent.

It was Yankee Bill the Elephant, and he came scooting in through the tent-flaps like a rabbit followed by ten hounds.

"Corday, hide me!"

"What is the matter?" I spluttered. His eyeballs, in the dimness, were popcorn, and his big frame was shaking as if some engine inside had come loose. I was having a private nervous breakdown of my own, and I was annoyed at this interruption. "What is the matter with you?"

The mad fellow gripped his rifle and bolted. Out through the back of the tent like a gust of wind, leaving me to wonder if he had ever been there. I crawled out after him, but the night might have swallowed him whole. Our encampment there was strung out along that river which came out of the canyon, tents and bonfires frontal to the river bank, the jungle like a black wall on three sides. Beyond range of the firelight there was nothing. The sort of pitchy blackness that makes one wonder if he has gone blind.

The American had vanished in that pitchy blackness, and I didn't like it. Clutching my rifle, I strained my eardrums to hear where the big one had gone, but the only sounds were the crackling of the campfires and the distant shouting of a corporal with the wood detail. Apparently the Yankee was hounded by some private terror of his own.

I was glad he had not returned to sit by our campfire, but I did not fancy the way he had faded into that wall of African blackness. Then I thought I heard him moving in the dark about a dozen feet away, and the way he was moving made a cold breath go over my skin. You know the tread of an animal stalking something dangerous? That was the sound conveyed to me by those movements in the dark. I froze in a crouch by my tent, waiting to see what it was.

Conceive my astoundment when Robbins the Englishman came prowling out of the night. For six paces or so, he prowled on the edges of the firelight, and then he saw with a start he was out of the night, and he prowled back into it again. Not before I had seen his face, though; or the grip of his fingers on his bayonet. Name of a name! He was clutching that bayonet as if to stab somebody, and his face was a cold white contortion that chilled my skeleton to the marrow.

After he melted into that wall of night where Yankee Bill had vanished, there was no sound at all. Do you think I was in any mood for that game of hide-and-seek? It just goes to show about imagination. Because at first glimpse of that Englishman's face as it had come from darkness into firelight—despite the Legion uniform—some twist of feature and shadow—I had thought it was Sugar!

CHAPTER IV.

DO YOU know, I was convinced I was going crazy? That head of Baptiste for a third time in my knapsack. Yankee Bill coming and going like a panic. A resemblance between the features of that British Legionnaire and the little pastry cook who had died in the fires of unrequited love in Sidi.

There was no logic, no reason behind any of those happenings; especially that game of tag between Robbins and Yankee Bill. I wanted to howl for the guard, and I did not dare. That English dog looking like Sugar—his expression green-eyed, white, as hers had been on the night she cut her wedding cake—but for a moment I thought it was the girl in Legion uniform.

And presently the American was back with the firewood squad, a little sweaty, perhaps, but hardly the mouse-chased elephant I had seen a few moments before. And later the Englishman, looking worried as he had of late, but no more girlish than he ever had.

All about me was the usual routine.

I waited for Yankee Bill to say something. Can you guess what he said? "Some lucky stiff is frying bacon." Then, after a gloomy sniff, the great ox rolled up in his blankets in the tent and shut his eyes.

That scared me into holding my tongue. All I could do was sit up all night on my knapsack, alternately hugging my rifle and clutching my hair, unable to drag my eyes from that terrible campfire.

It is not a nice sensation, to wonder if you are losing your mind. In the heart of an African jungle it is not.

By any manner of reasoning, the things which had been happening did not make sense. "But they did happen," I told myself. "I drowned that cursed head in a swamp. Then I flung it into a gulch. It is burning, now, to a cinder in that fire."

Then it occurred I was arguing myself out of it as a maniac would. Precisely. Suppose that talk of goats and bacon was hallucinary, too? *Mon Dieu!* Every time I said, "I am sane!" was not that proof I was going cracked?

But I repeated it again.

Turn me into a pepper mill! But when dawn flamed up over the jungle-tops at last, I did not know whether I was a lunatic or not. I did not know whether Baptiste's head had ever been inside my knapsack or not, and I was ready to believe I had chopped it off the sergeant, myself, if it had.

Then something happened that seemed to settle all of my doubts. Two days after I had burned Sergeant Baptiste's head in a campfire—two days and two million miles deeper into that weltering jungle—the head of Sergeant Baptiste came back.

You are surprised? I was not surprised. That jungle was hell. The vines were so thick we had to cut a clearing to pitch our tents, and the night was a cottony blackness that could hardly be breathed. Standing guard until midnight I had felt as if that silent blackness were crushing in my skull.

So I was not surprised to find Sergeant Baptiste's head in my kit that night. That time I did not even bother to speculate on the manner of its return. Simply and without ceremony, I took it out behind the tent and chopped it to pieces. Laughing to myself as I wielded the axe. Laughing as Landru and Doctor Cream and all those other demented Bluebeards must have laughed during their red moments.

Non, but they never hated their subjects as I hated that sergeant's head. I hated it because I had drowned it, thrown it off a cliff, burned it, and it had come back a fourth time to grin at me. I hated it because this time it was no bigger than a cantaloupe, shriveled and black, a thing mummified and dwarfed as if by some process of witch-doctoring.

I hated it because it convinced me I was crazy.

I WAS crazy, too, when I chopped up that head. I know it now, and I knew it then. A purple haze came over me, and I went on hacking and hacking.

When I was done with it that night it did not look like the head of Sergeant Baptiste. It did not look like anything. A sentry had called out to ask if I was chopping firewood, and I was still laughing. I had found out there were some kinds of fuel that wouldn't burn.

Chuckling all over, I went into our tent to say good-by to Yankee Bill. He wasn't there. Very carefully I put on my dress uniform. I waited a while for the Elephant to show up, but he did not. It was all part of my madness that the big American would not be in his blankets after midnight, and it made me laugh.

Then I went to Christianity Jensen's tent to say good-by to the little Dane. He was not there, either. There was a light in the colonel's big tent, and I wondered if my companions were there at headquarters, but I could hear no voices, and in that overpowering hush I could have heard a whisper. I waited by a fire, listening. The only voice I could hear was my own.

"You had better get it over with, Corday," it said. "You had better give yourself up before you go to work with that hatchet on the head of one of your *copains.*"

All right, I would go to Papa and tell him everything. I found myself walking to the colonel's tent to give myself up. I opened the unguarded tent-flap and looked in. But it would take me about two million curse-words to describe my sensations when I opened the colonel's tent-flap and looked in!

He was sitting at a camp table with a slush lamp in front of him, like a scholar late at night studying something that was clutched in his hands. Word of honor, I could not have looked crazier than he did. His eyes were bulging like a bullfrogs; sweat rolled down his cheekbones, watering his pigeonlike mustaches; his forehead was green as grass. He was so engrossed in whatever he was clutching in his hands that he did not know I was there until I coughed. Then, plunging around and flinging his hands behind him, he almost went back in his chair.

"Corday!" he gasped. "Do not tell—!"

My faith! It took my breath away. He looked like an assassin caught with a bloody knife.

"You saw?" he panted.

My nod was instinctive; I was not too crazy to know it is sometimes advantageous to let the *commandant* believe you have something on him.

The colonel had something on himself, all right. He screwed up his face as if he were going to cry. "I do not know where it came from," he whispered the moan. "Two nights ago I buried it in the jungle. The Thursday before that I left it under some rocks. When first I had it I threw it into a palm thicket. Either some fiend keeps finding it and returning it to my saddle bags—but I have watched like a hawk—or I am going mad!"

Sacré nom de Dieu! But he took his hands from behind him and put something on the table. And may my right hand drop off if I am lying! That something was the head of Sergeant Baptiste!

"WHAT?" you are exclaiming. After I had chopped it to mince? Some jackal might have snatched it out of the fire, scavenged it from the river, fished it from the swamp. Even passed it by sleight of hand to that colonel on those rare days when I did not have it, recovering it each time he threw it away. But after I had hacked it to cole slaw—*non!*

I am not asking you to believe that sergeant was a Greek myth with a couple of dozen heads. I am asking you to believe he was a Belgian scoundrel with one head only, yellow-haired, scar-browed, bent-nosed, grinning. I am asking you to believe I had chopped it to pieces, and there it was on that colonel's table again. Baptiste was not a Hydra, and you have not heard half!

"But it is impossible! It is impossible!" I pointed at the horror on the colonel's table. "An hour ago I chopped the thing to bits. How, then, can it be here?"

"An hour ago you had it?" the colonel gasped. "You chopped it up?"

I blurted out my own adventures with that piece of carrion, and the old man gulped like a bilious mudfish.

"It came here ten minutes ago," he panted. "I fell asleep reading the topographical charts. When I woke, it was there on the table." He was ogling the thing as one might look at an awful spider. Then he leaned at it, swearing. "Attend, Corday! See those stitches! By heaven, it looks as though it had been gathered by the pieces and sewed together again!"

Serpoletti! That could be the only answer. Naturally I had not made a close study of that head on its previous visits. Observed now under the colonel's lamp, it did not invite inspection, either. One could see it had suffered ill usage since leaving its owner's shoulders.

It was now not much bigger than a melon. Fire had left its mark. Yet somehow, in those diminished and distorted features, Baptiste's expression had been saved. I could see where the leathery fragments had been sewed together, and it made me sick.

"Then at least I am not mad," I whispered uncertainly. "But who can be playing these terrible tricks, *mon colonel?* Who could have pieced that head together in that short time after I shattered it?"

"We will find out!" he told me thickly. "I have said no word of this to my officers because I wanted to investigate, myself, and there is no telling who the madman is. The motive confounds me. I had wondered," his eyes on me were like cups of yellow flame, "if you, yourself, could provide the answer?"

"Me?" His meaning left me aghast.

"After I caught that whiff from your tent," he nodded. "But I am convinced now of your innocence. This shrunken blob! Only a doctor, one skilled with a needle, could have sewed those fragments together like that."

"A surgeon!" I caught his deduction. "But there is no surgeon with the detachment—"

Fiercely he spruced his whiskers, snarling, "There is one who has been a surgeon, you clod! Tell Jensen, behind you out there, to come in!"

In a night full of shocks, that gave me another. Not so much because I suddenly recalled the little Dane had once been a Copenhagen doctor. But because he was not behind me in the night outside of that tent.

"There is no one outside," I mumbled. "I have not seen the Dane."

"He is gone?" I tell you, the colonel jumped as if he had been kicked. His next move was to snatch out his revolver. "The rat must be found, at once! This proves it, do you hear? My orderly was sick tonight, and I ordered that Danish Legionnaire to guard my tent. *Sac à papier!* He was out there when I fell asleep. I noticed him acting queerly since Baptiste was murdered. And he was once a surgeon—the only one in the company who could have sewed up that head!"

No sooner was that accusation launched than it went up in smoke. Christianity returned. He came in out of the night as if forty devils were after him, pulled up short in front of Papa, opened his mouth to yell something, then staggered back as if he had been shot. The *commandant's* gun was leveled at him, too, but it was not that. Jensen's stare was fixed popeyed on that thing on the table.

"Baptiste's head!" I wish you could have heard the way he said it. "Again!"

Now all three of us were staring. The colonel had to pull a breath before he could roar.

"Baptiste's head, as you very well know, you Danish ghoul! Corday had it an hour ago, and gave it a chopping. You are the only ex-surgeon in this camp who could have sewed it together again."

"Sewed it together?" The Dane could hardly get his voice above a squeak. "Corday had it an hour ago? But if he chopped it to pieces, how could *I* have patched it up since then? When I was mounting guard outside the colonel's tent all evening up to the time, not fifteen minutes ago, when he fell asleep!"

THAT was the truth, and I could see the colonel realized it. Jensen's squeaky voice went on, and he waved his arms. "Then—it was when I could hear the colonel snoring in the tent—I thought I heard someone prowling along the jungle's edge in back. I ducked in back, and a shadow went by like a ghost. I was too scared to yell. It must have hit me over the head." He snatched off his cap; stood trembling. Myself, I could see the angry bump under his hair. "I guess I was knocked out," he moaned. "Or am I batty? That cursed dead coco on the table there—"

"What about it?" the colonel gurgled. Jensen's alibi had left everything in the air once more, and the Dane was glaring in a way that cooled that air to the atmospheric zero of a morgue. "What about it?"

"Yesterday I planted it in an ant hill," Christianity Jensen whispered. "Some monster had sneaked it into my blanket roll. And one day last week it was the same thing, and I pitched it into a bog where I saw a crocodile. What is it doing here—on the colonel's table—tonight?"

Before we could tell him, he had plunged to his face. Fainted.

Well, that gave us a turn. The colonel stared at me, and I stared at the colonel, and then our shocked stares fixed on that miserable cadaver-blossom on the table. It had done some traveling, apparently. One could believe from Jensen's ghost story that he had heard it on its way to visit the colonel tonight. Out there in the African blackness it had come floating along like a dandelion puff.

"And it has been chasing Jensen, too!" I groaned.

But that was nothing to what was coming. Sputtering like damp fireworks, the *commandant* dashed a canteen of water in the fainted Dane's face, and the little Legionnaire jumped to his feet.

"I tell you, I chased someone—some devil—out there in the dark! It must have been the werewolf who brought that head here! And as for the sewing job," he pointed shakily, "someone else besides myself could have done it. A surgeon is not the only one who can sew!"

"Who else?" the colonel wheezed, empurpled. "Who else could have hem-stitched a thing like that?"

"A sailor." Jensen's voice had sunk to his liver. "Sailors are handy with thread and needle."

"A sailor!" The colonel's face seemed to swell like a balloon.

"But there is one in the outfit who has been a sailor," Jensen husked. "Just last week I saw him stitching up his uniform, too. Yankee Bill!"

It rocked me back on my heels like a blow. Myself, I had seen the big American at work with needle and thread, and he had been nowhere in sight when I left those human fragments on the ground behind our tent. Could that *copain* of mine be behind this wizardish hurlothrumbo? Sacred stove! Of late he had been acting queerly.

But never as queerly as he acted when the colonel's bellow, echoing up like an explosion, produced him from some quarter of the encampment and he stood framed in the headquarters tent-flaps.

"You called out my name, *mon colonel!*" and then, his salute going awry as his voiced scaled upwards in a windy howl: "That there on the table? Holy Calliope! Where did you get that conk?"

YANKEE BILL, too? He was staring, shatterpated. The colonel, Jensen and I were staring, shatterpated. So was that reasty phrenological horror on the colonel's camp table.

The colonel said hoarsely, "What do you know about it? What have *you* had to do with this head, you American dog!"

"Do with it?" Yankee Bill stood as one appalled. "I didn't have anything to do with it, *mon colonel.* Some devil kept handing me the thing. I—I thought I was going nuts!"

"Handing you the thing?" the colonel echoed. "When?"

"Wuh-well," the big American stammered. "The first time was four nights ago. I was standing guard and it hit me in the back. I thought some lug had thrown a cocoanut. Cocoanut! Lord! I picked it up and walked toward one of the fires. When I saw what it was I nearly fell over. An officer was approaching, so I threw it away quick."

The colonel snarled, "What officer?"

"Lieutenant Rostand. That kid from Saint Cyr. He didn't see it. I threw too fast. Heard it land about a mile off. But it wasn't far enough," the big Yankee pulled a breath. "Later that same night it came back. The same way. Bounced off my shoulders. I jumped all around in the bushes, trying to find the skunk who was chucking that thing at me. Nobody there. 'I'll stop that!' I said. I took it into the jungle and buried it."

"You buried it, too?"

Green pallor crawled up the Yankee's jaws. "That wasn't all. I found a piece of dry timber and whittled a stake. Nobody was going to chuck that skull at me again. I buried it and drove that stake through it. Huh. It was there in the morning when we marched away; I crept through the vines to see. Next night it was handed me again. I was off with the firewood squad, in a thicket by myself. It was getting dark. I put my cap on the ground, and was cutting at a log. When I turned around, that sergeant's head was under my *képi,* grinning at me. There wasn't a mark from the stake!"

Listening to the words of that Yankee Legionnaire, I began to wonder if all of us in that tent were not a little mad. Expressions of idiocy grimaced on the features of the colonel and the little Dane. In the American's swollen eyeballs his thoughts were flicking and gibbering.

"There wasn't any mark from the stake!" he repeated. "The—wound had been fixed up. I was scared as hell. I know I should have reported, but I thought some fiend was after me. Maybe I was goofy. Anyhow I didn't dare report. All I wanted was to get rid of that non-com's conk. I—I dropped it in the soup kettle."

Hand flung to mouth, our colonel reeled back. His muffled voice gargled, "In the what—?"

"In the soup kettle," Yankee Bill confessed in a moan. "I—I didn't know what I was doing. I picked up that coco of Baptiste, and ducked. So the firewood squad wouldn't see it. I guess I was in a daze. Your orderly was making a stew for you that night, *mon colonel.* I saw the kettle over your campfire. He wasn't there. I didn't know what else to do with the head."

The old colonel was making gulping noises, and I had to gulp with sympathy. Jensen began to swear faintly, with picturesqueness. Yankee Bill, mustering courage to continue, perspired and swayed.

"But it wasn't long in the kettle, *mon colonel.* Ten minutes afterward I was back in that thicket where I'd dropped my axe and rifle. The squad hadn't missed me. It was pretty dark and the men had scattered. I couldn't find the axe and had to light a match. A man was crouched beside a tree—I hadn't heard him. Damn me, if he didn't have that head under his arm. Scared? He was worse than me. He went so fast I hardly saw his face. But I saw that head, no mistake about that. And I think," the big Yankee set his teeth together, "the man was that crazy sculptor, Robbins!"

Robbins! Thousand thunders! The name exploded through my consciousness like a bombshell. If anyone could be mixed up in all this ghoulery, it was that Englishman. That Englishman who had told us all about witchcraft in Senegal.

Jensen saw it from an angle more to the point. "Robbins!" he blurted with emphasis. "That is so, Yankee Bill—that Britisher did say he was once a sculptor—that last night we were at Sugar's shop in Sidi. And regard!" he wheeled on the colonel. "It would take more than a surgeon to rebuild a shattered mummy-head like that. It would take—"

"A witch-doctor!"

Intoned as though spoken in a tomb, the voice came tolling from behind Yankee Bill. All eyes swiveled from the table to the tent door. Robbins, the Englishman, was there.

CHAPTER V.

SACRED PIPE! He frightened me. Just his head was poked through the tent flaps; shadowed by the brim of his Legion cap his eyes glowed like a cat's; and to show you the state of mind I was in, I thought the fellow was there without his body.

The colonel didn't like that entry, either. He whipped up his pistol as if he meant to shoot.

"Wait! Don't shoot! I heard what the Yankee said! Great heavens! You can't believe I had anything to do with embalming that bloody napper!"

"Embalming!" Papa-the-colonel did not fancy the word. "Embalming, is it? Do you call this cursed death's-head which has been going and coming like some infernal plague—buried, burned, chopped up—made soup of!—do you call that embalmed?" He broke off, half choking; brandished the pistol. "Well, something around here besides Sergeant Baptiste's head will be embalmed in one minute. Explain, you sneaking clapperclaw! First: what do you mean, eavesdropping out there just now?"

"But I was going off guard duty," Robbins waved a hand. "Passing the tent, I saw the light and heard my name. Could I help listening when I heard mention of that head? That thing has been haunting me for a week."

Enfin, he blurted a story to match any confessed so far. Three times that incredible noggin had been in the Britisher's possession. He, too, had carried it in his pack for half a day, sweating lest the thing be discovered and a murder blamed on him. He, too, had buried it, burned it, and twenty-four hours after I had flung it into a gulch, thrown it into the same chasm.

"I thought I was going insane," he panted at us. "Each time it came back, I knew I must be going daffy. That time Yankee Bill saw me, I'd just picked up the thing. Some fiend hit me in the head with it. In the dark!"

Not ten minutes after the American, according to his claim, had dropped it in a stew!

"I imagined Yankee Bill had flung it at me," Robbins panted on. "I'd gone into that thicket after firewood, too, and I knew he was somewhere around. When he lit a match and looked at me it scared me daft. That was the night we were camped near that canyon river. I buried the head on a sandbar."

It was my turn to get back into the story, and I heard my tongue going before I could gag it. "Why, that was the place where I cremated the thing!" I blattered out. "Do you mean to say you had buried it earlier the same evening? And Yankee Bill had dropped it in the stew?"

"It is not possible!" from Jensen.

"Some dog of you is lying!" from the colonel.

"It's witchcraft!" Robbins groaned. "That proves it! Witchcraft!"

Then all of us were cursing at the same time, panting denials and accusations, shouting under our breaths, grimacing and gesticulating like a pack of fools.

Here, there, everywhere—that head could not have come and gone in such a fashion. In desperation we accused one another of complicity, of murder. That Englishman kept insisting on black magic.

"Listen! Wait!" Yankee Bill flung up a hand. "I got it!"

The way he did it sobered us. "Speak!" the colonel shouted. "What is it?"

"Colonel! Did you ever make love to Sugar?"

Picture Papa's face at that question. That question at such a moment! "What?" It almost blew the pigeons from his upper lip.

"Were you"—the Elephant had to loosen his collar to get it out—"did you ever make love to that little pastry cook at Sidi?"

It was amazing. And more amazing was the colonel's reaction to the question. Can you imagine him reddening? Reddening to the roots of his white hair? But blushing!

"And what if I did?" he spluttered like a cookpot on a stove. "It was never serious! Just a pastime! What are you getting at, idiot? What is it to you if I courted that girl six years ago?"

"Well, look!" in the effort for speech the big Legionnaire writhed. "Don't you see? Look! Jensen—Corday—Robbins—all of us here who've been haunted by that damned sergeant's head—we're the ones who one time or another made a play for that girl!"

We stared at one another. At that foul thing on the camp table. At the Yankee whose face was ashen. How we stared!

"Thunder of heaven!" The colonel was pale. "What is it you are trying to say?"

"I don't know," Yankee Bill shook his head. "Except she hated us same as she hated that Baptiste swine. She put a curse on him, and—"

"She put a curse on us!" Robbins finished the sentence left suspended in mid air. "An African curse! Now she's dead, but the black witch-doctors are carrying on for her. Only witch-doctors know how to cure and shrink a human head. Only witchcraft could make it follow us like this—"

The Englishman's eyes were shut and he was talking like a spiritualist in the middle of a séance.

Christianity Jensen interrupted with a startled oath. "Wait a minute! Our kid lieutenant!" He swerved his eyes. "He was one of us at the wedding party that night! Has anybody seen young Rostand?"

BLOOD of a hangman! It but needed that young Saint Cyr romantic to complete our circle. The circle of those Legion Romeos who were haunted by the memory of that girl.

The young lieutenant's name had hardly left Jensen's lips, when the boy came through the tent door. He came through the tent door as if blown through, the mouth screaming in his face, yet hardly making a sound. *"Mon colonel! Mon colonel! Mon colonel!"* Like that. Then he saw the thing on the camp table, and fell back clutching his forehead. Then he saw the rest of us rooted there, and if his voice was a whisper, it was his eyes that screamed.

"Hide me!" Exactly as Yankee Bill had once cried. "She is out there! In the dark! *She!"*

"Who?"

"She went right by my tent!" he waved his arms. "Not five minutes ago! I must have fainted when I saw her! *Sugar!"*

Sugar! That was something, was it not? A final madness to cap the whole insanity. Backed up by a choky holler from Yankee Bill:

"I saw her, too! That night I chucked the head in the stew! I was chasing Robbins, and I ran right against her in a thicket, and I got a dim look at her face, and I never told because I thought it was a dream—!"

"It was me!" The cry, then, came from Robbins. Holy Creator! Of any of the mad expressions in that tent right then—and I include that evil mummy-face on the table—that Englishman's was worst of all. Eyes of one crucified! Mouth a-twist! Face waxen, sweat-beaded, glittering! "It was me you saw!"

We stared at him.

"It was my face you saw that night, Yankee Bill. It was me you glimpsed tonight, Lieutenant!"

Do you know what I was remembering? I was remembering that time I had seen him and been reminded of Sugar.

"The girl burned herself to death," he was whispering. "You saw her in that fire the same as I did. She never knew about me. Why I called at her shop so often. She thought— But she put the witchcraft on me, too, the same as you other curs! Never knowing I truly loved her—where she got her talent—I was her father!"

Her father! One could glimpse it now it had been told. Around the eyes. Shape of the chin. Vague rumors we had heard in Sidi, and the fact this Englishman had been a sculptor. *Sacré*, how we stared!

"Her mother was an Arabian princess. I told you I had traveled in Africa. That is why I stayed, joined the Legion. Why I hired that French woman to rear the girl—have her set up shop in Sidi-bel-Abbes—"

One could glimpse other things in that crucified face. Something terrible. Beyond ordinary pain and anguish.

"You!" the colonel's voice shrilled. "You played those tricks with that head—on us! Because—"

"No!" Groaning, the English Legionnaire put his hands over his eyes. "I wish I had, that is all. I tell you, the girl had an African strain. There are mysteries the white race can never know. Her spirit—my own daughter—I can't bear to think of it influencing these Senegal headhunters. And it is!" he moaned. "It can't be anything else! Witch-craft!"

My faith! As if that speech was not enough to finish us off, it was echoed by a scream. *Dieu!* That scream had a jab to it.

Someone squalled, "Headhunters!" and somewhere a rifle went off. Then the night fell down and buried us as under an avalanche of coal.

HAVE you forgotten where we were located, then? In the jungly heart of Senegal? But a few days, now, from that Fort Défi outpost toward which we had been marching, yet a million miles from any glimmer of civilization, and all the fiends of Africa unchained in the night outside. *Oui,* like a coal-slide they came down. Like an anthracite avalanche. In the pitchy jungle silence around that camp those black devils had been gathering like the invisible forces of a storm, and they landed on that headquarters tent with the violence of a tornado.

Holy Sébastopol, what a charge! In that headquarters tent we were not only caught napping. We were caught mesmerized. We were caught with our emotions keyed to the highest C on the scale, transfixed on that stunning pitch by that hypodermic-needle scream.

I tell you, the battle was half over before I gave a thought for my gun. The tent collapsed, and those Senegalese butchers were on top of us like a stampede. Somehow I got out from under; found myself hemmed with the others who had been in that séance. About a million blacks were rushing in the dark around us—five hundred, anyway. Knives skimmed my ears, and lances flew. In the light of the campfires one caught the shine of ebony muscles, saw the egglike whites of their eyes, their grinning teeth. Whooping, leaping in the air, they spun around our huddle—a whirl of shrieking demons caterwauling for blood. Leopard skins, parrot plumes, necklaces of shin-bones—in that kaleidoscope of firelight and shadow they resembled the Furies out of Cagliostro's Box—creations of opium and sorcery—part bird, beast and human—and every one with a chopper as big as the moon.

They did not wait for any Legionnaires to come out of a trance. They did not! The fighting was brisk from the moment of their arrival. Attracted by that lighted tent, the fiends struck it first, cutting us off from assistance. Gunfire and yells from across the camp were no help. Caught on their blankets, the rest of the detachment had their own troubles and might have been five miles away. On the edge of the battle we were isolated, pinched off. Instantly we had to fight for our lives.

I was caught in the thick of it before I realized my only weapon was an axe. *Oui,* I was still carrying the axe I had used to such purpose earlier in the night, and I even found time in this last extremity to shudder as I gripped it anew. Of the battle after that I remember only fragments. Fragments dim-seen through darkness and red fire; glimpses as of objects whirled past one's eyes by a hurricane.

I remember Yankee Bill at my elbow firing his Lebel pointblank at screeching black faces; and the young Saint Cyr lieutenant, unarmed, crouching terror-stricken behind the American's legs.

Jensen was there somewhere, thrusting and stabbing with a scarlet bayonet; and Papa-the-colonel, plump and fierce-eyed, wildly firing his revolver.

Crash of rifles and tumult of screams. Canvas bursting into flame as the colonel's slush lamp fired the overthrown tent. Smoke rolling. Howls of the officers on the other side of the encampment. Crackling underbrush. Flamelight flashing on those chopping-knives that went around us like machinery. Black bodies leaping. Clang of blades against my axe. I was down. I was up. Hurled against Yankee Bill by the glancing blow of a spear.

"Look at Robbins!" the big Yankee bawled.

Will you believe I had to stop and look? That blazing tumble of canvas that had been the headquarters tent—Robbins was in the middle of it! I tell you, he was on his hands and knees on that carpet of fire, pawing around in the red flames with the light of hell on his face. About fifty Senegalese butchers were galloping around him like the horses of a merry-go-round, and that Englishman in the central blaze paid them no more attention than that! With all Hades broken loose around him, do you know what that British Legionnaire was doing?

"What became of it?" he was screaming. "That witch-cursed head? That head of Sergeant Baptiste?"

"Robbins! Robbins!" we screamed.

A PUFF of fire rolled over him, and the butchers, about to close in, jumped back. I have seen strange sights in the heat of battle, but never anything as appalling as that Englishman rising out of those flames like a swimmer out of surf, face scorched and smoking, uniform fringed with fire, but his hand aloft and that wretched mummified death's head in his clutch.

"I've got it!" Shouting like a diver who has recovered a pearl.

A dozen black men were dancing behind him with knives upraised, and we screamed at Robbins again, but he did not hear us. Snatching up his rifle, he dropped that head to the ground, and set to pounding it with his rifle-butt. Smash! Smash! Smash! *Dieu,* but of all that night's demonism, I think that episode was worst. That berserk Englishman pounding that evil head with his rifle-butt, beating it into the scorched earth, smashing it to a pulp while those black wolves behind him closed in.

Oui, that was the worst scene of all. Up to then.

"He's mad!" I heard Yankee Bill shout. "He hated Baptiste for jilting his daughter. He must hate the rest of us, too! He's behind all this voodoo! He— Wow!"

The American saw it happen before I did. All I saw was the knife flash. To spare your feelings, I will say it was as if a streak of lightning crossed the Englishman's shoulders, and his head simply vanished. I did not see it go. I remember only how his figure remained upright in the flamelight of that burning tent—how, for fifteen seconds, the lifted hands retained their grip on the upraised rifle—how, almost before I realized what was missing, the figure fell.

But wait. The guillotining, which had started with a cake bust in a Sidi-bel-Abbes pastry shop, was only getting under way. That English Legionnaire—Sugar's father—he may have been behind it, but his death did not end it. Even the pulping of that demonized sergeant's head could not end it. There were forces operating in that African midnight, violences unleashed which no minor terror could stop.

I saw Yankee Bill shoot the monster who slew Robbins, and then those Africans swept over us like a tidal wave. That group trapped by the colonel's burning tent, we were trampled flat. We were overpowered, disarmed and bound. Like trussed pigs we were rushed off that field of battle, and to this day I wake up hollering in fright, having remembered in my sleep, how I was captured by those Senegal headhunters—captured and carried off through the jungle, slung on a pole.

CHAPTER VI.

THE SLAUGHTER-HOUSE is the final scene of this story, and I knew it would be the final scene the moment I got there. It must have been ten miles from the unfortunate Legion camp, but, traveling upside down, I was too distressed to mark distances or direction. Sounds of gunfire died out behind us, that I know; and that jungle trail went on for years. Even so we reached that slaughter-house too soon.

That destination was the ticket office to Hell, comprehend. A great grass hut shaped like a giant haystack, central in a clutter of minor huts like beehives. One look at that witch-doctor on the threshhold, and I knew we were going to be murdered. He wore a festoon of skulls around his neck, and and another around his middle; on his chest there dangled a baby's skeleton. I don't know why Yankee Bill said something like: "He makes no bones about his job."

Bones about his job? That witch-doctor's house was floored with clavicles! We were carried in like sacks of meat, and we were left tied to chopping blocks—five chopping blocks that were ranged in a row, and our heads held by neck-ropes to the grooves.

Ten black devils tied us to the blocks with relentless efficiency, then backed out bowing. That bone-decked witch-doctor sauntered in with a basket on his arm; on his shoulder a headsman's axe. One or two of my companions did not seem to know where they were—the old colonel appeared to think himself in church, and the Saint Cyr cadet kept asking for his mother—and that monstrosity in the doorway made a little pantomime to show us what was up. Chuckling, he ran his thumb down the blade of his instrument as a barber might test a razor. Then, propping the big axe against a doorpost, he pointed at the graying sky, at the axe, at us and at an object hanging like an orchid in the doorway over his topknot.

That is the final scene of this story, *messieurs*—that cavernous African barn-interior—the doorway framing a glimpse of a native-village square, grass huts and graying sky in that barn, the five of us kneeling in a row, our chins stretched out on chopping blocks—that beast of a headsman pantomiming our finish in the doorway.

But it was that orchidlike decoration hanging in the doorway that gave it the final touch. Somehow at a time like that you keep hoping for a reprieve. Papa-the-colonel found solace in prayer; Yankee Bill and Jensen in profanity; the young lieutenant from Saint Cyr in calling, "Mother, Mother, Mother!" Me, I was pretending none of it was happening.

Do you realize what that orchid-thing was? It was a little dried head, a very triumph of the baking-and-shrinking process; leathery, cured and grinning, the face reduced to elfin size, the whole no bigger than your fist—one of those little baked heads.

In a wind that waffed from somewhere it turned slowly on its string. The sky grew lighter; one could see the mannikin profile and tiny ears. Did I say it was one of those little baked heads?

"Look!" the squall was from Yankee Bill, kneeling next in line. "Look at that thing in the doorway above that major-domo! Look, Corday!"

Name of a name! I was looking!

The sky was lemon-yellow behind it, now. The hair of that human miniature was yellow, too. *Oui,* it was blonde, and as the baked, midget face came around on the breeze, I hollered at the top of my lungs. For there again was that familiar scarred eyebrow, that familiar bent nose, that familiar Belgian grin. There again was the head of Sergeant Baptiste!

AND now you *will* say I am a liar, my friends. Now you will say that after what that head had been through, magic or otherwise, it has become too impossible, it has turned up too many times. I said that to myself, do you understand? I said that after the chopping, the cremating, the burying in ant-hills, after the pounding that mad Englishman had given the thing, it was not possible for that head to be in that witch-house doorway in a better state of preservation than before.

Now it was perfect! No stitches, no pox from ants, no decay. It was Baptiste's head reduced to pocket-size, yet no more distorted or out of proportion than one's photograph.

"Holy Mother!" Jensen the Dane saw it, too. "Then it wasn't poor Robbins after all. It is witchcraft, that's what has got us. Witchcraft!"

Witchcraft? Listen! A band of crimson flamed across the sky to paint that hanging bogey as with blood. In the village a rooster crowed. Like the thump of blood in my ears came the menacing *bum-bum-bum* of a kettle drum.

"He is picking up the axe!" the young Saint Cyr lieutenant had to scream. "The witch-doctor is going to kill us."

I tell you, that filthy headsman had not picked up his instrument as yet, but in response to the drum he was spitting on his hands.

"But look behind him!" Yankee Bill gasped wildly at me. "Great Lord! Corday! Look at that behind Mister Bones!"

The witch-doctor didn't see it; he was too intent on limbering up his palms. Neither did the collection of drummers, black men and crones gathered at one side of the village square. But coming out of the jungle, advancing in the dawnlight, was such a figure as I will not forget on the day they lay me in my grave. I will remember it when I am in my grave, and when I crumble to dust it will be in the last dust-particle of my memory.

AN apparition, *messieurs!* A ghost of all ghosts! Truly! A figure robed in white with a sheeted face and a big white sack on its shoulder. It did not appear to walk. It appeared to drift. Advancing in the dust and sunlight now pooling on that native square, it came as though drifting on a hurried wind.

By the blood of Napoleon and all his soldiers! I thought it was the messenger of Death come to claim us. But if it struck us in that slaughter-house appalled, it did something to those native villagers, too. The carnival spirit went out of them. Goggling, they stood. The drums stopped. Only that white-robed figure kept coming.

In his doorway, Monsieur Bones had to turn and see what had happened. He was a nasty devil with plenty of terrors in his repertoire, but he did not seem to like this new arrival. *Non,* apparently it was one of his ghosts, and he gave a startled jump that rattled his decorations.

"Great leaping Christmas!" my American companion panted. "It's come for us!"

So it appeared. Drifting straight to the threshhold of the witch-house, the apparition came to rest. It may have been running on feet, but its robes fell in white billows to the dust, and there was nothing so mortal as feet to that veiled figure. It had a hand, though; a pale, thin hand that slung its ghostly sack to the ground. And one eye that gleamed through a slit in the face-cloth, sending a glance through that doorway at us.

Attempt to imagine how we, in that death-house, felt then! How we felt when that ghostly figure from the netherworld gave us that one gleaming look; then, for all the world like an Arab merchant about to display his wares, set down its pack, and began to trade. To trade, do you comprehend? With that witch-doctor rooted in the doorway! That wizardish figure in white began to trade with that skull-hung African murder-priest, offering him a bargain.

It was all in pantomime, but the gestures were eloquent enough. That ghostly trader pointed at the five of us who were tied to the chopping blocks, then it pointed to itself. Then it pointed to the sack on the ground, and then at the witch-doctor. The finger went on to indicate the dried head hanging in the doorway; pointed to the sack, again. Then that ghost held up five fingers five times; waved its waxen hand at the sack, proposing a deal.

Can you see that mummery as I saw it in the dawnshine? That netherworld figure was trading for us! *Dieu!* Offering whatever it had in its bundle for five Legionnaires, and assuring Monsieur Bones he would come out on the better end of the trade. Only that witch-doctor was too astounded by the opportunity. In the yellow of early morning he stood hypnotized, as his drummer-boys and the whole village was standing hypnotized.

That didn't phase the white-robed figure. It wanted to close the deal, and to convince that black witch-doctor, the white-robed figure showed its wares. Listen to this! Opening that mysterious sack, that white apparition dumped the contents at the witch-doctor's feet. Exactly, as one farmer to another displays a bushel of prize vegetables.

Well, the contents of that sack poured out in bushels, but it was not vegetables. Never in the world! Tumbling, bouncing, bumbling out of that occult pack to heap up on that threshhold and roll on the ground at that stunned witch-doctor's feet, came heads! Baked heads, *messieurs!* Dried human heads! Little baked heads that were dead ringers for that one hanging over the doorway.

Murder! There must have been four dozen of the things. How that witch-doctor, beaten at his own evil specialty, glared. *Non,* but how we Legion dogs at our chopping blocks were glaring! Did you think I meant it as slang when I said those heads were dead ringers for the one above the doorway? But they were the same heads, can you understand that? Those four dozen heads from that white-robed apparition's bundle—they were all the same. All the faces were the same, and all were twins to that head hanging above the threshhold. Little bent noses, little scarred eyebrows, little Belgian grins—they were all heads of Sergeant Baptiste!

TO this day I can see them heaped like melons in that doorway. I can see the faces of my four doomed companions white as marble in paralysis. I can see that ghost-veiled trader standing back in anticipation of the deal; and I can see that popeyed witch-doctor as his stare reeled over that heap of similar heads, then jumped to that same head dangling above his own. Terror? That black Monsieur Bones went straight up in the air. Beneath a cosmetic paste of ashes and filth, his Negroid face went Aryan. He gave one howl like a steam whistle, and went express—fleeing across the village square, a witch-doctor out-witched. On the way he screamed something at his headhunters, and those Senegalese devils all went with him.

It wanted one final work of witchcraft to clear that village of every sign of life. Rushing through the slaughter-house door, that white-robed apparition that had won the deal, pulled a knife. Slash! Slash! We were cut loose, *messieurs.* The colonel and the fainting young lieutenant, Jensen, Yankee Bill and me. We were cut loose from those chopping blocks where we had been hogtied, and it did not take the cry, "Run! Run!" from that white-robed bargainer to get us out of that place.

As fugitives from a Chamber of Horrors, we fled. Dashed for the jungle. Tore in bunched formation through the underbrush. Ran blindly. Running blindly, I did not notice the white-robed figure was still with us until, somewhere, we halted under a great tree.

Oui, somewhere deep in that green welter we halted under a great tree, and that white-robed ghost from the dawn was still in our party. It was Yankee Bill the Elephant who brought our panic-stricken flight to a halt; turned to that white-robed figure and tore away the Arab face-veil. And there—in broad daylight—the sun glancing down through the tropic arches and the green wall ablaze with yellow—we had the greatest shock of all.

"Sugar!"

She merely stared at us. Her face was like stone under the thorny tangle of blonde hair. Like expressionless stone, with no light behind the eyes.

"But you are dead!" the young lieutenant screamed at her. "Go away! Go away—you are dead!"

"Yes," like her features, her voice and her nod were expressionless. "My heart is dead. But you see I remain alive—"

"But your shop! We saw you in the fire!" the colonel wailed.

"You saw a dummy in the fire," came the expressionless voice. "I made a dummy so that you would think I was dead. I made it that night after the wedding party—as I made those baked dummy-heads of Sergeant Baptiste!"

"You made all those heads?" I was the only one able to yell.

"Five dozen of them," her voice was like stone, too. "I hated him, do you understand? I hated all of you! You had stolen my heart, robbed me of love, I wanted to torture you all. I followed you to Senegal and I brought those dummy-heads I had made with me. I followed you on the march. I meant to keep putting those heads in your blankets and knapsacks until the lot of you lost your own heads, went mad." The stone voice broke on a sob. "I meant to start off by killing Baptiste. Him, I hated most of all. I had my pastry knife and I meant to take his mean skull, myself, but the very night I crept up on him some Legionnaire was in front of me. I do not know who did it, but it saved me the job. That Legionnaire threw the head into the bushes—the African hunters must have been there in the dark and taken it for themselves."

She sighed, and her voice was once more as stone. "I meant to drive you mad, you philanderers—but I could not see you killed. When I saw the Africans creeping up on your camp, I had to scream a warning. That is why I came to the village where they carried you captive. Not that I bear any love for you—never think that! But I could not bear to let the headhunters carry out my wish. After hiding in the jungle to watch the fighting, I saw what happened to that Englishman, Robbins—"

"Robbins!" Jensen blurted. "But, he was your—"

It was Yankee Bill's quick hand, again. Grabbing the little Dane's shoulder to shut him off. The rest of us got it, too, and kept silent. So that poor girl never knew the Britisher was her father; never knew where she got her talent for sculping; never knew the Legionnaire who killed the Romeo who had jilted her.

And that's about all of the story. Five days later, thanks to the colonel's midnight studies of his maps, we straggled into Fort Défi. There we found the survivors of our detachment—thirteen battle-scarred Legionnaires who tried to tell us they'd had a close shave saving their heads. What did they know, those lucky devils, about a close shave?

We laughed at them, shakily.

The little pastry baker went to the coast with the departing garrison contingent who knew nothing about her. I know she sailed for France.

But I would give a lot of money to know how she kept alive, trailing our column through that jungle of Senegalese headhunters. I would give a great deal of money to know. That jungle was Hell, and it must have been her Arabian heritage that kept her trailing us, untiring, on that march. Or perhaps she kept alive on French pastry.

OLD Thibaut Corday finished his story and the last of the *petit-fours* he had been eating with the same breath. In the darkness that had gathered under the café awning the American Express chap looked pale. The eyes of the young British consular agent were still fixed on the unopened cake box, but not so hungrily as before.

"By Jove!" the staring eyes finally lifted to the old French Legionnaire's face. "You're not one story-teller, Corday. You're the Brothers Grimm. No, I take that back. Those Grimm boys had imaginations, but their imaginations combined were nothing compared with yours."

"But it was not imagination," old Thibaut Corday said sharply. "There were times when I wished it had been, but it wasn't."

"But that fire in the pastry shop—the girl's charred face—and then all those heads! I mean, broad daylight—and you actually held them in your hand—"

"You mean, perhaps, that I could not have been fooled. That I should have known them for fakes, is that it?" Old Thibaut Corday waggled his beard. "*Eh bien.* I may grant you the imagination part of it there. There is a line from Shakespeare that may explain a little—'Our conscience doth make cowards of us all.' Is that it? *Alors,* our consciences were working overtime about that jilted girl, and after her retribution on Baptiste we had that head business on our minds. With something on your mind like that, it is easier to deceive the eye."

He gazed at us.

"But the hair!" the young British agent blurted. "The eyes of those heads! The—the skin!"

Old Thibaut Corday pulled a breath. "Well, to begin with, there was her own head in the burning shop. A dummy. Gingerbread only. It was charred when we saw it—in the midst of flames. If the firemen found anything, it was burned to ashes with the house, an obvious case of suicide—*fini!*

"As for the hair on those heads of Baptiste—her own. The eyes? Colored fish scales! The skin? Scraped hides from the meat market, peelings from a chicken. Put in teeth carved from dog bones, stuff with clay, and bake well. Garnish with garbage and drench with berry-juice—there you have the head of Sergeant Baptiste."

While speaking, old Thibaut Corday had let his fingers stray to the cake box, and now he was untying the string.

"I told you what that girl could do with pastry dough and flavored icings," he went on. "If she could make a flesh-colored angel cake of sherry and vanilla, hair of shredded cocoanut, ears from cut figs—*bleu!* If she could sculp in French pastry as Michael Angelo could carve in butter and marble—imagine what she could do with more fleshlike articles! But I will show you one of her French pastries; then, seeing it on the table, perhaps you can imagine those heads of Baptiste!"

There was silence as he opened the cake box, silence that was broken by exclamations as he held a match to show the little model it contained. Seen in matchlight, it was the head of old Thibaut Corday, a miniature bust in cake and colored frosting, wonderfully sculped even to the blueberry eyes and flowing cinnamon beard.

We stared silently a moment.

"Where did you get it?" the young British consular agent could not restrain a cry.

"From Paris." old Thibaut Corday said grimly. "She must have opened a pastry shop there. I don't know. But every year on a certain day comes one of these little heads by parcel post. I wrote to those others about it once, and they were getting them, too. Do you know what day it is they come, *messieurs?*"

The chap from the American Express and the young British consular agent didn't know.

"Valentine's Day!" old Thibaut Corday's voice was thick. "That was the day she was to have married Sergeant Baptiste! And, *sacré!* Now that I come to think of it, I have almost left out a most interesting irony to the story. Consider this for your amusement, *messieurs.* That little pastry cook's name, it was not Sugar. It was Salomé. And the sergeant's name was Jacques—Jacques le Baptiste!"

SNAKE-HEAD

PERHAPS, MESSIEURS, YOU DO NOT BELIEVE IN GORGONS WHOSE GLANCE TURNS MEN TO STONE. BUT HAVE YOU HEARD HOW THIBAUT CORDAY FACED A MODERN MEDUSA, WHILE HER SERPENTS SANG THEIR DEATH SONG?

CHAPTER I.

"THAT IS a great story!" Old Thibaut Corday shut the book he had been reading with an enthusiastic bang. "It is a pity *Monsieur* Bulfinch could not give to the characters their right names. And of course he has exaggerated in the American fashion, and added a little here and there. But in general it is true, and told in picturesque style. I must write to the author and ask him how he found out about me."

I said, bewildered, "How he found out about *you?*"

"I am surprised to see the story in print, because I never told anybody. *Eh bien,* perhaps the Arab girl has told it. In one way or another it must have reached America, for here it is in a book. An adventure in which I figured, you comprehend."

I stared at Old Thibaut Corday in astonishment. I stared at the book in Old Thibaut Corday's hand in astonishment. There was the blue-eyed, cinnamon-bearded veteran of the French Foreign Legion, eighty-five years old at the most, and not looking a day over sixty. There was the book in his hand (some scholarly tourist must have left it by accident on the café table)—*Bulfinch's Mythology!*

"Is it not"—he misread my look—"an unusual coincidence? I have never told it to anybody, I repeat, for who would believe it? Then it crops up in a book which somebody chances to leave on our table here. Yes, the author must have heard it from the Arab girl, and he has given her version; had I told it to him, he could have been more accurate as to details. This woman he calls Medusa—she was a snake charmer. He has failed to explain about the victims she turned into stone. Also I do not quite understand the American colloquialisms: the writer describes me as having wings on my heels; I suppose that is a way of saying I ran very fast. *Enfin,* he says I flew. Another

Let me live to be ten million, and I will not forget that creature like a living nightmare.

American way of saying I ran with great speed, I suppose?"

I cried, "You—you think that story is about you?"

He stiffened at my incredulity. "Certainly it is about me! He has given me the fiction-name of Perseus. The princess he calls Andromeda. Or perhaps those are the names the Arab girl gave him. At any rate, here is the whole amazing account—the snake charmer, the people turned into marble and all the rest of it—even to the fight I put up at the last. There could not have been two such remarkable adventures in the world!"

"But that book is *Bulfinch's Mythology!*" I blurted out. "The story you've been reading is a classic. Every high-school student knows the story about Perseus and the Gorgon's head. Medusa was a Gorgon—a beautiful woman who had snakes growing out of her scalp instead of hair, and terrible eyes that turned everyone she saw into stone. The princess Andromeda was carried off into captivity, and Perseus, the young warrior, went to rescue her. But to save her he first had to kill the Gorgon. He appealed to Minerva. the Goddess of Wisdom, and Minerva gave him winged heels so that he could fly. So he flew to the Gorgon's cave and killed Medusa—didn't look at her face, but watched her reflection in his polished shield, and cut off her head at one whack!"

"Only it was a mirror!" Old Thibaut Corday corrected fiercely. "Instead of a shield, I used a mirror. The mirror the old Kabyle woman gave me!"

"But I'm trying to explain," I cried, "that the story about Perseus and Medusa is a myth. It isn't an American story. You've been reading the translation of an ancient Greek legend that was told in Athens two thousand years ago!"

"Greek legend? Athens? Two thousand years ago?" The old Legion veteran brought his fist down on the table. "But it happened with me not ten years ago when I was in the *Premièr Régiment* of the French Foreign Legion, and it was right here in North Africa on the border of Algiers! This woman you call—what?—a Gorgon?—this Medusa! Well, she lived in a cave in the mountains not far from the pass of El Kantara in the territory of the Kabyles. This princess Andromeda was an Arab princess taken captive by an enemy tribe. And I cut off the head of that snake charmer, too—I, Old Thibaut Corday—in that very cavern full of people turned into stone!"

A two-thousand-year-old fable come to life in the French Foreign Legion! This leathery old French soldier of fortune in the role of Perseus, hero of ancient Greek mythology! An Arab princess as Andromeda, and a snake charmer living in a cave full of people turned to stone! There was a story behind the shine in the old veteran's eyes, and I wanted to hear it. I had an idea it would beat the translation in *Bulfinch's Mythology* a mile!

And Old Thibaut Corday had hardly begun before I knew Professor Bulfinch and the ancient Greek story-teller who invented the myth were going to be left far behind. Because they told the yarn as a fairy tale, and Old Thibaut Corday told it as truth—and just when I was about to call him a liar, he gave me a guarantee.

I DO not know anything about Greece or Athens (Old Thibaut Corday began, with a suspicious look at the book at his elbow). There was a Greek in my Legion company once, but he did not last long. His name was Rosenapopolous, and he was killed in a surprise attack his first week on campaign. An Arab crept up behind him, and the sergeant bellowed, "Look out, Rosenapopolous!" but before the sergeant could get out the name, the Greek was hamstrung.

Come to think of it, that was the very campaign of which I speak. On the border of Algeria near Tunis. In the territory of the Kabyles. These Kabyles are one of the fiercest of Arab tribes, which means they are the most backward and most superstitious—another way of saying the most holy. They are Mohammedans, and they are mountaineers, as fanatical as maniacs, as tough as the barren ranges they occupy, as merciless as vultures. When they are not fighting the other Arab tribes, they are fighting the French, and they keep in practice for both by fighting among themselves. *Alors,* now that France has pacified and cleaned up Tunis, Mussolini has decided that he wants Tunis for himself. The Romans once conquered Algeria and Tunis, and Mussolini likes to call himself a Roman. With this intent, he announces himself as a friend of the Arabs. Ha! The only Arabs who will associate with him are these renegade Kabyles. It seems Mussolini has forgotten it was the Arabs who threw out the Romans to begin with; it is only the Foreign Legion of France that can control North Africa.

So it is the usual uprising. Mussolini sends his secret agents among the Kabyle renegades, and tells them to fight a holy war. Do you think those mountain tribesmen need any urging? *Bang!* A train is dynamited. *Slash!* A French girl who has gone into the mountains to teach school has her throat cut. All this is very modern, our new diplomacy. Remains only for the War Department in Paris to put in a hurry call for the Foreign Legion.

Our detachment marched across Algeria, and we reached the mountain country of the Kabyles on the double quick. There the modern aspect of the campaign ended. Those mountains were old when the rest of this North African coast was cooling. They were old and burned-out and worn to the bone long before the Romans or the Arabs or Monsieur Mussolini or myself were ever heard of. Red iron crags and wind-swept ranges without a tree. Cliffs where the sun is a furnace by day, and one freezes at night. Peaks and canyons and boulders and rocks, and behind every rock a red-eyed Kabyle waiting to get a Foreign Legionnaire in the target sights of his gun.

Non, it was not the country to go marching in with a name like Rosenapopolous. Those Kabyle devils could strike like lightning and beat the echoes of their rifles on a disappearance. They jumped around on those rocky crags like goats. They vanished in the canyons like lizards going down a crack. We chased them, and we might as well have been chasing puffs of wind. We pursued them across precipices and into gorges, and we might as well have been pursuing shadows and ghosts. Rosenapopolous was not our only casualty on that expedition. Those Kabyle murderers made it hot for us from morning to night.

Even a name like Corday was too long. In a skirmish somewhere near the pass of El Kantara, I was captured. That was a hell of a thing, letting myself be captured by the Kabyles. We had been scouting up a canyon, and along in the middle of the afternoon I spotted one of those sharpshooting devils perched on a ledge up the canyon-wall like a hawk waiting for the mice to come along. The *salopard!* I let him have it. Lay on my stomach and trained my Lebel rifle on the speck of him visible up there, and let fly. *Bang!* That is war in the mountain country. What is it I have seen the children play in America—hide and seek? War in the mountain country is a game of hide and seek in which you must tag the enemy without ever giving him a chance to tag you.

But I did not kill the scoundrel. Instead of dying like a sportsman and a gentleman, he lay up there on that ledge and howled. Our heroes who stay home and draw the recruiting posters do not picture the enemy you have just shot as lying out in the sun somewhere, badly wounded and suffering. That Kabyle up there began to scream. He kept it up. I could see him sprawled as if his back were broken, and about every three minutes he uncorked a wail that did something to the muscles under my scalp.

I tried to walk away. I told myself that the devil deserved it. Besides, I had become separated from the rest of my companions, who had gone around a bend in the canyon and were busy with snipers around there. I could hear a lot of firing, and I started to join the skirmish, but the screams from the ledge came after me and held me back. *Dieu!* the fellow howled like a cat on a fence. It was hot up there on that cliff. He wanted a drink of water. Stuffing my fingers in my ears did not do any good. The trouble with me is, I am soft. *Non,* I am not a good soldier. I do not mind shooting at an enemy if he dies right away as he is supposed to. But if he lies down and screams from a broken back it hurts my conscience. At least I must return and finish the job.

SO I started across the canyon to finish the job, but that Kabyle scoundrel was not reasonable. He had fallen with his head behind a boulder, and I could not arrange him in my gun-sights. I had to climb the canyon-wall to reach him, and I did not like that. *Sacré!* I had to climb all the way to his ledge.

Now I am this kind of a fool. I can shoot a man from a half a mile away, but at fifteen feet it is something else again. At fifteen feet a man is no longer a target. Wounded with a bullet in his ribs and his rifle tumbled into a crevice, he is not even an adversary. *Non,* he is not even an Arab Kabyle. He is a man.

Worse than that, this brigand I had shot was a youth. Hardly with a beard on his chin. It did not matter if he had intended to murder me—*enfin,* he did not know any better. His parents had brought him up wrong, and his religion promised him a front seat in Paradise for every Unbeliever that he killed, and the agents of Mussolini had given him good Christian advice by telling him to dislike the French. For this he lay with his ribs broken by a bullet. Here was the result of his family training, his politics and his religion. He looked up at me with his big brown Arab eyes, and he begged in the Kabyle dialect for a drink of water.

"All right, here is a drink," I told him. "Also here is a bottle of iodine and a bandage, although I know very well that when you are back on your feet next month you will repay this silly sentimentalism by trying to kill me. I am sorry I did not shoot you through the head. With better luck I may be able to bring down your father."

I brought down his father, all right. *Sacré nom de Dieu!* Scarcely had I uttered the hope, when his father, his brothers, his uncles and about sixteen cousins came down from a rocky overhang above like an avalanche of demons on my head. Those infernal relatives of that Kabyle boy had heard his caterwauling, and they had come hot-footing to the rescue. *Thumpety-thump-thump-thump* their sandals landed on the ledge around me. I had no time to aim or even swing my gun. Those sheeted brigands jumped on me like spiders, and before I could budge a finger I was bound neck to foot in a web of leather rope.

I was sorry, then, I had pulled that little Red Cross stunt. You bet I was! That boy's father did not appreciate it. All he could figure was that I had shot his son, and he had a gleam in his eye as nasty as a tarantula. I was slung up and carried off like a trussed pig. Old Man Kabyle—he was a big black-whiskered pirate—carried his wounded boy in his arms, and off we went across the cliff-tops. I do not know where we went, but when evening came down we were still traveling. Up and down and over the rocky crags; in and out through narrow canyons; across a burned-out valley of huge boulders, and up a mountain wall as steep as the side of a building.

That was the hell of a trail. At every mile the mountains became more desolate, more barren, more like the middle of nowhere. Those tribesmen were taking me beyond any hope of rescue; taking me off the map. They were traveling like the wind, and pulling in their shadows behind them. And all the way along that trail, that black-whiskered Kabyle with his son in his arms kept turning his head to look at me. Sacred stove! what looks. His forehead knotted with rage. His black eyes coated with a shining enamel of hate. Ah, but there was a speculation in those black eyes, too. A thoughtfulness. An inspired cunning. I knew what he was doing, and the sweat poured out on my forehead like crème-de-menthe. He was inventing tortures, you understand. He was thinking up all the nice things he would do to me because I had put a bullet in his son. I knew it was going to go mighty hard with my arms and legs and nervous system when we got to that Kabyle camp.

YOU have heard the first rule of the French Foreign Legion? Never allow yourself to be taken alive by an Arab! Especially if that Arab happens to be a Kabyle. When it comes to torturing an enemy, a Kabyle can be twice as cruel as a Spanish aristocrat, and a Spanish aristocrat is the sort of man who can bomb a kindergarten and do it with a prayer. Only a Kabyle can be more cunningly savage. It was the Kabyles who invented burying a man up to his neck in sand and covering his head with honey to bring the ants. It was the Kabyles who invented stuffing a man's mouth with sticks of dynamite and lighting a long fuse that he could watch for three hours. I could see that my black-bearded captor was thinking up something new for my particular case. I was not wrong about it, either.

We reached the Kabyle camp at moonrise, and it was a picture I will not soon forget. The black felt tents of the Arabs pitched on a bare plateau. Purple mountains ringed around. Goats and mangy dogs and a collection of old hags waiting to see the show. My heart went through the bottom of my boots, I can tell you. When those old women saw that wounded Kabyle boy they set up a wailing that turned my blood to icewater. You know how Arab women can wail? *Hoo-hoo-hooooo!* Well, I found out something. Old Blackbeard was the sheik of this tribe! I had shot the son of the sheik! Not only that, it had been that boy's wedding day. His bride-to-be was the princess of a neighboring Kabyle tribe, and she was on her way through the mountains even then, due to arrive in camp for the marriage ceremony around midnight.

Figure to yourself what was going to happen to me for shooting the son of a Kabyle sheik on his wedding day! *Non!* but you could not figure it. The unconscious boy was carried into a tent, and then the lamentations of those women turned into foamings at the mouth. They wanted to claw me to pieces, but the sheik had a better idea. I must be saved for the wedding party that was coming over the mountains—the bride-to-be would doubtless enjoy stabbing me through the heart. Meantime I was to be made as uncomfortable as possible. Ah, yes. The sheik had thought up a number of ways to make me regret I had shot his son.

Presently I was pinned to the ground. Flat on my back with my hands and feet fastened to stakes. I believe the term is spread-eagled. My shirt was torn off, and in the process I had been scratched up a bit. Not fatally, of course, for the idea was to keep me fairly alive. With this in view, I was revived every time I fainted, and I fainted pretty often. I fainted when I realized my Legion comrades were miles away and never in the world could find this isolated mountain hide-out. I fainted when an old woman came out of a tent with a big brass bowl in her hands, followed by the sheik who arrived with a squeaking, biting rat in his grip. The bowl was placed upside-down on my stomach, and the rat was put under the bowl, and a little fire was built on top of the bowl. The invention was most ingenious. When the fire heated the bowl, it would get pretty hot inside, and the rat would start to dig. You will pardon me for fainting again.

Now you are probably wondering what all this has to do with a snake charmer and a beheading accomplished by a mirror and a cave full of people turned into stone. You are wondering what this has to do with this story of Medusa and Perseus. *Oui,* I see you are wishing I would get to that part of the adventure, and at last I am there. I do not like to talk of that rat-and-bowl incident, either.

To say the less of it, the bowl was just growing warm and the rat was spitting on his hands preparatory to picking up the shovel when there was an explosion of yells in the night, and the bridal party arrived. *You-wow!* They came into camp like that. Robes swirling, beards disheveled, the whole crowd hollering and leaping into the scene like a hurricane.

I was having my own troubles, but it came to me that something was wrong with this wedding bunch, something abnormal. The local Kabyles began to run around hollering to Allah, and Blackbeard the Sheik, who had been supervising my delicate operation, went over me with a bound, and rushed around in wild confab with the leader of the bride's crowd. Lucky for me, that tumult! In leaping my carcass,

Old Blackbeard kicked over the fiery bowl on my stomach. In the dust and excitement and uproar, *Monsieur* Rat scampered off hickory-dickory-dock. Sacred stove! But that was a close call for me. A terrible calamity had befallen this wedding party, it seemed. Through the bedlam I managed to learn that the bride had been kidnapped.

Perhaps you think I did not bless those kidnappers. Trooping through the mountains, the wedding party had been ambushed by an enemy tribe. Those Kabyles had more feuds on their social calendar than they could keep track of, and these enemy Arabs had shot up the procession and waltzed off with the bride. But this was something more than your ordinary kidnapping. I gathered it was a whole lot more. The captive bride was a princess, but she was not being held for ransom. The Arabs who had grabbed her were pretty sore at this particular Kabyle clan, and they were taking her to a witch of some kind—a sorceress who was going to give her the evil-eye.

"The Snake-Woman! The Snake-Woman!"

CHAPTER II.

THAT IS what the bride's party called her, and didn't those Kabyles howl to Allah at the mention of her name. *Dieu!* the whole camp got down and slammed their foreheads on the ground, and Old Blackbeard ran in a circle with his hands in the air, wailing to Allah.

"She is lost! The princess is lost! One look from the Snake-Woman's eye, and the princess will be turned into stone!"

Mon ami, I was just about done at that point, but when I heard Old Blackbeard yell that, I pricked up my ears. I told you those Kabyles were a superstitious bunch. So! And when Blackbeard yelled that business about the princess being turned into stone, there came to me a rumor I had heard in the Arab bazaars—one of those North African rumors that go whispering around the mosques and up the alleys of the *Kasbah* and in and out of the coffee dens to keep the population in a stew. What? A rumor about a wizardess who lived in a cave and had a stare that turned every man she saw into marble. A legend, of course. A yarn on the tongue of cameleers. But there was a little one-eyed rug merchant in Bou Saada who told me he had seen one of the victims this sorceress had petrified, and he swore by the three-fingered hand of Mohammed's wife that the story was true. I did not believe him, that liar! And I did not believe Old Blackbeard, the night of the kidnapping. But Blackbeard believed the business, I could see that, and I was mighty glad he did believe it. Running around in circles, he forgot about me. Those other Kabyles forgot about me, too.

"The princess will be turned into stone! Merciful Allah! The princess will be turned into stone!"

What a lament those devils set up. The women came out of their tents and tore their hair. The men ran up and down in their dirty robes, praying. In a sweat of terror and relief, I lay there spread-eagled, and I thanked heaven for this *brouhaha* which had thrown my captors into a panic.

"Save her!" The bride's father was leader of the ambushed party, and he howled at Blackbeard to do something. "How can we save her?"

"It is the custom to leave gold at the entrance to the Snake-Woman's cave!" Blackbeard moaned. "Much gold to appease the witch!"

"But it will leave me poverty-stricken," the bride's father wailed. "And when my brothers left such tribute at the mouth of the Snake-Woman's lair, their kidnapped children were never returned. Much gold have our tribesmen bestowed on this demoness. In the past to no avail!" He lifted his arms, squalling at his warriors in despair. "Five camels and ten hairs from the Beard of Mohammed to the man who rescues my daughter from the Snake-Woman's cave!"

"And I double the reward!" Blackbeard thundered. "Let the bravest of the Kabyles stand forward. As father of the warrior to whom the princess was betrothed, I double the reward for her rescue!"

Ten camels and all those sacred relics of Mohammed must have been a fortune to those mountain pariahs, but it did not bring the bravest of them forward. Those tribesmen swore and groaned and brandished their rifles, but I saw no volunteers. I began to comprehend that this Snake-Woman was a bugaboo of a pretty high order.

Alors, the father of the bride was on the verge of epilepsy. "By the Flames of Gehenna! is there no warrior among the Kabyles willing to chance his life for a princess of the blood of Mohammed? Is my daughter to pass into eternity accursed, spellbound in a bondage of stone? You!" he flung at Blackbeard, raving. "Where is this son of whom you boast? Where is this warrior to whom I gave my daughter in marriage—*aaaah,* that she was on her way to the wedding this very night! Is he son of a sheik or son of a jackal that he does not come forward to attempt his bride's deliverance!"

"Halouf ben halouf!" Blackbeard roared. "Father of a pig! Is my son to be blamed because he lies close to death with the bullet of an Unbeliever in his breast? The calamity on your house is only equaled by that on mine! If your daughter remains bewitched in stone, it is only for the wounding of my son—Allah save him—by the Infidel you see captive over there!"

HOLY Saint Catherine! That black-whiskered sheik pointed a finger at me, and the maddened crowd piled at me to shred me to pieces. "It is he! The Infidel, who has brought disaster upon us!"... "Allah's curse on this *Roumi* who has caused us this blight!"... "Butcher the French dog!"... "Cut out his eyes!"

Can you see me staked out on the ground, and that blood-thirsty wedding mob coming at me? Bones of the Little Corsican! I might have known those Kabyles would hold me responsible for everything. They had to wreak their vengeance on somebody, and I was it. If I wanted to live thirty more seconds I had to do some fast thinking, and I never thought faster in my life.

"Wait!" I screamed at Blackbeard, who was nearly on top of me with his knife. "I can save the kidnapped princess for you! I am not afraid of this Snake-Woman who turns your people into stone! Let me go to her cave, and I will return the princess to your tribe unharmed!"

How I ever got that out of my mouth, and in the Kabyle dialect besides, I do not know. But I screeched like a steam whistle, and the cry took effect. Those wolves stopped in their tracks, and Blackbeard came up short, his dagger not six inches from my nose.

"Pig!" he spat down at me. "Dog of a Christian, what do you know of this sorceress who changes men into rock with one look of her eye?"

"Only that the magic has no effect on a soldier of true courage! Behold!" I gave him. "I am unafraid! Tell me the lair of this witch, and I will go there single-handed where all your warriors fear to go. No woman as yet has been able to put the evil eye on me! Lead me to her, and I will return the lost princess to the tent of your son, in reward for which I ask only my life!"

That was a bold speech, was it not? The boldest I ever made. Also it was the sheerest bluff, one hundred percent bluff without a card in my hand to support it. But in a corner like that one must bid as if he held five aces. Too, I know Arabs. A plea for mercy is as useless before an Arab as a missionary's prayer would be on a tiger. Bluffers themselves, they are always surprised when they are met with bluff.

But surprised was not the word for it that night. They were stunned. There I was staked out on the ground like a carcass ready to be skinned alive, yet squalling that I was braver than they, offering to slay their witch-woman. It worked. By the very insolence, the unexpectedness of it, it worked.

"Hold!" That black-whiskered sheik flung up his hand. Rage on his face struggled with unbelief. "You hear what the Infidel has said?" he wheeled on the crowd. "Ha!" he flung at me. "You are willing, then, to face the Snake-Woman? By Allah's holy word! If you are as brave as you boast, perhaps we will give you this chance. Return the Princess Naja to her father unharmed, and my son's forgiveness for his injury will be assured. Attempt now to withdraw this bold offer, and you will be sorry!"

There was a glitter in his eye that convinced me I would be more than sorry if I backed down. And at the same time there was a gleam behind the glitter that suggested I was going to be sorry, anyway. That tarantula was accepting my offer a little too readily for my comfort. *Oui,* he was a little too quick on granting me this reprieve, and I had an idea that perhaps I had jumped from the frying pan into the fire.

But I had no time for subtleties, just then. All I wanted was to regain my feet from that spread-eagle posture. My stomach was on the verge of collapse from that rat-and-bowl business, and I was ready to grab at any straw to delay the murder that was waiting to pounce on me.

"Free me that I may start at once!" I bluffed, and louder. "Direct me to this evil-eyed spellbinder. But give me a weapon with which to slay her, and I will rid your people from her curse."

Old Blackbeard grinned at that. "You shall have my own scimitar," he assured me in a suddenly sweetened voice. "Up, dog of a Christian, and you will start at once!" Just to show me he was not quite my best friend, he spat in my face before giving his brigands the order to untie me.

I felt pretty blue when I was standing upright, however. Not for a minute could I stop bluffing, and I wanted to collapse from the strain.

Picture me bare to the belt, my britches torn to rags, my torso covered with welts, and a big red circle on my stomach where that brass bowl had branded me. I was plastered with dirt and my chin was bleeding. *Non,* I was hardly this hero called Perseus in the account which you say is a Greek fairy tale, but I will wager I outbluffed any Greek in any fairy tale that night.

"Lead me on!" I cried in the voice of a stage actor volunteering his life for Napoleon. "Where is this wizardess to be found?" I tell you, I swaggered in such a way that those Moslem devils stared at me in awe.

But old Blackbeard suspected a trick, and he was not going to give me a chance for any escaping act. He looped a rope around my neck, and clung to me as if I were a poodle on a leash. Never for a second was he forgetting I had put a bullet in his son.

"The Snake-Woman," he told me in that softened voice that was like poisoned sugar—"the Snake-Woman lives on the mountain, half a night's march distant. Do not think to evade us on the trail, for you go there as our captive until we reach the mouth of the cave. It is there I will give you my scimitar, and only for the sake of the Princess Naja will you proceed into the cave with Allah's blessing."

His black eyes glittered into mine as he gave me these instructions, and he concluded with a whisper that crawled into my ear like a cobra, "But I do not think Allah's blessing will avail. No man has ever returned alive from the Cave of the Petrified People."

WELL, that was encouraging, not so? To learn I had offered to visit a place from which no man had ever returned alive! It was a not cheerful prospect, just when I was trying to pump up a little courage. I did not like Blackbeard for telling me about the Cave of the Petrified People.

Even less did I like the looks of awe those other ruffians were giving me. There was a lot of whispering and hobnobbing, and a big murmur went through the crowd as Blackbeard gave a yank on my leash to signal the start. There was no doubt those devils thought I had taken the worse of two evils in choosing this Snake-Woman instead of ordinary death.

"The ignorant curs!" I said to myself. "They fear this woman, whoever she is, more than death, itself. Am I—a soldier of the Legion—to be unnerved by this superstitious Arab nonsense?"

Sacred pipe! I was lucky to be alive right then. It was no time to worry about witches. I told myself there was no such thing as witchcraft and men being turned into stone. North Africa was full of fake wonder-workers and hoodoo men, and some hag in a cave had fooled these primitive brigands into believing she had supernatural power.

Enfin, I must fool them, myself, and I squared my shoulders and tried to look like Saint George on his way to fight the Dragon. But as I stumbled off through the moonlight, on the end of Blackbeard's rope, I had a qualm. I was glad to be leaving that camp. You bet I was. Only it came to me that if there were such things as vampires, hoodoos and witch women, all of them inhabited those Kabyle mountains in North Africa.

Dead in daylight, those mountains at night were ghosts. In the moonlight the cliffs stood up white and sheer, while the canyons below were bottomless seas of ink. Pale peaks made a caravan of spectres under the stars; misshapen boulders were ghostly sentinels guarding the trail; fantastic black crags leaned down to watch us, like giants ready to pounce. A tremendous silence wrapped those mountains. As if every rock and stone and granite slab were holding its breath, listening. Once in Egypt I felt that same kind of hush come out of the Sphinx, and I would have given a thousand dollars to hear a bugle call in the middle of it as we marched from that camp that night.

But I did not hear any bugle calls, *mon gar'*. All I heard was the scuff of sandals, the whisper of Arab cloaks, the puffy breathing of my captors stealing along beside me, half invisible in the dark. That entire wedding crowd had come along to see the fun, and with Blackbeard tugging that rope around my neck, I staggered up the trail like a lost soul on his way to Hades with an escort of apparitions.

I did not like the walk old Blackbeard took me on that night. At places the trail followed the rim of a precipice, an abyss so black and deep that when a pebble went over the edge it was absorbed as if by a vacuum. There was a canyon barely wide enough to squeeze through, and a ladder of jagged crags where a misstep would have plunged one into an ocean of nothing. We saw no goats or jackals on that trip—they had all been killed by falling off those cliffs. It was a nasty piece of mountain climbing with a rope around my neck and that mob of cutthroats clinging to my heels. I began to wonder if I would not have been safer on the ground with my arms and legs tied to stakes.

"Where are the fiends taking me?" I groaned in my mind. "I can believe no man has returned alive from this witch's cave; what man could get there alive to begin with?"

The altitude was making me dizzy up there under the moon, and at the same time the silence was working on my imagination. Suppose this Snake-Woman did have some evil power? I had boasted a little when I declared that no woman had ever put the eye on me. Now that I was nearing the cave of the hag, my counterfeit confidence was failing me. I remembered how the little one-eyed rug merchant in Bou Saada had rolled his eye, describing the powers of this witch. Certainly the creature must have had something up her sleeve to frighten these bandits. As we neared her lair, my escort began to stare and peer as if they saw all the spectres of Tophet in the moonlight ahead.

"Slowly!" Blackbeard wheeled suddenly with uplifted finger. "We are almost there. Should the Snake-Woman be out of her hole, she might turn us all into marble at a glance."

ANOTHER time I might have laughed at the way those Kabyle gunmen hung back on the path. But I did not laugh that night. There was a witchery in the silence of those mountains, something that made me break out in goose pimples. I could hear the father of the kidnapped bride moaning prayers to Allah. Around me my captors muttered in fear. Blackbeard gave a jerk on my halter, and ordered me to walk ahead of him. I walked ahead, and the sheeted crowd came creeping at my heels like hunters moving up on a lion's den behind a decoy. I was the decoy, and I did not like the part. The trail climbed on and up through a jungle of silent rocks, and every few feet Blackbeard would give me a kick to hurry me up. I cursed myself for having sniped at his son, I can tell you. I cursed myself double for the Red Cross-nurse act that had invited my capture.

Alors, the path made a sudden upward twist, and Blackbeard gave a yank on the leash. "There is the place!" he snarled from behind me. "Go up the mountainside and look in, you dog. Demonstrate the courage of which you brag." He was paying out the rope in his hands to let me go forward, and I saw in the mountain ahead an opening that looked like the door of a coal mine. If you think I wanted to look into that opening, you are wrong. But it was either that or Blackbeard, so I took the opening.

Do you know how the entrance of a coal mine looks at night? Well, that mouth in the mountainside was like a mine-shaft. A square door shored up with slabs of granite, and then a shaft that dipped down into the mountain at an angle of ninety degrees. Moonlight fell down into the shaft as far as darkness at the bottom, and there was a tunnel down there, and the blackness in that tunnel was the darkest black I had ever seen. I got a whiff of air that smelled as though it had been buried about ten thousand years, and I pulled back my head with a gasp of fear.

"The tunnel," Blackbeard called to me, "leads into the Cave of the Petrified People. Lucky for you the Snake-Woman was not out."

"But how can I go down and kill her?" I asked hopefully. "There are no steps to descend."

"We will let you down on the rope," Blackbeard snarled. "That is how the Snake-Woman's victims are brought to her. They are let down on a rope, and then the rope is cut so they cannot climb out. Shots drive them into the tunnel where the Snake-Woman seizes them. They never return."

That black-mawed cave sucked in his words and echoed them. A hundred voices seemed to mumble, "Never—"

The father of the kidnapped girl wrung his hands. "Hurry, hurry!" he cawed at me. "There is yet a chance the Snake-Woman has not transformed my daughter. It is written that one is safe while the Snake-Woman sleeps, for the magic is in her eye. *Mektoob!* It may be she is still asleep."

"The shots always wake her up," Blackbeard said grimly. "She catches her victims in the tunnel and turns them to stone. I have gone down to spy in the tunnel, and I have seen."

"And how am I to get out when the witch is slain?" I asked.

Blackbeard nodded fiercely. "We will wait for you. I have given my oath, and we will wait until sunrise. Return with the Princess Naja, and we will haul you out. Fail, dog! and you remain here to eternity."

Nom de Dieu! it was either remaining in that hole until eternity, or going to eternity then and there on the mountain-side. Any way I looked at it, eternity was staring me in the face, but I decided I would rather be petrified than chopped to pieces. So I went down.

CHAPTER III.

I DID not go on winged heels as in the Greek legend. The wings on my heels came later. I went down that moonlit mine-shaft on a strong piece of hemp, and when I reached the bottom I learned where that expression comes from—to be at the end of one's rope. I was at the end of my rope when I faced that black tunnel, I can tell you. All the way up the mountain I had been wildly planning how I might hack my way out of the mob at the moment Blackbeard gave me his scimitar, as promised. But that sheik was too smart for me again. He told me I would receive the blade when I reached the bottom of the mine-shaft and the rope was hauled up, and he went on to add that some day he would come down and get it out of my marble hand.

He was afraid to go near that mine-shaft, you comprehend. The rope was looped under my arms; twenty feet from the mine-mouth, Blackbeard and his crowd stood back to pay it out; I went down with a series of jerks that almost broke my neck. Then when the rope was hauled up, Blackbeard sent his wife to throw down to me the scimitar.

Picture me at the bottom of that shaft—when I looked up and saw the wrinkled face of an Arab woman peering down at me. "*Roumi,*" she called in a low, hoarse voice. "Here is the blade!"

That did not surprise me, for I know how Arabs treat their wives. But instead of a blade, she was clutching a piece of glass in her downstretched hand. A little round piece of glass that reflected the moonray. I thought Old Blackbeard was playing me some trick, and my heart went through the soles of my boots. Then I heard the old woman's whisper.

"Catch the mirror, *Roumi.* Do not let it break. You tried to help my son after you shot him, and now I will try to help you. A mirror is your only chance against the Snake-Woman."

Well, that surprised me a bit. I had been cursing myself for that Red Cross stunt, and I was staggered by the old Arab woman's gratitude. I was so surprised that I caught the little mirror as she let it fall. I gripped it tight and tilted my face to hear her speak again.

"Do not look at the Snake-Woman," came her low-voiced call. "Do not look at her face, but watch her in the mirror. One stare from her eye would change you into stone." She pulled up her face-cloth hurriedly. "The Black Sheik would kill me for helping you, but you saved the life of our son."

Then she threw down the scimitar. The big blade struck near my boots with a clang, and I snatched it up and spun at the tunnel-mouth, expecting God knew what to rush out at me. Nothing rushed out.

Nothing but blackness and a silence that made the hush on the mountainside din-like in comparison. I lifted my eyes to the opening overhead, but the old Arab woman was gone. Can you see me at the bottom of that moony shaft, scimitar clutched in one hand, mirror in the other, staring up at a little patch of night and stars? In front of me was that tunnel, a black throat breathing stale air. I did not want to go into that tunnel after a kidnapped Arab princess, my friend.

But if I was not back with the princess by sunrise, I would stay in that hole till eternity. Clutching scimitar and mirror, I said good-by to Thibaut Corday, and I crept into the tunnel.

NOW that tunnel was a detail they left out in the story of Perseus. Me, I think this Perseus had it soft. There was no time-limit set on Perseus, and he did not go through a tunnel. I wish I could describe to you my feelings as I went into that corridor in the earth, but it would take a nerve specialist to describe them. Consider what I had been through before I started that underground stroll. But that rat-and-bowl incident and the close shave from being flayed to death—those were pleasantries compared to the nerve-strain of that tunnel.

I do not suppose they had tunnels like that in Greece. Only in North Africa would you find such a thing. They talk of the St. Goddard Tunnel in the Alps. Well, that subway in the Kabyle Mountains was dug a few years before the St. Goddard job. Quite a few years before! My boots in that passage stirred a dust as thick as smoke, and the air was staler than the atmosphere in a pharaoh's tomb.

Black? It was so black in that passage that I thought I had gone blind. I put out a hand and groped along the wall, moving like a mole. The tunnel zig-zagged and bent, and at each successive bend I expected something terrible to happen. But nothing happened. Every few seconds I would stop to listen. I could hear nothing. A few steps farther on I would halt to peer. I could see nothing. There are times, my friend, when nothing is worse than something, and that was one of the times. The suspense was terrific. Sweat poured down my forehead, and blood pounded in my ears. After about twenty minutes of creeping along like a blind man in a haunted catacomb, I would have welcomed anything. A dozen times I started to turn back, but the thought of seeing sunrise over that mine-shaft pushed me on.

"There is no such thing as witchcraft!" I kept saying to myself. "There is no such thing as a woman's eye which changes men to stone."

And another thought bolstered my bluff. Perhaps I could find a side-passage, an exit, an escape from this subterranean hole. Hope springs eternal in the human breast, not so? I grabbed at that idea as a drowning man at a straw. *Dieu!* I fumbled along that invisible wall praying for an exit like one of those drainage mains which are offshoots of the Paris sewers. Funny how the wish is father to the thought. The more I wished for it, the more I became convinced I would find such an exit. The hope stiffened my legs. I hurried my pace. Presently I was walking faster. In that blind tunnel of zigzags and bends, I began to run. I was getting away! I had bluffed myself out of the Black Sheik's clutches, and I was going to get out of this tunnel.

Perhaps I even laughed a little at how easy it would be, for I have a memory of laughter that mocked the blank walls. The scimitar sweated in my hand and I told myself, "You'll find the way, Corday!"

Then, *bump!* Headlong I ran into an obstacle that hurled me backward in the dark. Solid rock that got in my way. A wall? Blindly I put out my hand, groping. The passage made a bend, there, and I had collided with a projecting boulder. The thing jutted out to block my path like a knee. Cursing, I ran my hand over the smooth curve of stone, trying to squeeze my way around. My blind hand went over the stone, and froze. It was a knee!

My friend, I jerked my hand away and stood there in the dark with every hair at attention on my head. In the blackness I had palmed a woman's knee! Do you think a soldier of the French Foreign Legion could mistake such an article? But no Legionnaire had ever come across a knee like that one! That was a stone knee—a marble knee! There was a woman there in that black tunnel, and her short skirt was blown back above her knee, and she was running. Only she wasn't running. In that pose she did not move an inch. She was frozen in stone.

And for the wink of an eye I, too, was petrified.

Who wouldn't be?

Monsieur believes that I collided with a stone woman there in that tunnel? Too polite, *monsieur.* I see you are skeptical, but I tell you I am speaking the truth. I was skeptical, too, at first. Recovering from shock, I groped out again, and caught an arm. I figured this was my imagination, also. Until I put my hand on her face. That convinced me, on my oath! She had been running in my direction, and she was running still—in rock.

"The princess!" All the breath leaked out of me at that. The woman was wearing an Arab robe, and that was stone, too. "It must be the Arab princess, and the Snake-Woman caught her trying to escape."

Can't you hear me mumbling those words as I jittered there?

NOW we are coming to the part where I had wings on my heels. The panic that came over me gave me wings. *Oui,* I flew. But in terror I failed to realize that I had squeezed past the woman and was running in the wrong direction. That tunnel had so many twists and bends I did not realize I was going toward the Snake-Woman's cave. The shock of that woman in the passage had put out of commission the compass in my head. I had not gone fifteen bounds before I ran into another obstacle. *Slam!* Head-on, I collided with a fat man.

He was dressed in Arab robes, too, and he was carrying a spear and he had a curly beard. I know he had a beard, because I tried to grab it. But it was not a beard of hair, my friend, and his stomach was not soft like the stomachs of other fat men. It was a beard of stone and a stomach as hard as concrete, and he was standing there at the side of the passage as stiff and stupid as a Prussian guardsman on parade.

I leaped back from him with a yell that made the echoes a hundred wailing banshees. I leaped and ran.

I do not know what direction I went after that. Terror robbed me of my senses. That tunnel was a black, insane nightmare, and I fled like a sightless idiot through a crowd. *Oui,* there were other figures in that passage. Men and women running, crouching, doubled in postures of agony or standing rigid in fear. I collided with them at the turns; brushed past them on the straightaway. They did not move, those creatures in that tunnel. They were so much stone. I ran full-tilt into a child, and my blade clanged sparks against his face as if I had struck an anvil.

I went mad with fright in that tunnel. It is bad enough bumping into people in the dark, but when you know those people are not flesh and blood, it is something else. *Mère de Dieu!* I rushed on in a daze of terror, and then suddenly I was in a place where I almost lost what remained of my sanity.

The tunnel made a sharp leftward bend, and I rushed out into the middle of it before I could stop. Into the middle of what? Into the middle of a great domed cavern, a vast underground room as big as the interior of Notre Dame. It was lighted like a cathedral, too—which is to say, dim and shadowy with hushed blue shafts of light slanting down from above, corners shrouded in darkness, arches indistinct in gray dusk. But there were no gentle candles to relieve this gloom. The illumination was moonlight sifting through a great crack in the ceiling, an eerie incandescence from half a million miles overhead. And, as in a cathedral, the cavernous hush was broken by a low, murmurous buzzing; but the sound did not come from people telling their beads.

Non, the people in that cavern were not saying their prayers. They were not saying anything. There must have been a hundred of them there in the dimness, and their silence was the silence of the deaf and dumb and dead. It was a silence more extraordinary than death, for those people were posed in attitudes of life. Robed warriors there were, poised to throw uplifted spears. Women hugging children in their arms. A nude girl with an urn on her shoulder, looking sideways in fear. An old man bent on a staff, peering near-sightedly over an upraised lantern. In a far, dark corner a half-naked man—a porter evidently—in the act of escaping around a pillar with a huge round bundle on his back. A staring fellow with a pitchfork in his hands.

All these and more, a company frozen in dread, stood guard in that whispering chamber of horrors.

Word of honor, there were animals in it, too. A deer had somewhere wandered into that place, and the huntress who had followed the beast had just laid her hand on the animal's neck. It had happened a long time ago, I could see. The huntress carried a bow and arrow, and judging from the cobwebs, she looked as if she had been there for ten thousand years. All those people were covered with cobwebs, coated with dust. *Oui,* they leaped and crouched and ran and brandished spears in a hundred different poses of action, but their gestures were motionless; dust coated their bulging muscles and straining thighs. They had been caught, you comprehend. Like Lot's wife who had looked back and been turned into salt, those people had been petrified. Only they had been turned into stone.

Seeing those stone corpses, I almost turned into stone, myself. No such thing as witchcraft? Well, I wish you could have seen those people posed there in the gloom, their expressions fixed in marble, their gestures trapped in stone. *Dieu!* It needed but a key to unlock that spell—a magic word to bring them back to life, the spearmen throwing, the huntress catching that deer, the women running with their babes. A terrible sorcery had mummified those people into solid rock. You would have believed in sorcery, too, had you seen that crowd in the moon-shadowed dimness of that vast, eerie cavern, *monsieur.*

And the murmuring buzz that was like the muffled droning of prayer? Well, that murmuring buzz was the warning signal of a congregation of reptiles. Listen! That cavern was alive with snakes. As my vision cleared a little from the first daze of shock, I saw the floor of that cave was crawling. Did this fiction character, Perseus, have anything like that? He did not! The only snakes he had to contend with were in the Gorgon woman's hair; me, I saw a whole den of reptiles, hundreds of snakes. Fat snakes and thin snakes. Long snakes and short snakes. Rattlesnakes, *monsieur!* Everywhere! That rock-walled cavern was a perfect breeding ground for the things; they hung from every cornice, coiled in corners, writhed out of cracks in the wall, wriggled around the ankles of the stone people.

I tell you, that cave was humming and droning like a beehive, and those snakes were getting angrier by the second. Something in a distant corner had disturbed them. Heads up and buzzing, they were swarming around a stone pedestal like a mass of cooking spaghetti, and when I saw what was on that pedestal the last bit of bluff leaked out of me. There was a figure on that pedestal, a white-robed woman standing rigid with her hands up over her face. At first I thought she was stone like the other figures in the dimness; then I saw the figure was alive.

A girl! A flesh and blood girl, in a pose of terror, too frightened to move. *Ventre bleu!* when I saw the gleam of moonlight on her dark young hair, I could feel my own limbs numbing. About sixty snakes had surrounded her pedestal, and there was enough poison in that stewing batch to have killed every girl in North Africa.

CHAPTER IV.

"JUMP!" I screamed in Kabyle. "The snakes are climbing up the pedestal! Jump!" That was a fool thing to do because it woke up every snake in the place. The murmur became a tremendous rattling, as if a horde of unseen voodoo doctors were shaking their skeletal beads.

The Arab girl's scream, smothered by her fingers, hardly reached me. "I cannot jump!" she wailed. "I dare not take my hands from my face. The Snake-Woman will see me!"

That gave me something to choke on. You bet it did. I was not afraid of those rattlesnakes. I had on my elephant-hide Legion *brodequins*—those big nail-studded marching boots that come up to the calf and are thick enough to ricochet a bullet. Snakes were something within my experience. What I could not cope with were those people of stone, the wizardry that had petrified them.

"Where is the Snake-Woman?" I bawled. Believe me, I was peering into the glooms ahead of me, expecting any second to be stacked up in marble. I did not see any demoness there, and the anticipation was something I could not stand. "Where is she hiding? Where?"

Then, before the Arab girl could answer, I saw her. I saw her in the mirror which I was clutching in my numbed left hand. She was behind me, you comprehend. Emerging from an aperture in the cavern wall; stepping through a curtain of gray cobwebs out onto a big marble platform furnished with a marble throne. *Oui,* she came out through the spiderwebs like a queen from behind a portiere, but the wickedest ruler in history never made such an entrance. Never!

Let me live to be ten million, and I will not forget the creature who walked out on that platform. Just the sight of her in a mirror made me wish I was back in that Kabyle camp with a bowl-prisoned rat on my appendix. That witch was twice the bulk of an ordinary woman. Built like an Amazon. But then, from throat to ankles cloaked in an evil purple mantle, a billowing shapeless robe that might have been robbed from the shoulders of a long-dead monarch, heavy with mildew and green decay.

This Gorgon called Medusa in the story of Perseus—at least she had a figure. My North-African witch was a bloated monstrosity. Only in her face was there the semblance of anything feminine—a dead white face expressionless as a plaster death-mask save for bulging, cruel eyes that rolled between hooded white lids like the eyes of a crocodile. Then around her neck, like a fur, a coiled rattlesnake! Another looped over her left shoulder, and a third wrapped around her left arm. But those were nothing to the viperous mass of her coiffure, the writhing tangle of little rattlesnakes that hissed out of her scalp, wriggled around her ears, hung down over her brow like a tumble of curls. *Dieu!* that creature was a figment of delirium tremens. The Gorgon of Perseus was a beauty alongside the one I saw. And the Gorgon of Perseus was fiction, whereas the one I beheld that night was real!

I could see her coming across that platform like a living nightmare. I could see the vipers coiling in her scalp. I could feel the penetration of her eyes on the back of my neck. That hoodoo did not know I could see her. Stealthily she moved, skirting the marble throne, down the stone steps of the platform, toward me on soundless feet. *Brrrrrr!* I was freezing. There was a flash reflected in the mirror—scimitar coming out of her cloak. Silently she produced the blade. Crept up on me to do murder.

NOW I know you will not believe this, but I could feel the marrow stiffening in my skeleton, the muscles hardening in my heart, the cement setting in the arteries of my arms and legs. The cement of terror, you will say. Perhaps. I am still not sure. I have an idea that if the Arab girl had not screamed when she did, I might today be rooted in that cavern, a mummy in stone, petrified and dust-covered like those fossilized figures which stood around me.

But the Arab girl screamed. That saved me. That, and the mirror.

One of those snakes had oozed up on the pedestal where the girl was perched, and she gave a scream that would have broken the spell on the Sphinx. It kicked me out of paralysis just in time. *Oui,* I whirled just in time to dodge the Gorgon's blow, and that monster, not realizing I had seen it in the mirror, was taken by surprise. The scimitar aimed at my skull missed me by a hair. I do not like to recall that big blade slicing past my face. If it had sliced down on my skull, it would have halved me like a sausage, and I would not be here to tell you what happened after that in the Cave of the Petrified People.

But I am not exactly certain of what happened after that. That blade zipped by me like a streak of dark lightning, and something snapped in my head. I do not know what it was that snapped, but the human mind can stand only a certain amount of terror. Go beyond that point, and a man begins to laugh. I laughed when that butcher-blade missed my skull. I shrieked a laugh to match the hideous death-mask look on that Gorgon's face, and I cut at that snaky head with my own scimitar—*zaff!*—a slash which missed, but made that snake charmer scream.

That Gorgon screamed and drove a blow at my middle that would have felled a pine tree. I can show you the scratch made by that Gorgon's scimitar where it was aimed to cut me in two. It bisects the circle branded on me by Blackbeard's heated bowl. My stomach had a bad time of it that night, my friend. A very bad time. *Slash, slash, slash,* that Gorgon's blade took three cuts at me before I could recover my wind, and each slash made me jump backward like a frog in reverse.

The last jump sent me crashing into one of those stone figures, and then I went berserk. Do you understand why? Well, there were a hundred people in that cavern around me turned into rock, but that Gorgon had not petrified me at first glance. Rushing me, its eyes were glaring like the eyes of a charging rhinoceros, but something had gone wrong with the magic, and that monster knew it. I knew it, too. Clutching my scimitar in both hands, I sprang to meet the rush. Blade for blade, I met the fiend. Slash for slash, the scimitars clashing together in midair. Sparks showering. Steel ringing on steel. Step by step, I drove the Snake-Woman back. In the center of that cavern we fought like maniacs, *monsieur.*

Can you visualise such a battle in that gloomy crypt? The smashing moon-curved blades? That snaky-haired Gorgon whirling, dodging in a swirl of purple robes? One Legionnaire mad as a hatter, swinging wildly to decapitate that monster? That silent audience of stone people standing around? Snakes hissing from every crevice in the floor. The Arab princess screaming on her pedestal? That Arab girl's screams got into my heart, *mon ami,* and pumped new blood into my exhausted arms. I was fighting for two lives in that terrible cave, and I battled as that hero in this fiction story never did.

Oui, I could see that Arab girl from the corner of my eye, a big hamadryad inching its scaly length up the pedestal to reach her. I fought the Snake-Woman then! Lashing criss-cross with my scimitar, I made the monster dance. I saw fear come into those sorcerous, cruel eyes. Heard the wheeze and whistle of the creature's tiring breath. Screeching, she dodged behind the stone huntress with the deer, and I hurdled the animal to get at her. In and around the petrified people we duelled, circling the frightened girl with the urn on her shoulder, the staring fellow with the pitchfork, the motionless mothers hugging their children, the posed warriors immovably gesturing with their spellbound weapons.

It was one of those poor stone creatures that came to my aid in the end. A kneeling woman whose outstretched supplicating hand caught a fold of the Gorgon's robe and held the creature fast in a grip of granite. For a piece of wizardry, I give you that, *monsieur.* That a woman of stone should have captured and tripped the Gorgon! Yanked backward, the monster thought I had caught hold of the robe. Whirling with a squall, she slashed out wildly and whanged the stone woman a tremendous cut across the face. Sparks blazed as the ringing weapon shivered out of the Gorgon's grasp. At one bound I was on her. I drove a cut at that viper-wigged woman which would have sheared the head from an ox. All the fury of madness was behind that swipe, and I did not miss that time. The Gorgon did not have time to duck, and I did not have time to miss.

BLOOD sprayed in a geyser, and when I opened my eyes to look, I saw the Snake-Woman salaaming, headless. Never will I forget that headless, bending body, or the thing that rolled around on the floor at my feet. I give you my word, the basket-robber who attends the guillotine would have blanched at sight of that head.

Can you guess what had happened to that Gorgon's head, *monsieur?* There is nothing similar in this tale translated by Bulfinch. What had happened to that Gorgon's head was something extraordinary, even for a Gorgon! On the shoulders of that Snake-Woman it had been the head of a female. In leaping from those shoulders it had sprouted a man's beard. It had sprouted a set of black whiskers, I tell you, and when it hit the floor that woman's face had come off like a leaf shucked off of a cabbage. The white, plaster face and the coiffure of curly snakes had shucked off, and underneath that woman-faced death mask was another, a black-whiskered death mask—the face of a man!

I got out of that cavern then. I kicked that black-whiskered Gorgon's head under the stone woman who had captured him, and I grabbed up the woman-mask and rushed to rescue the Arab girl. The snake-headed thing in my clutch was merely plaster, but the snakes attacking the Arab princess were not, and I snatched her off that pedestal only in the nick of time.

"The Snake-Woman!" she screamed when she saw that thing in my hand. "Name of Allah! you have slain the Snake-Woman!"

I did not bother to disillusion her, you comprehend. I carried her across that cave of rattlesnakes and stone people; raced her through the tunnel. Wings on my heels? Airplane propellers, *monsieur!* Dawn was pink and blue in the mine-shaft when I got there, and how those Kabyle brigands shouted when they hauled me out with the Gorgon's head and the girl.

I did not bother to disillusion them, either. They carried me down the mountain on their shoulders, whooping and dervishing and firing salutes with their rifles, and promising me a great celebration as soon as the Black Sheik got back.

"And where is the Black Sheik?" I asked.

"He went off scouting by himself in the night," the bride's father told me. "He wanted to trail the kidnappers who ambushed our wedding party. He did not believe you would return from the Cave of the Petrified People."

The Kabyles were sorry when I explained that I could not wait for Blackbeard to come back and celebrate. I wish you could have seen my triumphal return to civilization. They carried me on their shoulders to within sight of a Legion outpost—me, clutching that snake-headed plaster mask aloft—and when they set me down, the kidnapped bride wanted to kiss me.

"Conqueror!" she called me. "Warrior of warriors! Killer of the Snake-Woman!"

WHO was I to tell her I had merely slain her father-in-law? Far be it from me to disillusion a Kabyle tribe about their sheik. Ah, that black-whiskered rascal! Many a pot of gold he must have gathered as tribute for his Snake-Woman act, sneaking down into that cavern by means of some secret entry, collecting the offerings of his superstitious tribesmen, consigning his kidnapped victims to the rattlesnakes. Do you think an Arab might not order the kidnapping of his intended daughter-in-law? But those Kabyles had banded in friendship with Mussolini—all men are known by the company they keep.

Neither did I explain to the colonel how I had managed my escape. There is an insane hospital for Legionnaires, and I was not anxious to be stationed there. When the colonel asked me how I had escaped, I told him a snake charmer had sneaked me through the Kabyle lines.

"You must have used your head," the colonel guessed.

But he did not guess which one. Only one other person saw that Gorgon's head, and quite by accident. You recall the Greek, Rosenapopolous, who had been killed at the start of that campaign? His father. The father of Rosenapopolous, come to Algiers seeking word of his son. He wanted the boy to return to Athens, and when the colonel informed him I had been at the action, where his son was killed, he came wandering into the barracks to question me. I was alone in the billet. Unpacking that plaster mask to hide it in my blanket roll. That Greek spied it with a yell.

"Praxiteles!"

"What is that?" I asked.

"It means I will give you five thousand dollars, *monsieur,* if you will take me to the place where you found that mask!"

I looked at him drearily. Not for fifty thousand dollars would I have gone back to that cave. Not for fifty million. Besides, the father of the kidnapped bride had ordered his tribesmen to blow up the place with dynamite, and on reaching the Legion outpost where those Kabyles had delivered me, I had heard somewhere in the distances a tremendous explosion. So I did not go back there with that Greek who was so quick to forget all about his dead son. I have never been able to find out what he meant by *Praxiteles,* but if he meant all the gold in the world, I would not have returned to that Cave of the Petrified People.

There was witchcraft in that cavern, my friend. Perhaps Blackbeard the sheik was a fake, but the wizard who had transformed those people into stone was no fake. I wish you could have seen those figures coated by the dust of centuries, spellbound in the midst of action. Instead of calling me a liar, as your eyes are calling me now, you would believe every word of this story. That it did not happen in Greece two thousand years ago does not signify that it did not happen ten years ago to me in the country of the Kabyle.

OLD Thibaut Corday brought his hand down, *whack!* on *Bulfinch's Mythology,* and reared to his feet in stiff-shouldered indignation. My apologetic, "Wait!" was answered by a snort, and the old Legion veteran was through the door and gone in the Algerian twilight before I could salve his wounded feelings.

But presently he was back—having marched the distance to his *pension* in a surprisingly short time for his rheumatic legs—back grim-eyed, panting, a bundle wrapped in newspaper under his arm.

He surveyed me with a glance that had scorn and triumph burning in it to fry away my feeble grin. Upon the drink-ringed table he placed the bundle, and stood back with a gesture that Salome might have used.

"Skeptic!" he snapped at me. "You Americans! Always skeptic! Well, here is something for your skepticism, my friend. Regard that!"

I regarded it, all right. Wrappings torn off, it stared up at me with its sightless, empty-slitted eyes. Medusa's snaky head. A plaster mask in perfect preservation. A livid, life-like beauty!

I expelled a fervent breath.

Old Thibaut Corday was right; he *had* seen witchcraft in that cavern. The sorcery of a wizard who could, indeed, capture men and women in stone. But I did not tell the old Frenchman that the Romans (as boasted by Mussolini) had once conquered those mountains of North Africa. That the Romans had carried with them the looted treasures, the culture, the legends of a previously conquered Greece. That among those legends was the story of Perseus and the Gorgon (which must have been incorporated in Arab lore), and among the treasures were those figures he had seen in that underground cave: the marble Gods of ancient Athens—Diana the Huntress—Poseidon with his tines—Atlas weighted by the world upon his shoulders—Dionysus and Aphrodite and Hermes.

"There is no mistake about it," I agreed, staring at the plaster mask. "You are right, Old Thibaut Corday. It is sorcery."

But I did not tell him it was the sorcery of Praxiteles, greatest sculptor of all time. I did not want to disillusion the old Frenchman. When those Kabyles dynamited that cave he had discovered, they blew to pieces about ten million dollars worth of ancient Greek statuary.

THE WONDERFUL LAMP OF THIBAUT CORDAY

LISTEN WHILE THE BEARDED SCHEHEREZADE OF THE LEGION SPINS THE TALE OF THE WEIRDEST ARABIAN ADVENTURE THAT MAN HAS EVER LIVED TO TELL. HERE IS THE LAMP THAT ALADDIN MIGHT HAVE OWNED, HERE IS THE GENIE OF MIRACULOUS GIFTS, AND HERE, FOR GOOD MEASURE, IS THE GREEN-EYED WOMAN WITH A SONG SWEET ENOUGH TO LURE A LATTERDAY SINBAD TO A THOUSAND DEATHS.

CHAPTER I.

"I WAS reading the other day about the memory of man." Old Thibaut Corday tapped his forehead significantly. "How amazingly far back it goes. *Par example,* dragons. In this modern age we say, 'Pouf!' to stories about dragons; then some explorer digs up the bones of some huge animal sixty feet long. Some ancient ancestor saw this monster and called it a dragon, and the story came down through the centuries in the memory of man, so many centuries it finally was not believed. So with other wonderful things we disbelieve as myths. Like sea serpents, or the Little People."

"What about sea serpents and the Little People?"

Old Thibaut Corday scowled learnedly. "Why, there were such things. Have not our scientists reported huge marine snakes in the far Pacific? As for the Little People of Ireland, it has recently been discovered that the original inhabitants of Ireland were dwarfs. Three or four feet tall, they roamed the island long before the Celts arrived. Today these extinct dwarfs are remembered in legends, old wives' tales told in every Irish hut."

"Corday," I explained to the young British consular agent, "is propounding this new theory that most of our traditional myths have a scientific basis in fact. Bedtime stories aren't told at bedtime these days. They're discussed in the laboratory and placed under examination."

"Exactly." Old Thibaut Corday thumped the table. "They are not in our history books, these legends. But what child has not heard of giants, witches, wizards? A fairy story, the child is told. Yet now we are discovering that these legends are more than imaginary. These legends are recollections, so to speak. Of long-extinct marvels. Of one-time actualities."

The young British consular agent smiled. "Next thing you know, Corday, you'll be believing in Old Mother Hubbard and the Arabian Nights?"

"About Grandmother Hubbard I do not know, but I do believe in the Arabian Nights!"

The old Frenchman's eyes blazed with conviction, and I had to suppress a chuckle, myself.

"You think they are so fantastic?" He glared. "You laugh at my credulity. But I think the Arabs have their memories, too. And what is an airplane, then, but a Magic Carpet? Who knows but what some sailor named Sinbad, many centuries ago, traveled about on some manner of flying kite? Today there are doors that open from the vibration of a voice. Who knows that the door to Ali Baba's cave did not open by some such vibration trick?

"Mind you"—Old Thibaut Corday raised a finger—"I do not say they were miracles without an explanation. I say they came down through the ages as *seeming* miracles. Such things happened and were remembered. Like the marvelous tale the woman with the emerald eyes told me."

"And did you live happy ever after?" The Englishman grinned.

"It was not so funny as you think," the old Frenchman snapped. "It was one of those Arabian Nights stories, and I thought it was only a nursery tale. Then I found out differently, and I was lucky to live afterwards at all. What? Have I never told you about the genie who came at my summons? The genie who gave me a wish, and the wish came true?"

And there they were, that howling Arab pack, ravening to send us spinning down to death.

Round-eyed, the young British consular agent stared. At the old Legion veteran across the table, then at the wine bottle at Corday's elbow. "Genie? Came at your summons? Gave you a wish—?"

"—that came true!" Old Thibaut Corday nodded. "I was in Arabia, and I wished I was out of there, and that curst genie waved his hand—*Sacré!* the next thing I knew I was on British soil. It was exactly as the woman with the emerald eyes had promised, exactly as she had told it in her story from the Arabian Nights. If you think I am drunk, I can prove to you I am not. It has to do with this business of the truth behind nursery tales, and I can prove it with the story of the green-eyed woman and the genie. A bottle of Dubonnet I can do it to your satisfaction."

The young Englishmen said it was a wager because it would take a lot of satisfying to convince him there was such a thing as a genie. In the twilight under the café awning the old Frenchman's eyes glinted fiercely. Lubricating his throat with the last of his wine, he leaned forward in his chair, and sprinted off from a gun-shot oath to win the Dubonnet....

MORBLEU! (Old Thibaut Corday was off) it started innocently enough with a fight aboard a troopship steaming down the Red Sea for French Somaliland, miles south of the Suez Canal. The World War was two years over, but the Legion must go down and fight Somali bandits. The Foreign Legion is always fighting. On the troopship there was nothing to do, so the Legionnaires fought among themselves.

I acquired the hate of a Spanish scoundrel named Balderos, an evil bullfighter who had taken to jabbing his dagger into people instead of bulls. He had a nose as sharp as a blade, and I dulled it for him one night when he was bragging too much. The weasel swore he would get even. It was a good place to do it in, too. That Red Sea is a moat to keep civilization out of Arabia, and from the look of the coast there it has done a good job. Balderos decided it would make a nice shore for my body to rot on. A treacherous rascal. I was ordered up on deck to stand a midnight watch, and the villain sprang at me from behind a ventilator. Quick and silent he sprang; in the gleams from a distant port hole I had only a glimpse of his face. *Mon Dieu!* he meant to murder me—just in time I dodged the knife. I flung up my arm to fend the blow; the blade only pared a peel from my Adam's apple; but the collision flung me overboard, knocked me over the rail like a sack of beef.

When I cleared my eyes the ship was waddling off into darkness; I was alone in the black, warm brine of the sea. My first yells were only gargles, and by the time I pumped my lungs free of salt water the transport was gone. I had an idea the Spaniard would not ask the captain to drop a lifeboat. Somaliland was as far as Mars; the nearest coast was Arabia, and it looked as if I had to swim for it.

I swam and swam. Somehow I kicked off my shoes and juggled out of my tunic; and I struck off for what I hoped was the coast, and kept swimming. *Bleu!* that Red Sea was black. I could see nothing.

After a few hours I began to tire. If that Red Sea was not so salty and buoyant, I would today be rubbing elbow-bones with the charioteers who tried to follow Moses.

But along about morning I hit a strip of beach, and the sun was coming up as I hauled myself up on the salt-crusted rocks to dry. That beach was hardly the place to recuperate, and I knew it the minute I looked around.

Inland I could see nothing but sandbanks rank with thorny desert-brush; the beach was no more than a clutter of heat-cracked rocks. Under the blazing sun I began to fry like a herring. *"Ma mère!"* I groaned. "In five minutes I will die of thirst, and there is no drinking water within a million miles. This is surely the coast of hell."

THEN I saw the woman. I was lacing on the boots which I had hung around my neck, and when I looked up—pouf!—she was there. Not fifteen feet away, she was lying atop a big yellow rock, watching me, intent. I do not say it was magic, though so it seemed at the time. I suppose my brine-stung eyes had not noticed her at first. She was posed so superbly motionless that her bronze figure melted into the scenery the way an umber lioness melts into African veldt.

Oui, I thought her a piece of bronze statuary that some sculptor had put up on top of that rock. Reclining on one elbow, head up-lifted, langorous, she watched me. Picture the face of Mona Lisa on a figure of burnished curves clad in no more than a string. But it was her eyes that convinced me she was not real. Never had I been fixed by a stare of such vivid green.

"Emeralds!" I exclaimed. "Now I know I am in Hades."

I got up and started toward her but I did not get far. Three steps through the sunrise, and I fell on my face. That firebrand sun hit me over the head, or it may be the woman's gaze felled me; at any rate I dropped unconscious, and I came to, groaning for water.

I stopped groaning when I discovered myself in the green-eyed woman's arms. She had pulled me into a shady recess behind the big yellow rock, and she was soothing my forehead with a hand as cool as mint. When she saw I was awake, she pressed a little stone jug to my lips and gave me a drink of fig wine.

"Do you feel better now, *Ferangi?*" she murmured. "You were almost drowned, and you were dying of thirst. Do you feel better now?"

"Much better," I gasped. Ah, I could have swooned there drinking that matchless nectar with that woman stroking my forehead. I closed my eyes again, and she gave me another drink. Her fingers were like brook-ripples and the drink was wonderful.

"And now you eat."

From a crevice she took a brown cloak and unwrapped a piece of bread. There were dates in the bread, and I lay back on the sand, munching it and staring at the woman and thinking of Omar Khayyam. The woman reclined beside me, and watched with emerald eyes.

"I am glad the Spaniard threw me overboard," I told her finally. "Where am I? It is not bad here. How long have I been dead?"

"But you are not dead," she gave me with a soft bronze smile. "You had swallowed much salt water, but you are far too strong to die. This," and she pointed down the coast, "is that part of Arabia known as Asir. You were swimming out there in the Red Sea when I saw you just before dawn. I ran to this end of the beach where I saw you were going to land, but I dared not aid you until I saw you were an honest man. Honesty I read in your face while your mind was asleep just now. But do not talk, *Ferangi,* you are tired." She laid cool fingers on my eyelids. "Rest, now. Rest—"

I rested. With those mint-tipped fingers on my eyelids I felt as drowsy as if I were in a hammock under a tree. The woman was not any ordinary Arab, I was certain. To begin with, she had spoken in English—soft-throated English with an Arabic accent—and there was an alloy of gold in her hair and complexion, and she was twice too beautiful to be the daughter of some Bedouin camel-thumper. Part Egyptian or Circassian or something like that, she would have been a beauty in any language, and she was a big surprise on that burning, barren coast.

But I kept napping off instead of asking questions, and each time I woke she would give me more wine and date bread.

Eh bien, the day passed so, and I was sorry to wake up at last in late afternoon. Blue shadows were pooling among the rocks and the woman sat beside me, wrapped in her cloak, portioning out the last of the bread. Also she had found my cigarettes in my belt and laid them out to dry. Matches, too. When I finished my rations and leaned back, smoking, I decided I had met the one perfect woman in the world.

"You saved my life," I told her. "I would have died had you not come to my aid. Is there any way I can repay you?"

Her green eyes regarded me thoughtfully when I said that. Regarding me, they gave me that feeling I had as a child when I would lean over the stone rim and look down into the depths of my father's well.

"You would like to repay me, *Sidi?* You would really like to do something for me in return?"

"I would, indeed," I assured her, feeling the pull of those bottomless green depths. "I am only a castaway, a soldier of the Legion; but for you I would do anything. Anything at all."

"How would you like to help me recover a fortune?" she asked.

So casually she asked it that I was shocked bolt upright, *messieurs.* I stared at her lips to make sure I had heard it. "A fortune—?"

"A great fortune," she nodded, "one of the greatest in the world. Diamonds are nothing beside it. Rubies, pearls—it is worth them all. Just to hold it in your hand for one night would make you a millionaire forever, *Sidi.* How would you like to help me recover it?"

"Where is it?" I cried. "Where can such a treasure be found?"

She looked at me for a long time as if trying to make up her mind, and then her voice came low above the whisper of the Red Sea waves that were sporting in the twilight on the sand.

"In a lamp."

CHAPTER II.

THAT IS how I met the woman with the emerald eyes; how she came to tell me the story of the wonderful lamp. She told it to me there on that twilight Red Sea beach a million miles from Nowhere, and I was not as prepared to hear that marvelous story as you have been.

She began by drawing a picture of the lamp in the sand, the sort of big Arab lamp that you see in the native bazaars, shaped like a ten-gallon pitcher, but small at the neck like a jug, with a wick in the spout. She was a good artist, too. But her words were better. She moulded that lamp with words that gave it curves like a woman's hip. She gilded it and filled it with the oil of her voice. Lit it with the blaze from her eyes. Its flame, she said, was pure brightness, a handful of incandescence from the sun. I almost forgot the point behind her story in the desire she created in me to see so splendid a thing.

"And it doesn't smoke?" I asked. "You never have to trim the wick?"

"It does not smoke and you never have to trim the wick. Think of it, *Sidi.* The shape! Made of gold! A flame like the sun in darkness!

From the shop of the world's greatest lamp-maker! Would you not like to own such a lamp?"

"I certainly would!" said I, a Legionnaire who had never owned a lamp or a window to throw one out of—*non,* nor ever wanted to till then. That woman made me feel as if I had missed the greatest treat of my life, and I voiced my wonder at the spendthrift plutocrat who would hide a treasure in such a magnificent vessel.

"But the lamp, itself, is the treasure!" the woman cried. "It is priceless, *Sidi.* Beyond the reach of any pocketbook! Men have died for a chance to see it; kings have sold their thrones to own it for an hour. Rich and poor have cut one another's throats, traded their souls to Shaitan in attempts to get that lamp in their possession. It is ten thousand years old—twice ten thousand!—and from the day it was made, men have cut the East in bloody strips trying to get their hands on it. Listen, *Sidi*—"

I listened, all right. That lamp had a history as well as a pedigree; and as the green-eyed woman recited it to me, I listened as a schoolboy listens to the exploits of Napoleon.

What a saga that was. It seemed that lamp had been made in the workshops of Araby before Bagdad was built. The pyramids over in Egypt were still on blue-prints; the East was a pretty dark place up until that lamp was put on the market.

That lamp brightened things up a bit. It was just as much of a novelty as your grandfather's Mazda bulb, and the Arabs, who had known only stars and torches, sat around and blinked at the thing in wonder. The lampsmith gave it to the king as a birthday gift; but the first thing the king knew, he was murdered in his bed by some neighboring *ameer* who wanted to brighten up his own dark evenings.

From then on, it was a dogfight to see who could keep it. Shieks stole it from sultans, and khedives stole it from shieks. Thieves made off with it; princes killed their brothers to inherit it; moguls hanged their children to make them tell where it was.

For century after century the Arab world was in a turmoil over that lamp. Marauders carried it to Persia, and an army went from Mecca to fetch it back. It was owned by Ahmed the Mighty, by Suliman the Conqueror. Zoroaster wrote the great *Zend-Avesta* by its light, and Mohammed the Prophet tore half the hairs from his beard because it disappeared during his lifetime and his generals could not find out where.

From Turkey to Palestine, it went. From palaces to pawnshops. When it was lost, the East was perfumed by the corpses of adventurers who had lost their lives hunting it. Jenghiz Khan charged all the way from Tartary seeking the lamp; Tamerlane hid it in India; it was owned by Abdul the Great.

BUT the story needs that barren beach, the desert stretching east, the Red Sea stretching west, twilight spinning gray cobwebs among the rocks, the silence of Arabia around. It needs that bronze-skinned beauty with the emerald eyes. She chanted me that history in a mixture of quaint, Arabic-accented English that I could not hope to copy; some of her phrases were a little hard for me, a Frenchman, to understand.

But I could understand the rise and fall of her tones. Her eyes. Her gestures. Her voice struck chords as haunting as a balalaika. In her eyes I could see the battles and murders, all those thieves, shieks and sultans she was talking about. I figured she was exaggerating—what woman does not?—and I counted on—how do you call it?—poetic license. Nonetheless, I comprehended what she meant to convey.

This lamp was worth more than just gold. It was a priceless relic, a most rare antique—like the belt of Buddha, or Cleopatra's bedroom slippers.

"It is something more than that!" she cried when I spoke out. "Does it mean anything to you, *Sidi,*"—she threw wide her arms—"when I tell you this lamp once belonged to the great prince, Allah Deen?"

"Allah Deen," I pronounced the name after her. "No, I have never heard of this prince before."

"But he was one of the greatest of Arabian princes," she cried. "Known all over the world! Almost as famous in Islam as the Prophet!"

"I am not so well educated in Arabian history," I apologized. "But I understand. The lamp is a priceless relic, having belonged to so great a historical character."

"More than that! More than that!" In exasperation at my ignorance, the woman burst into a barrage of excited Arabic. Then even her native tongue seemed incapable of evaluating this curio, for at the point where she tried to price it, her vocabulary seemed to wear into holes and tatters. "Only you would not believe what I try to tell you." She shook her head at my incomprehension. "The English words—I cannot find them to tell it in. You must rob the lamp to find out what it is worth. Do you understand? You must *rob* the lamp!"

"I see." In truth, it startled me. "You want me to steal it."

"Steal! Yes! That is it!" She leaned at me, breathlessly. "Once we have it in our possession the world is ours! Power! Riches! Travel! It is a treasure that can bring you anything you wish!"

"But who owns it now?" I panted. Her expression made my pulses pound, but I still had a spark of conscience. Stealing a candle is one thing, perhaps, but one's conscience is apt to prick at the thought of snaffling a lamp worth millions.

She snuffed that out of me, though. She dropped her voice to an alto that made prickles tiptoe down my spine as I realized she was betraying a secret every robber in Arabia would have butchered his mother to hear.

"It is in a den of thieves," she said. "A stronghold of rascals, rogues, marauders. Chief of the stronghold is the wicked Caïd El Azrek, whose name strikes terror to all who hear it along this coast. For years, undiscovered, he has held the lamp secure in this walled fortress of assassins. It was thought to be in Bagdad, but El Azrek murdered the Caliph who owned it, and fled with it here for safe keeping."

"And why do you tell me this?" I asked.

Serpolette! her face went hard. At my question it went from bronze to iron. "Because I hate El Azrek!" she spat. "You do not know how I hate him! I was his wife in Bagdad, favorite of his harem—until he seized the lamp. The fortune went to his head, *Ferangi!*

"He left me for riches; fled with his treasure to this desert stronghold where he thought to hide it in greater security. For ten years I have been hunting this wretch who prizes riches more than my love. Only yesterday I found his hideout; I knew it by the lamplight, by Allah! The walls are high and well guarded, but there is a back door, and I saw the room where the Caïd sleeps with the treasure he chose in my stead." Her voice dropped a shivery octave. "It would kill him if the lamp were stolen. It would break his evil heart!"

"How do you propose to steal it?" I stammered.

Softening her features, she regarded me gently with her deep, green eyes. "I have made a plan which I can tell you when we get there. I could not carry the gold lamp alone; but where one could never enter, two can slip through. There is danger, but you are brave. There is risk, but much to gain. Remember! Only to rob this lamp and it will bring you any luxury in the world!"

For that green-eyed look of hers, I felt willing to risk anything.

"How far is this bandit stronghold?" I was on my feet.

She gripped my arm and pointed at the sand hills where the dusk was gathering up the last pink patches of sunset light. "We can be there by midnight if we start at once."

Her eyes met mine, and we started at once.

CHAPTER III.

PERHAPS YOU wonder how I could follow a strange woman into unknown desert like that, and sometimes I wonder myself. Was it the sea water I had swallowed? Fig wine and the woman's eyes? The saga she had sung about that lamp? I think it was all those together; and I had nothing to lose, nowhere to go, and I owed the lady something for her rescue act.

At any rate, I had caught the treasure-fever, and caught it bad! Treasure-fever? Well, the sanest citizen is a fortune hunter at heart—and Foreign Legionnaires are not quite the sanest citizens. Ha! It seemed to me that night as if Fate had washed me up at the feet of Lady Luck herself. I followed her, itching, like Cortez on his way to Eldorado.

That desert had Eldorado atmosphere, too. We tramped southeast across the sandhills, and the night came down in black silk curtains that transformed that Arabian wilderness into a patch of real estate from a dream.

The hills were black crêpe crested with splashes of lemon. The sky was a purple velvet canopy pinned back by a yellow crescent moon with a star at its tip, like the trademark on a package of Turkish cigarettes. Warm air whispered in the thorn clumps, and there was a tang in the darkness that reminded me of the spice-cake my mother used to make. It seemed like just the country where a jealousy-maddened woman would set out to steal from her husband a relic worth a few million dollars.

The woman walked fast, striding through the brush with the sure-footed swiftness of one who knew her ground and purpose. I could discern no trail, but I think her eyes could see in the dark.

When we topped a moony rise I would glimpse her face, and her features were cast-iron when she thought I wasn't looking. Her eyes gleamed green on some fixed point in the night ahead, a gleam that telegraphed shivers down my neck.

"Dieu!" I thought to myself. "That El Azrek was a lumphead to jilt this lady for any lamp. I would suffer a lifetime with Mother-in-Law Poverty before I ditched a wife with such eyes!"

Myself, I would not have picked the fort of an Arab bandit as a place to attempt grand larceny. But every time I had doubts, the woman would sense them and demolish them with her magic words.

"Remember, it is the lamp that belonged to the great Prince Allah Deen. Any shiek in Arabia would pay a fortune for the wick, alone, of this lamp!"

Well, it took little urging to hustle me over those sand hills. I knew a little about curios, understand. In Algeria and Tonkin I had seen high prices on ancient knick-knacks; in Syria there had been some antique-merchants digging near our Legion outpost, and an old image without a head—a piece of baked mud, merely—had been shipped to America with a price-tag of staggering extravagance. That hunk of mud was nowhere near as old as the woman said this lamp was. And the lamp was solid gold!

I saw the bankers and museum-collectors of London, New York and Paris opening their purses to buy that relic. No more drill and foot-slog in the lousy Legion. I'd buy Renaults and two wine cellars and a box of cigars, and I'd bribe the War Department to send that Spaniard Balderos to the terrible Battalion d'Afrique!

For five hours we hurried across those dreamy sandhills, and at the end of that time I was lounging on divans in air-castles, richer than Croesus.

We were many miles from the coast when the woman finally halted in the lee of a high purple ridge directly under the cigarette-package moon. "We are almost there," she breathed. "El Azrek's stronghold lies in a valley the other side of this ridge. Take care to keep in shadow. The bandits who guard the treasure-house of the lamp have eyes like jackals."

IT was all I could do to keep from bolting up over the hill to see the place. As the woman ascended ahead of me, my hands itched, my tongue poked out. The night was like an ambush up ahead, but I was too busy mentally fingering a million dollars to worry about the hazards of attainment.

At the ridge-top the woman clutched me down into the shadow

of a thorn bush. "There it is!" she panted. "Look! The lamp! Down there—!"

Believe me, I was looking. How I looked! It was a great scene the woman showed me from that high place, the greater because in the back of my French mind I had been skeptical of seeing anything at all. What I saw then gave the knockout punch to my skepticism. Arabia, *messieurs!* One vast sweeping stretch of silent sandhills, etched in moon-yellow and stripes of black night, a landscape like a tiger's pelt spread out to the edges of the world. And on the sands below our high place, a black-walled, sullen fortress with a light in its lofty watchtower glowing as one fierce, livid eye.

It was a tiger asleep with one eye open....

The fortress resembled a bunch of piled-up dungeons, black as coal, but that light in the upper tower was just about the brightest glare I had ever seen. What is it from Shakespeare—How far that little candle throws its beams? Huh! The flare in that turret was about two million kilowatts beyond Shakespeare. It was all of a mile distant, but even at that distance it made me blink. It was as if that tower room was filled with a white-green fire. I thought I had never beheld such a radiance.

The green-eyed woman gripped my arm. "I told you it was the brightest lamp in the world. You would have seen it from the coast had not this high ridge come between. Ah, that husband of mine! That hyena, El Azrek! Back here with his treasure he thought to be safe, for no caravans cross that waste you see out there, and the Arabs of the coast, who quail at his name, dare not cross the ridge at night, and have not seen the lamp!"

"But blessed Sébastopol!" I gulped. The glare in that tower was holding my visionary muscles hypnotized, but I was not too blinded to catch the white-hooded figures of Arabs moving sentrylike along the battlements beneath. "The place is guarded like a citadel. It would take three regiments of Legionnaires to storm those walls. Why, stealing that light would be like trying to take the torch from the Statue of Liberty."

My companion murmured: "Hear me. In a little while that light will go out. *Mektoob!* It is written that he who would keep the precious lamp must light it for an hour every midnight. My pious husband is keeping the tradition, but by Allah! he shall not keep the lamp. Soon he will blow out the flame and carry it down to his chamber where he thinks it is safe for the night. That wolf's den will be in pitch darkness; then we strike!"

"But those brigands guarding the wall!"

"As I told you," she pointed, "last night when I crept around the place I discovered a back door. I saw El Azrek at a window beyond with his cherished lamp. *Ins'allah!* I would have climbed the wall to claw out his faithless beard, but to steal the treasure-lamp would be six times the revenge, so I retired and walked all night by the sea, thinking."

Her eyes refracted gleams from that mile-off incandescence, and I was glad the lady hadn't walked the beach all night cooking up something against me. "Observe." She pressed my knee. "That back door opens into a little palm garden. Beyond is an archway, a flight of stairs. The stairs lead to the Caïd's bed chamber, but the scoundrel sleeps in an alcove and the room may be entered unseen. So much I learned from the guard who stands nearest that rear entry—a beardless boy! I sang to him a soft love song, and boys can be made to talk! One has but to enter the fortress; then—? Easy!"

"Easy!" I gasped. "How do you open that door to begin with?"

"Leave that to me," was her answer. "The boy expects me tonight; I will lure him a distance away. Follow me to within a stone's throw of the walls; I will open the door; then I will go to a corner of the wall and call off the boy. That will be your chance. The lamp—such a treasure as you never dreamed—but waits your hand for the taking, *Ferangi!*"

Aunt of the Devil! just as the woman said that, that light went out as she had promised. And I think my reason was extinguished with it.

Fantastic as that lamp-story sounded, that stronghold in the middle of Nowhere with that light in its tower confirmed it. That was no common Arab stronghold! I could smell bandits in that place the way you can whiff a den of rattlesnakes, yet your ordinary bandit chief doesn't set off an acetylene torch at the top of his citadel. And when that light blacked out, Belief hit me over the head and raised one big bump of credulity.

THE woman started down from the ridge, and I went after her. The fortress, after that glim was doused, was black. *Lamp* black! The walls reared up like a masonry of ink and silence, and as we reached desert-level they loomed like a silhouetted animal, couchant but ready to pounce. It had shut its bright eye, but it was a wary sleeper, you could tell. I felt as if I were treading on its fur, and I moved across the sands very softly, you may believe.

Not as softly as that bronze lady, though. The sand was waved up in low dunes—it was the shadows between the dunes which gave the desert that striping effect—and the woman crept over the moon-washed crests with a protective coloration that was wonderful. She could flatten and melt on the sand as a chameleon melts itself on a wall; and watching her, I learned how it was that Arabs could surprise a Legion outpost by charging as if from mid-air.

In the black stripes between she could disappear completely! Twice I thought she was a dozen yards ahead, and bumped into her in a dark spot where she was waiting, invisible.

"Do not do that!" I begged.

"Hush!" She touched my lips. "The walls of that place have ears. All would be lost if those guards heard us approaching."

We had a mile of sand to cross before we reached that sleeping stronghold, and before we had covered half the distance I wanted to sit down and howl. At least, my nerves did. The rest of me wanted to rush that treasure-house and get it over with.

Alors, we got there soon enough. My nervous system was blowing out a fuse when the woman halted in a thorn clump and turned to give me final instructions. Close up, that fortress looked bigger than the Bastille. Walls thirty feet high enclosed a massive, dark-windowed keep, a veritable Rhineland castle save for the crenellated ramparts and square-topped Arab tower. I could make out a little door facing us that might have been imported from the Tower of London. Also I could make out Arab turbans and a glint of rifle barrels moving up and down the palisades above, and my teeth, which had more sense than I did, began to chatter.

"Wait here." The woman squeezed my hand. "It will take me but a moment to open that door; then I will run to that corner of the wall to draw the attention of the guard. I will sing to him a love song that will blind him with desire. Enter when I drop the wine jug. That is your signal."

Was there ever such a campaign-plan to enter such a fortress? Contemplating that stronghold, my treasure-fever chilled down a degree, and I turned to ask the woman if she couldn't blind that guardsman with something a little more interesting than a song. Holy Saint Anselm! She was gone! In the shadows at my elbow she had vanished. I didn't want to be left by myself just then. I grabbed around in the thorn scrub, but she wasn't there.

Do you know where she was when I saw her next? She was halfway between that clump where I was frozen and that fortress door. And then she was at the door—as quick as that! I tell you, that woman was like a draught of air, all moonlight and shadow and dust. At that door she was as hard to see as a phantom's silhouette.

I would give much to know how she opened that door in the wall. I believe she said, "Open Sesame!" It looked like that kind of a door. Anyway, it was not ten seconds before she crept to a corner of that battlement; and the door was unlocked when I got there.

The green-eyed woman sang and a young Arab looked over the rampart above her; and when she dropped her little jug, I raced to that door and darted in. You believe? Too generous, *messieurs.* Had you known that woman you would believe me capable of such folly with more conviction. I do not know what she sang to that guard—but I know how she had sung that lamp-yarn to me, and she had drugged me with a desire that made me rush in where angels would fear to tread.

I must have been mad when I ran through that unlocked portal into that fortress—! Think of the chances I took! The woman and her guard were not a hundred feet away, and the whole place crawled with watchmen like a mangy dog with fleas.

I did not stop in the high-walled garden, either. It was a dusty courtyard, Arab style, where a couple of date palms drooped glumly over a well. I crossed this patio to an onion-peaked archway that gave view to dark steps mounting into the Bastille, and I went up those sinister steps as a man would climb a stair up into a catacomb.

Gumshoe I went. With thudding heart and baited breath. Into a black hush at the summit that was like a funeral. Conceive me creeping into that fortress while that woman serenaded the watchman outside! Picture me shaky-legged in a dark upper corridor, peering, sweating, almost suffocating in the bandit-musk. Imagine, then, a near doorway, an inner chamber blue with moonlight, the sound of someone snoring. Whew! I took one peek into that moon-lit room; turned to run. Then—? Then I saw the lamp!

CHAPTER IV.

WHAT COULD I say of that lamp? At that moment I could not talk. Nor can I now, for when I try to tell of it as I saw it, my vocabulary wears out and goes to pieces. So high—so wide—shaped like a big water-pitcher, but narrowed at the neck like a jug with spout and wick—that sounds like a lamp you'd see in any Arab shop in the Kasbah. Ten-gallon capacity sounds like a milk can. It was there in a corner?—So is your old umbrella stand. I am reduced to the one word, "Gold!" Which is feeble description for a thing which gleamed like butter in the shadows, big and yellow as the prize at Rainbow's End.

Now I was on that bonanza in one bound. I had it on my shoulder and out of that snoring room in a trice. As far as the stairs it was all according to schedule, but at that point Providence set out to teach me a lesson. As I started down those steps there was a screech at the bottom that shattered the silence like a factory whistle.

"Waaaah!"

I thought it was an elephant charging in from the courtyard, but it was only a seven-foot Negro waving a scimitar. That giant must have seen me as I whisked the golden lamp past a window, and he had come bounding from his post to find out what it was about. When he saw me on those stairs, he trumpeted another blast and started up to me. The six Prussian guardsmen who once caught me on a chateau staircase at Rheims were not quite as ugly as that customer. I took on those six Prussians—I would do it again—but that Negro looked like a Senegalese army coming up the stairs, and I wheeled in immediate retreat.

Too late! That screech had roused the house. Snores in El Azrek's bedroom had turned to howls. Men were bursting from doors down the corridor. That fortress was roaring like a four-alarm fire. Up the steps came that black giant while all the fiends of Gehenna were rushing me from the corridor; I had to pick the Negro and let fly.

Wham! With the only weapon I had, *messieurs.* That sacred lamp! With all my might I flung it; dived down after it as it cleared a path. *Whankety-whang-whang-whang!* It made a racket, I can tell you. Bouncing like a beer keg, it took that black man across the shins and sent him tumbling. I jumped him, and we bounced down together—

myself, the black giant and the lamp. Wow! that fortress came into action with the roar of an exploding cannon foundry on Sunday. As I rolled out into the courtyard with lamp and giant, I saw Arabs running and shooting from all directions.

I slugged that huge gorilla-man with every fist I had. He laughed when I hit him; jumped up and grinned like a slice of watermelon. He slashed out with his scimitar and would have cut me in half if he hadn't tripped over the lamp and gone floundering headlong into the well.

Water shot up like a fountain as Negro and scimitar disappeared, but they were instantly replaced by a dozen Arabs who jumped me through a dust-cloud. I had a scrap on my hands then, my friends. The worst kind of a scrap! Like demons they were on me.

I snatched up the spinning lamp and flailed like a maniac at those leaping devils. Knives flashed by me. Guns fired. Sheeted bodies, bearded faces boiled around me in the dust-swirl. I dented a few heads with that crushing antique, but it was far too heavy for in-fighting.

Back and across that court I fought, like a dog in the middle of a wolf pack, while more and more Arabs leaped down from the walls. Their number hampered gunfire, but they would have knifed me to ribbons under a pile-up, if the woman hadn't rushed in to my aid.

Like a Goddess of Fury she charged into that pack, cracking heads with her stone wine-jug, spitting and biting like a wolverine. I think the surprise scattered those Arabs as much as anything. Not expecting her, they jumped back to their wall stations to see if there were any more coming.

"The lamp!" she screamed, arriving at my side. "I knew you could get it, *Sidi!* Run now! Run!"

I needed no second invitation. Lamp aloft, with the green-eyed woman acting as rear guard, I streaked out. All hell was loose in that bandit-hive behind me—a tumult of whistles, yowls, shooting, torch-flares and trumpet blasts. Somewhere a drum was booming and in the tower they were pounding a brass gong, but I did not wait to see the fun.

The woman got me out of that little door. I believe she could have gotten me out of anything. Outside she took the lead, screaming at me to follow, and I chased after her while a bullet-blizzard chased after me. I was not surprised to see the young Arab guard tied hand and foot at the corner of the fortress wall.

"This way! This way!" she called. "Keep in the shadow!" She had reached one of those valleys between the dunes where the wall snipers couldn't see us, and she raced down the furrow invisible as a rabbit in an underground hole.

She knew the Arabs would not chase out of their fortress after us on foot—your Arab never walks when he can ride—and by delaying to saddle up, those devils gave us the chance she wanted.

"Three miles south there is a bridge," she cried. "Over a canyon of boiling mud. If we can beat their horses to the bridge I can stop them!"

"How can we beat their horses to the bridge?" I gasped.

"They will think us headed for the coast where the brush is thicker," the woman cried. "They will ride that way to head us off. By the time they find our tracks we will have ten minutes' start."

SURE enough, a moment later I heard hoofbeats thunder out of the fortress and fade in the direction of the coast, and I ran for my life. Ten minutes is not much start on a batch of Arab horsemen. I ran like Nurmi, shifting my burden from right to left shoulder to keep it from raising a blister.

"Courage, *mes braves!*" I addressed my legs. "Get me away with this prize and you have put an end to marching with haversacks forever. By its heft this gold lamp should purchase a chair on the stock exchange at least!"

Ten minutes later, as the woman had predicted, the night was full of echoing hoofbeats. I had to concentrate on the business of running. That can be a tiresome business, too. The green-eyed woman ran like a fluid streak, and I had to strain to keep up with her.

Those hoofbeats behind us thundered closer and closer. "Faster!" the woman screamed. "We are almost at the canyon!" She raced up and over a dune patched with thorn scrub, and then I saw something that dead-stopped me.

That vast cleft in the desert with the boiling mud river at its bottom—that is something you will have to take my word for. The devil's cauldrons of the Yellowstone and the fire bogs of Tannu Tuva are on your maps, but that chasm I saw in Arabia is not, and neither is that part of Arabia. I suppose that gulch is one of the undiscovered wonders of the world; let me tell you, I was not too happy about discovering it.

My boots were palsied on its edge. Fifty feet across the top, it dropped a thousand, sheer-walled—a terrific zigzag abyss that looked as if the tropic heat had cracked the globe and left a fissure so deep it drained the earth's core.

I could see the drainage far at the bottom—a winding, writhing river of brown, bubbling, spitting; a snake of boiling slime that crawled down that earth-bowel, jetting up vapors and spattering its walls with mire. I hollered when I looked down into that sewer of hell, and I hollered again when I saw the bridge that spanned that abyss.

That was no cantilever trestle!

It was just a flimsy rigging of timber and bamboo duckboards some fool had thrown across—time had rotted the underpinnings and there weren't any handrails, and it hung above there like a cobweb terrified of the gust of wind that will knock it down. A spider wouldn't have dared to cross on it, and I froze as the woman screamed at me to start.

"Better fall than be caught by my husband." She shoved me. "He would torture you for a year if he caught you alive with the lamp!" Do you know what she did? She snatched the relic from my arms; pulled a stopper near the wick-spout, and poured out a stream of oil. "Run first!" she cried. "Go on! I will set the bridge afire as I follow!"

I told you that lady was cool.

Fierce yells burst out in the night; over the dune charged El Azrek's riders led by what looked like the Four Horsemen of the Apocalypse; the woman gave me a push that sent me reeling out on that bridge, and, pouring oil, she labored after me.

The trestle gave a sickening sag, and I felt the bones melt in my knees as I looked down. My boots went so fast they did not seem to touch those lurching duckboards. After me toiled the woman, spilling oil from that ponderous lamp, and striking and dropping matches—those matches she had salvaged from my pockets on the beach—with the other. Bent almost double—her face sweat-streaked....

Leaping from their horses, our pursuers howled when they saw her arson—that web of timbers caught fire like straw, and a trail of flame jumped up at the woman's heels. Those Arabs just stood fumbling their knives and guns. I reached the other side of the abyss two jumps ahead of that woman; the bridge was an arc of flame behind her—and if you can picture that, try this!

Leaping to safety, the woman heaved the lamp back into my sweating hands, pushed me into a brush-clump and turned to give our pursuers a laugh that trilled into a cry of fear. "Name of Allah!

Keep running! Here they come!"

Those weren't Arabs, they were daredevils! Was that fiery bridge going to stop them? *Non!* Out on that trestle of fire they were creeping single file, beating at the flames with their cloaks, swaying and balancing in the sparks and blazelight and smoke like demons.

I ran when I saw it, *messieurs!* Praying for the bridge to crash, I shouldered the lamp and ran after the woman at express speed, but the bridge delayed crashing just long enough for the Arabs to get across, and again the hue and cry was after us in the night. I asked my legs to move me, then. I was certain, now, I was carrying off a gold mine in that lamp.

AH, but I was soon to learn how much a gold mine can weigh! I was soon to learn that getting a fortune is one thing, enjoying it another! In the race I ran with that lamp across that desert in Arabia I learned a number of things, my friends.

We ran into a dawn where the sun came up like Saint Anthony's fire, and I learned about heat. We ran into a noon where the fig wine was gone from the woman's little jug, and I learned about thirst. We ran on into an afternoon where I learned about foot-blisters, heart-fatigue, lung-strain. All day we fled across the burning dunes with that lamp, and all day those Arab hounds pursued us.

We ran blindly, wearily, heavily and more heavily burdened. They ran steadily, tirelessly, like machinery. Looking back I could see them a quarter-mile behind, rifles and knife-blades flashing up and down in the sun like the pistons in a harvest reaper.

It had given me a stimulus to see the lamp at sunrise—inscribed with Arabic characters and fine filigree, it was a goldsmith's masterpiece if I ever saw one; it had blazed like a bonfire in my arms, like the Gold Pot from Rainbow's End. But the woman grabbed it from me to wrap it in her cloak—I wish you could have seen the way she ran with it, hugging it to her bosom, patting it, talking to it as if it were a baby—*oui,* she made a sling for me to carry it by, also hiding its golden flare. But the Arabs following us could see it, all right. Sacred blue! They never let up for a minute. *Enfin,* when my back was breaking the woman would take the lamp from me and carry it for a little while, but it was too heavy for her to carry far, and I did most of the toting. That lamp took on poundage at every mile, too. Seventy pounds at first, by mid-afternoon it seemed more like seventy tons. I learned why millionaires have stooped shoulders as I stumbled with that treasure lamp across those scorching sands.

As we fled toward the end of that day, that Arab mowing-machine still behind us, I was done to bones and rags. The woman's bronze skin was immune to the sun, and those fiends behind us were sired by camels, but I was ready to lie down and play banquet for the vultures.

It was the lamp that kept me going then, *messieurs!* Only that lamp! When my legs broke down, the woman would crank them up again by unwrapping that *kickshaw* and giving me a look. When I croaked in thirst, she would give me a drink of that lamp-story. I forgot my sprained muscles, my shriveling stomach, my crippled back. "Remember, *Sidi,* you are carrying the most priceless relic in existence," she would say in a soft whip-voice that drove me on. I guess I was too brainless to catch sunstroke under that furnace sun. I had traded my brains for a lamp.

But I will shorten the rest of that grueling race across the desert—I promised you a tale of the Arabian Nights—and bring it to that tea-time when we arrived once more at the brink of that terrific crevice. I do not know if we had run in a circle or whether the canyon made a tangent to cut across our course, but we raced at sundown over a hill of brambles, and suddenly that chasm reappeared in front of us. El Azrek's harvesting machine was not far behind us, coming *plut, plut, plut* down a sunset-reddened slope, and it looked like the end.

Those Arabs thought they had us then, and they charged, yelling their savage heads off.

I went sick. They were so close I could see their hate-scribbled faces, bulging eyeballs, teeth clenched fiercely in wind-parted beards. The two in the lead resembled the creatures of a nightmare—that Nubian headsman, and a big shiek with orange whiskers that billowed back like blowing flame. The Devil and his bodyguard from Sheol!

"My husband!" She pointed at Orange-beard. "El Azrek, by all the fiends! We must never let him take us! Fly! Fly!"

Fleet as a *kudu* antelope, she raced off down the chasm-brink. Somehow I gathered the gristle to sprint after her. A misstep would have meant instant death, and I expected any second to step over the edge of that trench and spin down to the boiling mud below.

It was the woman who stepped off into that gulch, not me! *Sacré Nom de Dieu!* Before my very eyes! Figure to yourself the shock when she disappeared with no shade in that vermillion sundown to aid her usual vanishing act. I howled when she stepped over that ledge. I skidded to a halt with locked kneecaps, and leaned out over that abyss, expecting to see her falling body.

But she was not falling down that gulch. Nothing was falling save long shafts of twilight and some pebbles my boots had kicked over. "Yow!" I wailed. "Right in thin air she has made herself invisible!"

Then I heard her, and jumped. "The ladder!" her voice was calling. Up from the dizzy emptiness beyond my boots, like an echo she had left suspended in space. "*Ferangi*—the rope ladder! There beside you in the bushes!"

CHOKING. I looked down. The ledge was undermined at that point, its rim overgrown with brush. She was under the overhang, clinging like an acrobat to a heart-sickening Jacob's ladder which dribbled like a skimpy vine down that smooth-polished canyon wall. Only that particular rope ladder went to hell! I turn cold to remember it—a precarious rigging of hemp moored to the clifftop by a couple of shaky posts. It must have been hung there by the engineers who had tacked up that careless trestle, and it looked ten times as insecure. It was horrible.

The green-eyed woman waved up at me, crying to hand her the lamp. Am I sweating as I tell about it? But my forehead was snowing as I leaned out to lower that heavy antique; saw her grab, catch, hold on. "Now come down after me!" she shrilled. "El Azrek and his fiends will not see us down here. Before they discover where we went, we can reach the bottom!"

No time to wonder what we'd do when we got down there. Swinging over that brink on those creaking ropes, I had an idea I would not live long enough to find out. I started down.

I made the mistake of looking at my feet as I fumbled to find the ladder-rungs. The depths below made my brains spin, and the gravity of that drop grabbed me by the ankles and tried to pull me off the crossropes.

Have you ever heard a ship's rigging crying at the strain of windy weather? Those hempen cables in my clutch cried out like that. When we were quarter-way down they were stretching to a groan; and halfway, the thing began to swing.

Visualize that—myself and that woman five hundred feet in the air!—that ladder swooping in wide, swishy arcs like a pendulum. Don't talk to me about ladders! Today the sight of any ladder makes me ill.

Just last month I saw some sailors climb down a ship's side on a Jacob's ladder, and I went to bed for a week.

"Descend! Descend!" the woman called up faintly. I was paralyzed on those swinging strands, and she was going down the rungs like a trapeze artist. "Plant your feet in the middle of the crossropes and it will not sway! Do not be afraid—!"

"I can't! The ropes are breaking under me!" I sobbed.

"They are not breaking under me!" her voice came back. "I am heavier than you—I am carrying the lamp!"

I called that woman a trapeze artist, but she was something more. To scale down a ladder with a seventy-pound load slung on your back—that is something beyond mere skill.

She saw I was stalled in panic, and she started to sing me that lamp-yarn again. But I think I was becoming a little cynical on that ladder—beginning to realize that a fortune may cost more than it is worth. Praise that lamp as she would, the woman could not lure me past the halfway mark of that aerial descent. It wanted more than a sales talk to budge my numbed knees, and it got it!

"Merciful Allah!" the woman's chant broke into a shriek. "They have seen us from above and they are running to cut the cables. Come down! Come down—!"

Those brigands had failed to spy the rigging in the bushes at first. They had dashed along the clifftop quite a distance beyond those mooring posts; then some vulture had looked over and spotted us, and now they were rushing back to hack at the guy-ropes with their choppers.

I went down that ladder, then! How I went. I left the palms of both hands on those hampen cables; took the arches out of my boots on the rungs. A hundred feet from the bottom, the woman screamed out that Old orange-beard was chopping at the top-shrouds, and I had a vision of Gabriel getting ready to play taps for me on his horn.

"Slide! Wrap your arms and legs around the guy-ropes and slide!" the woman screamed. "You are almost at the bottom—!"

I pulled an icy breath, wrapped my arms and legs around the guy-ropes, slid! I burned my chest on that descent. But I reached that canyon bottom just one foot ahead of Gabriel; the woman jerked me sideways under a rock; there was a roar like Niagara breaking loose from an ice jam—*swish!*—*crrrrrash!*—then it seemed as if a year went by while that avalanche of rope kept coming down.

Knots whiplashed past my face and hawsers coiled up in writhing piles; I don't know how long I crouched staring at that mass of lunging hemp—one year, a decade, perhaps a century.

Then something slapped me in the face, something that wasn't rope. Something hot and sticky that smelled like sulphur. Only then was I aware of the fuming fog around me, squirts of flying goo in the air, a splut and gurgle as of a million kettles boiling. Only then did I realize I was at the bottom of that canyon on the bank of that hellish river.

"We are lost!" I groaned at the green-eyed woman, pointing at the brown tide which galloped past the bank where we crouched befogged.

"No," she stood up calmly. "Those fools have cut their ladder, now they cannot descend to follow us. Bring the lamp, *Ferangi.* There is our boat!"

CHAPTER V.

MESSIEURS, I will remember the boat trip I took down that canyon until I die, and I think as I lie in my coffin I will still remember it. And I will laugh at Satan's Netherworld; I will tell him his subway of horrors is just second-class.

"Listen," I will jeer. "There is a big trench somewhere in Arabia that beats any of your infernal drains all hollow. I took a barge ride down that stream which makes your tour up the River Styx seem an excursion on the Seine in comparison."

I will tell him about the mud bank where the trip commenced; about the scow beached there in a stink of mire. I will tell him how the woman and I pushed off with the lamp; how the barge went swirling downstream on that torrent of bubbling glue. He will paw brimstone with his hoofs when I describe the wild bends of that channel; and when I tell how that muck-flood hissed and spat, he will turn from red to green with envy.

"Corday," he will bow, "I have met my match at last. You are the bigger liar." And if lies are half truths, then the Old Scratch will be right, for I couldn't describe that raging river of mud by half.

Non, I couldn't do justice to that mud stream any more than I could explain how the green-eyed woman knew about that barge, or account for any other of Mother Nature's alarming wonders. It was in a class with Stromboli, volcanoes, earthquakes, things like that.

We went down that goo-flood like a chip in a millrace of lava. It bombarded our scow with gouts of muck. On the sharp bends, it threatened to capsize us, drown us in turkey-gobbling swirls of mire. Our little barge plunged and wallowed, splattering through storms of semi-solid surf, *tubbedy, bub, bub, bub!*

That was no *Maid of the Mist,* that barge. It was just a raft of palm-trunks with planks whacked up for sideboards and a sort of crude rudder at the stern. The green-eyed woman crouched at the steering oar, and I huddled in the center of the deck, my arms around the lamp, ducking bursts of hot slime.

Bursts of slime? The whole surface of that river was popping, exploding. Geysers spouted thirteen feet in the air. Blasts of steam spurted from the muck, hurling mud-balls with the force of shrapnel. Weird clouds rolled across the thrashing channel, stifling as the smoke of burning rubber—and the canyon walls were obscured.

Any second I expected the barge would crash, provided it was not first blown to pieces by a geyser or swamped by the liquid sludge slopping over the sides.

Parbleu! as we shot down that canyon in that batter of scalding mud I felt like a bug on a potato peel going down a gutter of bacon grease. How long that excursion lasted I have no idea. I only know the canyon zigzagged like a chain of lighting, and we followed the zigzag at a tremendous rate of speed. *Le bon Dieu* only knows how the woman steered that punt.

Around zooping bends where we buried our beam ends under—through fogs of sticky steam—over rapids of cooking mucilage—between scalding geysers and fusillades of bursting mire she steered as though she held the helm of a gondola. Such a cruise could not be measured in minutes or miles. It might have lasted an hour, yet it seemed to me like an eternity.

The end? The sort you would expect of a cruise with such a beginning. A place where the canyon widened into a great rock-rimmed basin, a vast pot-hole of the gorge where that wild muck-torrent returned to its volcanic sewers. Goulash in a kettle, stirred to whirling circles by an unseen spoon. A hole at the bottom of the kettle sucks the center of the whirl down into a cone. Any fly in that swirling soup would be drawn faster and faster into that suction cone. That, magnified, was what we came to at the end of that mud river—a mile before we got there I could hear that whirlpool roaring—and our barge was the helpless fly.

Sacré bleu! we flew out of that canyon and were twice around the basin before I could make out what it was.

"A maelstrom!" I screamed at the woman. "We are caught in the current of a maelstrom!"

Round and round we went in mile-rimmed circles while I gaped in stunned horror at the hub of the awful thing. Five times we made the circle, each time a little faster as we neared the inner whirl. Any second I expected some spiral pull of suction to grab the barge and yank it spinning into that death-cone.

"Help! Help me hold the rudder!" The green-eyed woman's cries shrilled faintly through the boiler-steam roaring of that vortex. "We must steer the barge into the outer currents! Our only chance is to jump for shore—!"

I FLUNG myself to her side; jammed my shoulder against the steering oar. I could hear the tiller post cracking as the scow swung over a little. I didn't see any shore. From what I could see through the dusk and vapor, the walls of that pot-hole were like the walls of a quarry, bowl-shaped by the whirling maelstrom, slippery as the sides of a crock. Where the canyon flood rushed in, the whirlpool was churned to a wild surf. But at the far side, the wall flattened into a sort of beach where a boat, if it escaped the whirlpool's vortex, might ground.

"We must jump there!" the woman shrieked. "The current is too swift for us to make fast. Next time around I will steer in as close as I can. You must take the lamp in your arms and jump!"

I wanted to curse at the woman for that. I looked at that lamp in the middle of the barge-deck, and I looked at that breach in the basin-wall as we shot past. It was just a muddy ledge, not much wider than a table. Jumping from the barge to that ledge was on a par with leaping to a baggage platform from an express train as it took a curve. Then I saw that sucking maw in the whirlpool's center. Even a flying jump for the moon would have been preferable.

"Next time around!" came the woman's cry. "Get ready! Take the lamp!"

Leaping from the tiller, I grabbed up that confounded antique and crouched ready to spring from the side of the barge. Why did I add the hazard of an armload? Well, I had not learned my lesson yet. Amazing, is it not, what we mortals will endure for a million dollars? "All or nothing, Corday," I was gritting to myself. *Oui,* I did not believe the lamp would make the difference between missing or making that ledge; it did not even occur to me to throw it.

Shoving with all her might, the green-eyed woman steered the barge along the outside rim of the whirlpool. The canyon-mouth whisked by, and we swept around the turn so fast the wall-curve was a streaky blur.

"Ready!" the woman shrilled. "I am holding as close to the wall as I can! Here it comes! Now! Jump! Jump!"

I sprang. Soul of Saint Sebastian! I put my last ounce of power and nerve into that spring. Lamp hugged to chest, I made a wild leap; hit the ledge on two feet, upright; skidded as though on a shelf of ice; crashed into the caved bank and sat down. By the time I got to my feet the woman was coming around again. The barge was nearly opposite when she dropped the steering oar, ran to the side and crouched to leap. I could see the emerald gleam of her stare as she marked the timing and distance. Like a panther she was crouched—a bronze flash through the steam, and she landed lithely at my side.

I won't forget to tell the Devil how that barge sped away, how it swept around that whirlpool in smaller and smaller circles; how finally it was gulped down that roaring, sucking throat. That is another thing I will remember after I am dead—and this!

The green-eyed woman took my arm and conducted me up the caved-in side of the maelstrom-bowl. At the top I saw desert, blue sand hills, evening stars. The cigarette-package moon was on the horizon again, and there in the western distance under a haze was an expanse of silver sea. I stared at that vista of sand, sky and sea, and I began to cry. I was so glad to be out of that canyon and maelstrom that I dropped the lamp and sat down beside it, and shook and wept like a baby.

"Look." I unwrapped the lamp and sobbed. "We are safe with it at last."

My companion was looking, that is so; but not down at me, not at the lamp. She had turned to stare off at the hills which enfolded the canyon, and she was staring with a squint of such emerald-fierce intensity that I jumped up to see what she was looking at.

Merely a dust cloud, *messieurs.* A little moon-tinted dust cloud that was traveling down from a distant ridge toward the lower levels where we stood.

"What is the matter?" I asked. "Why do you stare at that dust puff?"

"That is El Azrek," her toneless voice was a knell. "Allah curse him for a fiend, he has crossed the chasm somewhere, and his men have regained their horses! They know the boiling river ends at this whirlpool! They are riding hard to find us!" She wheeled at me, white-lipped, sobbing. "Pick up the lamp, *Ferangi!* We must run on—!"

I COULDN'T do it. If that lamp had been made of feathers I couldn't have picked it up. I sagged there glaring at the lamp, at the woman, at that down-rolling dust puff, and I couldn't have run another step if Shaitan and all his Black Uhlans were charging down at me. For twenty solid hours I had been on the run, and I think you will agree I had taken a beating in those twenty hours.

In that scrimmage in the fortress I had lost three teeth. I had shredded my nerves on that canyon bridge. A day in the desert had scorched me to a fig; I had torn my soul out going down that Jacob's ladder; the river had parboiled my remains, and that maelstrom had removed the stuffing and left me ready to serve.

Oui, I was done. Broiled, baked, grilled; smoked dry and covered with a gravy of mud. From head to foot I was thorn-slashed, blistered, dripping. Swaying there in the moonlight I would have made a splendid centerpiece for a platter of garbage.

"I can go no farther," I croaked at the woman. "I am used up! Through!"

Echo of hoofbeats spattered through the moonlight, and the green-eyed woman spun at me. "Only a little way farther!" she begged. "Carry the lamp as far as the sea! Once we reach the sea we can run in the surf and they will never find our tracks! We are saved once we reach the sea!"

"Be damned to the sea," I moaned. "I cannot move!"

"Think of the lamp! All the riches it can bring you—"

I was thinking of that. *Hein!* All those rainbow visions, they had gone before my eyes; in their place I was seeing mirages of myself chopped to hamburg by El Azrek and his boys.

"To the devil with the lamp!" I raged. "These are the riches it has brought me—a broken back, parboiled eyes, a burning throat and hands. It has led me here to die a rat's death in the desert. Would God I had never seen the thing!"

Ah, suddenly I hated it. I turned and kicked it as if it were a cuspidor. But you should have seen the way that woman flew at me when I kicked it. "No, no!" she screamed, pulling at my arm. "Rob it, *Ferangi!* Rob the lamp! One chance you have to rob it, and it will bring you anything you wish! Close your eyes and do as I say! Hurry! There is not much time!"

"I am through with robbing it!" I snarled at her. "I would like to throw it into that whirling crater of mud and you with it!" I struck her off with my elbow, sent her reeling back with such violence that she dropped that empty wine jug she had somehow clung to throughout that race. "Get on!" I shouted at her, sinking to my knees. "Take this cursed junkpiece with you! *Va-t'-en!*"

"But you do not understand!" she swayed back at me. "You do not comprehend! I mean *rob* the lamp! *Rob* it! Like this!"

Thunder of heaven! she polished her knuckles against her arm, and for the first time I caught what she meant. I tell you, it crashed over me like one avalanche. The whole fantastic nonsense of it crashed over me. Her Baghdad-accented English which had been fuddled by my French ear. Her lamp-yarn which I had construed as fact! The flowery phrases I had thought mere exaggerations. The "Prince Allah Deen"—"Bring you anything you wish!"—"Rob the lamp!"

Do you get it, my friends? Do you get it as *I* got it—there between the eyes? Well, she meant *rub* the lamp! She meant literally it would bring me anything I wished! Allah Deen—that was the Arabic pronunciation of Aladdin! Name of God! she had told me a fairy story—a nursery tale I had swallowed as actuality! I had bartered my life, suffered the tortures of the damned, to steal Aladdin's Wonderful Lamp!

CHAPTER VI.

SO! YOU knew it all along, *messieurs,* but I did not know it until that moment in the adventure when I petered out there at trail's end.

"Infernal woman!" I squalled. "Is this what I am going to be butchered for? Your crackpot legend about the lamp of Aladdin which I took to be true—*true*—!"

"But it is true! All that I have told you is the truth!" the woman cried. "Scrub the lamp with your knuckles, *Ferangi!* A *djinn* will come—yes, yes, the genie in the lamp! Close your eyes as you scrub and a genie will appear and give you anything you wish! You will see!"

By the bones of Saint Philip of Benguela! I was so mad I went almost blind. I was wild. I wanted to wring the woman's neck for spinning that Arabian Nights yarn, and I wanted someone to wring mine for believing it.

I started up to carry out the first of these two desires, and it looked as if the horsemen racing down from the ridge would carry out the second. They were not far away—maybe two miles. If I intended to throttle that female—

Then I stopped! Stunned by another brain-shock! After all, here was this lamp! Gold! An antique! Certainly treasured in that fortress of Arab thieves! Would bandits risk burning trestles for an antique only? Would a woman of such savagery and steel risk her life's blood on a fairy story? Maybe I went crazy, then. Maybe it was her eyes. Maybe it was that a man condemned will grasp at any straw, but I fell to my knees and rubbed my knuckles on the shoulder of that lamp.

"Harder!" the woman screamed. "Keep your eyes tight shut and rob harder!"

I ground my knuckles into that lamp. Clutching it by the neck, I held it upright in front of me and squeezed shut my eyelids and massaged that big piece of bric-a-brac so hard I could smell the hot metal.

Now you will not believe what I am going to tell you; I did not believe it, myself, at the time. Try to picture it there on that patch of moonlit desert—me, scrubbing that golden lamp—the woman screaming at me to rub harder—then a squeaking!—a jittery, monkeylike squeaking at my elbow, as if a kinkajou had jumped out of Nothingness and landed at my side!

I spun back on my knees with popped eyes. A man was there! A mite of a man! A tiny creature not over twenty-four inches tall, black as tar with catlike ivory teeth, wee white-slitted eyes, a wizened gnome-face wrinkled like a raisin. Squeaking at me like a monkey, dressed in red fez, yellow bloomers, long curly-tipped slippers of blue leather. Rings flashed on his bird-claw fingers; jewels sparkled in his vest—an imp for the bottle!—a genie from the Arabian Nights!—a conjuration straight out of Abracadabra. *Dieu!* I wanted to fall on my face when he raised twelve-inch arms and gave me a salaam.

I jumped back and stared like a strawless scarecrow at a blackbird. Behind me the green-eyed woman murmured, "Make a wish, *Ferangi;* ask the spirit of the lamp of Allah Deen. One chance you have to shut your eyes and make a wish, and the wish shall be gratified. What is it that you wish for most in the world—?"

My brains were so stunned I could scarcely think, much less wish. Staring at the imp beside the lamp, I was shatterpated. I knew I must be moonstruck, dreaming. But at that moment I heard a wild whoop from those horsemen pounding down through the night—a whoop too bloodcurdling for any dream—and I shut my eyes and bellowed my wish.

"I wish to God I was out of Arabia!"

Whack! Blackness swept over me! Spinning, rushing blackness, as quick as that! Through that lightless night I was whirled like a leaf in a vacuum. For miles I seemed to whirl, breathless, blinded, dumb—on and on across limitless space—a void full of wind-rush, motion, watery sounds, blurred echo of far-off voices. Then I was sinking. Sinking into a soundless blank. Then nothing....

THE first thing I saw was the bottle of Johnny Walker. Then someone said, "Now how did that blighter ever get here? By jove, he's a French Legionnaire—"

I sat bolt upright, blinked the grogginess out of my eyes, gave a yell. I was in bed in a room! I saw white walls, window-casements, a door, table, chairs—

Even after my vision cleared everything swayed, tipped and swam. Sunlight kept climbing up and down the wall in a way most incredible as I stared at a picture of King George on the wall; at the bottle on the table; at the men in white talking in a corner; at the officer in the doorway. He wore khaki and looked at me through a monocle.

"Hello! The chap's awake. Only a Frenchman could survive a bop like that."

Only a Frenchman could survive such an impossible awakening. "*Sacré!* You are English?"

"Right you are. And now," he said, stepping over the doorsill, "do you mind explaining yourself? We aren't quite used to having Foreign Legion deserters here on the Picadilly."

I opened my mouth to tell him Foreign Legionnaires weren't used to finding themselves on the Picadilly, but a muscle stuck in my tongue. The room swam. Everything tipped and swayed. One of the men at room's end turned and walked toward me, chuckling. He had a red, roast-beef face, and he was shaking drops of water from a fever thermometer.

"Pukka fellow," he told the officer, aiming the thermometer at me. "Hundred and five a while ago, but you can't kill the French. You should have heard him carrying on. Thinks he's Sinbad or somebody. Keeps mumbling about Aladdin's lamp—"

"Aladdin!" I gasped. "The lamp! I rubbed it! The green-eyed woman told me to rub it! She said the genie would appear and—"

"What's this about Aladdin's lamp?" a voice rumbled. The figure of John Bull in a naval commander's uniform stepped in through the door behind the khaki Sandhurst officer. "So the scoundrel admits the theft, does he? Speak up, fellow," he roared at me, "what do you know about this job?"

"I was in Arabia!" I panted. "I—" My tongue jammed again. It jammed when I saw another figure coming through the door. A big Arab shiek whose presence crowded the room and made the walls tilt every which way. I screamed, "Orange-beard! That's him! The green-eyed woman's husband! He's followed me here!"

Hands caught me as I tried to leap out of bed. The white room spun. I must have put up a brisk tussle. Afterwards there were pillow feathers all over the place, the Johnny Walker was smashed on the floor and I was pinned down like Gulliver under an army corps of Englishmen.

"Now," the one with the John Bull face was roaring down, "if you're sane enough to talk, just what does this nonsense mean?"

I told my story. Graphically and as best I could without the use of gestures, I told it. Those Britishers were not as skeptical of my account as you are at the present moment, *messieurs.* One by one they got up off my legs, arms and diaphragm, and when I reached that climax where the genie appeared, they were not skeptical at all.

They winked and blinked, made faces, shot quick glances at Orange-beard. All sorts of British expressions they wore when I gasped to a finish, but unbelief was not among them. The man whose features were like red roast beef jabbed the thermometer into my mouth when I was through. He said, "George! The chap's really normal."

"The French are never normal!" John Bull snapped. "Who but a Gascon would try to steal Aladdin's lamp?"

"Who but an Englishman would stand there belching, 'Haw!' if I did?" I shouted. "Someone is whisked from the Arabian desert to the Picadilly, and the British take his temperature! *Non,* and there stands El Azrek—that woman's husband!"

I WISH you could have heard the sound that came out of Orange-beard's whiskers. An Arab can belch like nobody on earth. It is the equivalent in insults of a British stare, and Orange-beard gave it to me when I hollered and pointed at his face.

"Lucky that's only curry and the Caïd understands no English." The grizzled, fat navy officer frowned. "Have a nice international situation in Asir if it got around that woman was in El Azrek's harem. I must say, Corday, you've strained his relations enough as it is."

"But he left her!" I gagged. "In Bagdad where he stole the lamp—"

"Bagdad be blowed! Stole the lamp, be blowed!" the John Bull roared. "El Azrek bought that lamp in the bazaar at Jizan—"

"Bought it!" I choked. "He didn't murder a—and hide it in his—but I tell you, I saw it there! In his Arabian fortress of thieves!"

"Fortress of thieves is right!" came the bull-lunged answer. "Listen, Gascon! That fort is a prison! The Caïd is in charge of that place and it's full of the toughest batch of caravan raiders and Red Sea pirates you ever heard of. For a year El Azrek has been working alongside the British Government to police this coast—why, he's one of our most trusted allies! The woman didn't know that when she sold him that cheap lamp in the bazaar!"

I was strangling. I whispered, "She sold him that lamp—?"

"She's sold them by the dozen! Goes from town to town, palming off those brass lamps as antiques. Told you it was Aladdin's lamp, eh? That's a new one! What she didn't tell you—it's worthless brass covered by fake gold leaf, with a small oil reservoir at the top, air holes in the bottom and a trap door in the side that springs like the lid of a Jackinabox."

Room, Englishmen and El Azrek swam around me, and I did not want to hear any more, but John Bull's voice boomed on. "Well, that woman sells those trick lamps into some sheik's palace or rich merchant's house, but she doesn't sell 'em into prisons. I suppose she heard El Azrek was rich, but she didn't know he ran a jail, and when she found out where he had gone with the infernal lamp she must've had a fit. Prison was just the right place for that piece of junk, too, if only you hadn't helped her sneak it out of there like an idiot! Do you know who that woman was, you fool?"

I made weak sounds of not knowing.

"That woman was one of the cleverest jewel thieves in the East. Kedija the Key! As for what she called the genie in the lamp—that's the blasted pigmy boy she teams with—Little Hamid! In the lamp—my God! That pair have cleaned out the coffers all the way from Cape Town to Constantinople working that lamp trick.

"With that midget hiding in the lamp, the woman sells it in the bazaar. Buyer takes it home; then the pigmy sneaks out at night and robs the house. Aladdin's Wonderful Lamp! Well, that pigmy couldn't get out of it in that prison, so Kedija got you to fetch him out; not only that, made you lug him on your back and take the worst part of the risk. El Azrek thought you were trying to pull off a prison-break. Wait till he hears!"

I whispered faintly, "Kedija the Key! Little Hamid! He was in that lamp when I stole it out of that fortress! I—I carried him all that time on my back!" Somehow I was on my feet. Swaying. Cursing. I caught the table; screamed. "Where is she? Where is that jade?"

"El Azrek threw them both into a mud hole," the John Bull snapped. "I can't make out from his description what kind of a place it was—some sort of bloody mud whirlpool in the desert, it seems. Anyway, he caught 'em near it and chucked them in. You'd have gone in with them if you hadn't been a white man. He thought you might be English so he brought you here for us to look at on the Picadilly. You're lucky you're alive, man. That woman slugged you over the noggin so hard with a wine jug that she shattered it into a thousand bits. The jug, I mean."

He thought I was stupid for believing the green-eyed woman's story; he thought no Englishman could have believed in Aladdin's Wonderful Lamp. He did not see that vixen's emerald eyes, nor did he hear her sing that Arabian Nights tale on the Red Sea beach.

They bandaged my head, those British, and put me back in bed. Six weeks later they returned me to the French Foreign Legion. I still possess the scar where that woman struck me from behind while I made a wish with closed eyes. I? It makes to me no difference whether she was Kedija the Key and that imp was Little Hamid. *Non,* that only convinces me. Such jewel thieves as that, *messieurs*—such a prison-break—such a lamp—well, if it was not the lamp of Aladdin, it was every bit as wonderful. I do not laugh at the Arabian Nights, you comprehend. I went through one of them....

OLD Thibaut Corday grunted an exclamation point, and leaned back in his chair to let us know the story was over. Algerian twilight was stretching its blue-gauze veils across the Boulevard Sadi Carnot, and the tootle and thump of the Kasbah dance joints came sifting under our café awning to replace the echoes of Arabia. The young British consulate agent stared at Old Thibaut Corday, started to say something, swallowed.

"Alors," the ancient Legion veteran reminded him, "do I win the bottle of Dubonnet?"

"Right." The Englishman nodded. "If you'll explain how that pigmy or whatever your genie was—how it kept alive all that day in the desert. The sun beating on that lamp like that—nothing to drink and—"

"And why didn't it kill him when I flung the lamp down those stairs?" The old Frenchman shook his head grimly. "Ah, I wish I had fractured every bone in the little rat's body, but I suppose he did not even feel the jolting, like those devils who go over Niagara Falls in a barrel. As for heat, he was an African pigmy. Recall, too, how the woman wrapped her cloak around the lamp? How she patted it and talked to it as she carried it now and then? That *poissarde!* She must have been telling him to enjoy the free ride and sneaking him drinks of that fig wine. When I think of how I lugged that little monster! The woman knew he could never run fast or far on his twelve-inch legs. She used me for a camel. A sacred camel!"

"Twelve-inch legs or your legs!" the English boy cried. "What was that light you saw in that tower, and if it wasn't a magic lamp how did you get from that desert in Arabia to the Picadilly?"

"The light?" Old Thibaut Corday grunted. "The Caïd's radio station. His favorite plaything, I found out. Turned it on for an hour every midnight, as the jade probably learned. I saw the flare of the generators. And the Picadilly?" The old veteran grinned. "Orange-beard lugged me there over his saddle. Did I not say at the beginning how one minute I was in Arabia and the next thing I knew I was on British soil? *Eh bien,* I woke up on a British patrol boat, a Red Sea cruiser named the *Picadilly.* A British boat—not so?—is British soil."

He gestured with finality.

The young English consular agent was already fumbling in his pocket. Old Thibaut Corday nodded approvingly. "I think I have made my point fairly clear, *messieurs.* Which was—if you recall—that nursery tales have a basis in fact. You see, then, the basis behind Aladdin's Wonderful Lamp. Perhaps there was no such thing as magic lamp and genie, but I will bet you the woman got hold of the right angle to that story.

"Somewhere in ancient Arabia there was an Aladdin. He traveled around with a midget in a lamp, and he was one damn big jewel thief!"

The young British agent ordered two bottles of Dubonnet.

CORDAY AND THE SEVEN LEAGUE BOOTS

JUST TRY THEM FOR SIZE, MONSIEUR LE LEGIONNAIRE—THEY WILL NOT PINCH OR CHAFE, BUT IF THEY CARRY YOU ON FABULOUS FLIGHTS INTO THE REALM OF MANIAC ADVENTURE, YOU MUST NOT BE SURPRISED. FOR HE WHO TAKES BIG STEPS WILL STUMBLE....

Walk Softly, Go Far—
Old Oriental Proverb

THE YOUNG British consular agent said he had done a lot of walking that day and his shoes pinched him. Old Thibaut Corday said the Englishman did not know anything about walking, or shoes either.

"Regard!" the old Frenchman thrust out a foot. "Observe that for a shoe! There is what one wears in the accursed Foreign Legion—what Legionnaires call a *brodequin.* Is that a dancing pump or oxford? You behold it is not. That is an engine, a ten pound galley to enslave the toes!"

The Englishman remarked he had worn a similar boot playing Rugby.

"You did not!" Old Thibaut Corday declared. "A Legion *brodequin* would make your British football shoe look like a lady's slipper alongside. Today this boot is old, decayed, thin, the sole a mere tissue and the hobnails worn down like the stubs of an old lion's teeth. Years ago when that boot was new, it was a rock-crusher! That leather is hippopotamus hide; that bunion-bulged toe could have kicked to bits a brick wall; the sole was thicker than a carpenters plank, and if in a fight I stamped down on a ruffian's hand the iron studs would have flattened it to a pancake.

"As for walking—?" The old Frenchman eyed his shoe with the veneration of the master praising an old hunting dog. "*Non,* but in the Legion we did not walk. We marched! On hard earth. In mud. Tough gravel. Hot sand. A Legionnaire must teach his boots to drill,

From the darkness they sprang up, and the night was suddenly alive with Touaregs.

slog, parade, charge. They must trot him quick-step, *pas gymnastique,* or pace endless routines of sentry duty, or stand still on guard when there is a noise in the dark and his feet want to go.

"Sometimes, with the bullets nipping their heels, they must run like the wind, those boots. They are to a Legionnaire what a horse is to a cavalry man. It is not for nothing they call the Legion the Cavalry-on-Foot, and I would like a *centime* for every mile these clogs have carried me. Twenty miles a day was nothing—thirty!—even forty these hellions have marched. That expression, 'die with your boots on'—that is from the French Foreign Legion, too. I would like a *centime* for every mile these boots have run to save me from dying in them. I would be a millionaire!"

The young consular agent asked Corday to tell him in seriousness the longest distance he had ever run in his boots without stopping. "I mean how far in one stretch, say, in a day?"

Old Thibaut Corday studied his shoe thoughtfully. "I will tell you," he agreed, pulling up an extra chair, propping up both feet and grimacing at his boots as if he had suddenly contracted the gout. "There is a story about a pair of boots—not these, but some others I wore—and I will tell it to you if you listen through to the end without blurting out that I am a liar. You agree?"

"Fair enough." The young Englishman grinned across the café table. "Forward march."

The veteran raked his cinnamon whiskers clear of his lips and stared at his footwear gravely. "I will strain your credulity at once," he advised. "The longest day's run I ever made in a pair of boots was from Tunis to India. That was only the halfway mark.

"From there I ran to China, Persia and Japan, pausing for breath in Cambodia and taking the long way around by Madagascar. In the end I landed in Hell.

"There were bullets nipping my heels all the way, and I could not have done it if each stride in those boots I wore had not carried me one hundred and eleven thousand and eighty feet!"

The young British consular agent looked worried. The Algerian sun blazed hot outside the café awning, and Old Thibaut Corday had walked in without his hat. He murmured, "I say, old boy. Now really!"

The old Frenchman gave him a glare. "*Zut!* Already you think I lie, although you are bound by contract not to say so. But I am not lying, and my scalp is too thick for the sun. I promise this is a true story—"

CHAPTER I.

NEW BOOTS SWEEP CLEAN.

NOW NAPOLEON was the world's greatest general, perhaps, and who am I to criticize his military tactics? But he made one error in his record, *monsieur;* he said an army marches on its stomach. Every soldier knows an army marches by its boots. A regiment can dispense with food for a week, but where could it march to barefoot, I would like to inquire? If I remember my schoolbook history, the American patriots who had the chilblains at Valley Forge could answer that. So could the men of MacMahon who died at Sedan, ill-shod in the patent leather boots and spats invented by some dancing master in the War Department of 1870. So could the grenadiers who killed their feet on that stroll back from Moscow.

An army is no better than its shoes.

Boots are as important to a soldier as hoofs to a horse. Give him a good dry pair. Roomy enough for a circulation of air between the toes, but snug, so that one's heel does not slide and blister. Staunch as a ferryboat for fording swamps, yet light as a canoe for speed. Armor-leathered to turn a ricochetted bullet, yet cool for marching in the desert. Hobnailed for cobblestones. Gum-soled for stealthy corners. Tough, but easy on the instep. Blunt-nosed, but not liable to stumble. Serviceable, yet smart. Where in the world is such a pair? Nowhere!

What do you get in the army? In the French Foreign Legion you get these *brodequins.* And a kick from the rat-faced supply sergeant who gives them to you.

"Here, Blue!" he calls when you enter the barracks at Sidi as a recruit. "Break these in on your pumpers!" Flinging a pair of those bull-killers at you.

You tell him your feet are size nine. "Nine, be blowed!" he roars. "Do you think this is a shoe shop on the Rue de la Paix? I am all out of nines and you are lucky to get eights. Do not worry, you will learn to march in them! Your toes are too long? You will see how those boots can cut them off!"

Or suppose that your feet are small; then you are swamped in those boats, size eleven. "Too big for you, Blue? Your tootsies slide around? Never fear, little man; your feet will swell into them!"

You are not issued socks in the Legion, either, and breaking in a pair of those hobnailed, hippopotamus-hide boots is like trying to tame a couple of rhinoceri lashed on your feet. If you are not dead after five years' service, you may re-enlist and get another pair. A batch of Legionnaires marching off in new boots resembles a parade of cripples hobbling to a hospital. Believe it, there will be plenty of growling and limping. Everyone tries to exchange with the next man, and everyone prays for a battle. Stealing the boots from a dead man is a little game long played in the Legion. You mark him off, if his feet are anywhere near your size; and there is a common understanding—first come, first served.

THAT company stationed at El Hamma in Tunis was a typical example. I think when I go to Hades I will see a close resemblance to El Hamma. It was not the place where you could repair your corns or cool your heels. Not that town of dirty Arab houses, twisty alleys and evil bazaars roasting under the North African sun on the edge of that fiery desert called the Grand Erg Orientale.

That was a villainous village! Hot? Merely to lift an arm caused you to break out in perspiration. The alleys were choked with blowing sand and dirty smells and a scum of Arabs and Negroes good for nothing but wickedness.

The thermometer was permanent at a hundred and ten in the shade, only there was no shade. No tree-cooled boulevards and pretty promenades in that town. You could not baby your feet in that place. It did not go in for footwear. There was one old blind cobbler in El Hamma.

I am all for giving Tunis to Mussolini after seeing that part of it. France ought to let him have it. He would probably make a lot of friends there; El Hamma would be a congenial spot for him to live. Besides heat and heathenism, the place was a hellhole full of drugs. Hashish and opium was the local diet. The Government would not have cared, but these narcotics were being streaked to the tribal chieftains out in the desert, along with advice to fight the French.

Those Arabs who infested the Grand Erg Orientale were ugly customers at best; give them a whiff of the poppy, and they were dangerous as dynamite. Inspired with hashish and rebellion, the desert tribes were becoming unruly. Trouble was brewing in Tunis even in those days—El Hamma was the cookpot of the sedition. *Voilà!* The French Legion was sent down to police the place. We marched there, you comprehend. All the way from the railhead at Kairouan. In new boots.

You never saw a detachment of men as footsore. Groaning and cursing, we hobbled into the outpost at El Hamma.

"By the grave-slippers of my dead grandmother!" I remember Yankee Bill the Elephant swearing. "My clogs are killing me! Why does the supply department torture us this way? We spend five years breaking in a pair of brogans in Algeria, then the outfit is ordered into new shoes and told to make a forced march across half of Africa! I am crippled for life!"

"You think *you* are crippled!" That from Christianity Jensen the Dane. "I am walking on boiled lobsters. Last night I had to cut the laces open with a knife. My toes refused to enter prison again this morning. I had to stuff them in with a spoon!"

"That is nothing, pigeon-toes!" cried another man. "Look at my heel! Achilles, himself, never had such a blister!"

"It is something new in the Legion! We are to bind our feet like Chinese women. Mine grow smaller every year. In this pair of sabots they will be reduced to stumps!"

"I am marking you, my friend," came the laugh. "Those eights of yours will be a relief after this boy's size I am limping in."

"Dirty German! You would like to kill me, yourself, just to get my shoes!"

"No danger of that," was the warning from our corporal, himself sitting on his cot with a foot in a tender hand. "The colonel will kill you fatheads before you know it. You think your hoofs are hurting you now, but wait! You do not know Papa Rolant!"

Ha ha, but we did know Papa Rolant. His reputation in the Legion was of the best—or of the worst—depending on how you looked at it. His personality was a blend of Tiger Clemenceau, Madame Dufarge, two bottles of cognac and a novel by De Maupassant. He was as French as the Three Musketeers. And he resembled Santa Claus, as plump as a chuckle, with merry red cheeks and a white-winged mustache and twinkling blue eyes.

But do not be mistaken about that little package. It could be explosive. All of us pretend we are someone else, and Papa Rolant had a secret yearning to be Napoleon. Emperor and Soldier—he fancied the role: genius of the battlefield, and dashing boulevardier! About anything military he had Napoleonic ideas. Honor! Valor! Discipline! He rubbed it in.

Twinkling and merry, he was nevertheless the very devil for military rules. In a battle he was as cunning as a fox, following orders from above to the letter, but in such a way that he never wasted the lives of his men. In the outpost he was murderous. He had a passion for pomp and circumstance. For bugles and drums. For military display. He loved dress parades!

Full-dress parades! At any time of the day he was liable to order one. Every Legionnaire must turn out completely equipped, down to the last trenching tool, the last sacred button. Uniforms must be perfect to the uttermost detail. Collars hooked. Buckles shining. Knapsacks ready for the field.

Woe to the soldier whose rifle wasn't clean. Let his *képi* be askew, and he would not soon forget it. A grease-spot on a tunic meant a week in the guardhouse. To be late for lineup or slouchy on the march meant such punishments as were ordinarily meted to criminals. Funny, was it not? A man could be a coward on the battlefield, and Papa Rolant would forgive him. But he would not forgive anything at parade.

"It is the high point of soldiering," he would say. "It keeps the men on their toes. It impresses the Arabs. It is excellent for morale. It keeps the Legionnaires from going *cafard.*"

Cafard—that is when men go a little crazy from the sunshine and monotony of a desert outpost. The Legionnaires would have risked it a thousand times in preference to those parades. How they hated them. To line up at full regimentals in the blazing North African heat! To drill and wheel in the dust like West Pointers, like Prussians on Unter den Linden, like cadets at Saint Cyr! To march through those dirty alleys of El Hamma, colors flying, in a fanfare of bugles and drums, precise as tin soldiers! With Papa Rolant reviewing us from his horse, pretending to himself he was Napoleon! Even the under-officers loathed those daily parades, but that was nothing to the men. And do you know what that colonel was most stern and particular about? That the parade keep exactly in step! And that every man keep a shine on his shoes!

NOW that was a nice situation—our boots being what they were, and Papa Rolant being what he was! Figure to yourself those Legion cripples keeping in step to begin with, much less putting a polish on their clogs. And then parading every day because the colonel liked military pageants. It was enough to have the whole garrison wild as a zoo.

Our happy colonel was patient at first. "I realize this company is in need of drilling," he announced during one review. "It is my intention to make this El Hamma garrison the finest company in the Legion. I will tolerate no clumsy-footed marching, no slovenly uniform. I understand there has been much grumbling about the order for cleaning boots. Boots are as much a part of the uniform as cummerbund or tunic. You will learn that I ask no more of my soldiers than I demand of myself. *Allons!*"

He referred to his own uniform which, for all his pudgy pod, was as smart as starch. He delighted in fine uniforms. I know. I had to brush them. I was his orderly.

After about a month of dressing up and parading, the garrison was savage. It began to seem as if something worse than drug-running and native insurrection might blow the roof off El Hamma. Those daily parades were brutal. The season got hotter. The colonel more strict. The Legionnaires madder.

"The garrison will mutiny," Yankee Bill the Elephant raged one night. "That dumpling colonel will drive us to revolt with these infernal parades. He thinks we are tin soldiers."

"It is not enough we must patrol this sink of iniquity for dope-runners," Jensen snarled.

"He expects us to look as trig as the King's Household Guard in these rags. Marches us quick-step through the sun for three hours, then yells because our boots are not like his, all polished up."

"As if he did not have a batman to dust him off twice a day. That pompous comedian! Do you ever see him marching? No, he is glued to the saddle like the statue of a general that he thinks he is!"

Well, we stumped and marched and paraded around that cursed Arab town until the colonel, himself, without lifting a foot, went a little lame. Corns did not dampen his passion for military reviews, but only put him in a temper. And that is where that old blind cobbler of El Hamma came in.

Imagine my lack of sympathy when I reported at headquarters one night and found Colonel Rolant sitting with his feet in a pan of water.

"They are blistered!" He glared at his swollen toes. "It is the perspiration! I am stout and I suffer from the heat! Do you know, orderly, I believe my shoes are too tight. Is there a cobbler in this mishap of a town who could stretch them for me?"

"There is a blind Arab cobbler in the Lane of the Three Thirsty Camels."

Presently we were on our way, the colonel puffing behind me as I led him through the evil bazaar, taking the long route around in the hopes that his touchy feet might teach him a lesson. Do you think it did? *Non,* he saw no connection between his own toes and those of common men. He was an officer. *His* feet were special. Corns were an indulgence not permitted to lowly Legionnaires.

As we entered the shop of this miserable cobbler the colonel's eye fell on a pair of remarkable riding boots that gleamed with fresh polish. Shinier, even, than the colonel's own. Unusual for a dingy Arab shop, they stood out in a litter of shabby sandals, scuffed clipper-cloppers and old native slippers as surprisingly as though they had just walked in from an expensive bootmaker's in London.

Papa Rolant was on them at once, admiring them, testing the leather, turning them in is hands. The soles were at least an inch thick, yet the boots seemed light. The workmanship was extraordinary. The calf was soft and pliable as buckskin. They were not as short as Arab riding boots, nor as tall as British riding boots, nor as thick as cavalry or field boots. A beautiful pair!

NEXT to wine and women, your average man has a weakness for good leather—there is something about its smell of leather, its feeling. Those beautiful boots had them both. I would have given my soul to own them. I could see a hungry twinkle come to Papa Rolant's eye. Those boots were just made for him. Such boots any general might wear. They were magnificently military.

"Corday, I want to buy these boots. Strike a bargain."

That was funny. As the colonel spoke, the old blind cobbler who had been sitting cross-legged at the back of the shop jumped up as if he had been kicked. Dropping awl and thread and a piece of leather, he somehow glared at us with alarm in the vacant sockets of his eyes. He was an ancient and withered scarecrow, more a skeleton in rags and turban than a man; and his voice came out like the yell of a ghost.

"What boots do you mean, Sidi? Which pair would you buy?"

"I want to buy this fine black pair," the colonel puffed. "I am the *commandant* of the garrison here. How much for these black boots?"

Sacred pipe! the ancient blind man tottered forward and snatched the boots out of the colonel's hand. "No, no! Do not touch them! These boots are not for sale!"

Papa Rolant looked astounded. He was not used to having a native snatch anything out of his hand. "How much are they, old rascal? Quick, I have no time for your Arab bargaining. I offer one hundred francs!"

"A hundred francs?" the blind cobbler wheezed. "No, no, Sidi. I could not sell them to you for five hundred francs. For five thousand!"

"What is the matter with this crack-potted scamp?" the colonel yelled at me. "Does he not know who I am? Speak to him in Arabic, Corday. Tell him I want to buy those boots, and mean to have them! Nor will I pay him any such fantastic price. Does he think they are made of gold?"

"But I cannot sell them," the old scarecrow wailed, hugging them to his chest. "They are not for sale, Sidi! They were only brought here to be polished. I do not own them."

Disappointment sulked across the colonel's face. His corns gave a twinge, and he snapped, "Who owns them, then? Who in this dirty desert town could afford such a pair?"

"Ah, Sidi," the old cobbler bowed, "I do not think the owner would sell them to you, either. He is so fond of them that every evening he brings them in for me to polish. It is the Italian, Sidi. The Italian who rides every day from El Hamma to dig in the sands of the desert, seeking the Past."

A jealous gleam came to Papa Rolant's eye. He knew who was referred to. The archaeologist living in El Hamma, a pale scholar from Rome who was digging excavations a few miles from our outpost in search of Carthaginian ruins. Papa Rolant had been annoyed by him, for it was the duty of the French Government to afford such people protection. The Italian had refused any military escort, saying he would risk any trouble with the desert tribes and preferred to work alone.

"So he owns these fine boots? *Zut!* Where did he get them?"

"He bought them from an Arab trader," the old cobbler whined. "At a tremendous price from a caravan sheik out across the sands."

Well, the colonel could not have that. He wanted those boots, and he pouted like a woman who had missed a bargain. He was the *commandant* of El Hamma, and it would not do for someone to wear a better pair of boots than he. Particularly some fool scholar, some Italian.

"Attend!" Papa Rolant ordered the cobbler. "If I cannot buy this particular pair, I will have a pair as good. I want the same quality of leather and workmanship. You can make me a pair exactly like those?"

The blind cobbler bowed. "With my eyes shut I can copy them, Sidi. You wear the same size? That is well. By Saturday you may have a pair of such likeness that you could not tell the difference. The price at only five hundred francs."

Who could have guessed what astonishing things were in shoe-leather? And that is when the real trouble began. That Saturday when the colonel ordered a dress parade and turned out to review us in his fine new boots.

CHAPTER II.

BOOTMARKS IN THE SAND.

I WISH you could have seen the faces of the men when the colonel stalked out that morning in those boots. Even the captain and the two lieutenants looked as if they would like to cut his throat. *Sapristi!* it was the hottest day of the year. That, or any year.

Since sunrise the garrison had been on patrol, and that was warm and nasty work. Divided into squads, the company scouted along the edge of the desert looking for suspicious guerilla bands, or combed the town, examining and searching suspicious characters for drugs. Since every tribesman in that desert was suspicious and every native in town was equally suspect, you can figure the job.

Looking for narcotics in an Arab town is like hunting a wisp of straw in a haystack. We found plenty of hashish and opium. Those natives were full of it. But it was inside them when we found it, and where it came from and how it reached them was something else again. It was dangerous work, too, searching those wolves. Your Arab drug-fiend will go berserk with a knife as soon as not, and those dope-maddened desert chiefs were just waiting for a signal to start a revolution.

Very good! After you spend a few hours searching a batch of African drug addicts in a place where such dope is dynamite, you are hardly in the mood for a parade. *Tiens!* There was the bugle tootling the assembly. The sun almost at noon. Orders for full regimentals and all equipment. Parade call!

The men were ugly that noon, I can tell you. Lined up on the drill field in full marching equipment, they were weighted down like camels. Who wanted to carry extra cartridge belts, water canteens and kits of food just for the exercise? Already they were footsore from patrol; sweating like horses in the heat. But you had to scour the dirt of the bazaar off your *brodequins* and play tin soldier for Papa Rolant. And then to have him stalk out for parade inspection in that pair of beautiful boots!

On my word, there was not a sound on that field when the colonel stomped into view. A hundred pairs of eyes were on his feet. Angry eyes. Envious eyes. Bitter eyes. You could see them following his steps as he advanced down the line to front and center. Those men were like tigers fascinated by a pair of taunting black cats.

Have you ever seen a small boy showing off a new pair of shoes? The colonel was like that. He was brisk and jovial. He pretended he did not care about his new boots, but he could not help looking down once a minute and admiring them. He would stoop and flick off a speck of dust. He could see his apple-cheeked reflection in the toes. The toes were like hlack mirrors; the night before, I had spent three hours polishing them.

The blind Arab cobbler had promised delivery Saturday morning, but the colonel had not been able to wait. Friday midnight he had been there at the blind cobbler's shop to try them on. Ah! What comfort! He had wanted to break them in so they would not squeak, but those boots were wonderfully pliable from the first. All night he had kept them on, as a child sleeps with a delightful toy. He had scarcely been able to wait for the parade. Now he strutted out like a gamecock. He was playing Napoleon to the hilt. All he lacked was the paper hat and the wooden sword.

Silently the men writhed and snarled. Their own boots were torturing them. He enjoyed them so much that he wanted to walk in them. Instead of riding at the head of the column as was his custom on parade, he walked at the head of the column. I followed at his heels, leading his horse.

OUT of the barrack-ground we marched, and down through the twisting bazaar of the town. Flags flying. Drums rolling. Bugles blaring out *La Casquette de Père Bugeaud.* The colonel was putting it on, I can tell you. You would have thought he was leading a crack Chasseur regiment down the Champs Elysée to the Arc de Triomphe. He wore all his medals, and his braid gleamed in the sun. He held his sword at half salute off his pouting chest, and he lifted his new boots high. He would show this stupid Arab village a thing or two, and he went through the whole parade routine—company, right oblique!—left oblique!—column right!—column at fours!—company at quick-step!—halt!—squads left!—company march! If only French marching regulations included the goose-step, his happiness would have been complete.

Behind him came the sweating color-bearers, and behind the sweating color-bearers came the sweating buglers. Then came the sweating drummers with water flying off their wrists; and behind the drummers, the sweat-soaked column of marching men, with sweat-soaked officers up and down the line and bringing up the rear.

Through the stifling alleys of El Hamma the parade wheeled and pivoted and executed pretty maneuvers, for the benefit of sneering Arab merchants, sullen riff-raff and barking dogs.

Drums and bugle tunes drowned out the cursing and complaining, but I had only to look behind me to see every dripping face enraged. Yankee Bill told me he heard one of the lieutenants snarling, "The vain little popinjay would march us to Hell just to show off his new boots!"

So it seemed.

At the south end of El Hamma there was an Arab gate—a Moslem arch that gave view to the miles of emptiness and sand, that burnt-copper wilderness of the Grand Erg Orientale that stretches down to the Nowhere of the Sahara. Ordinarily our good colonel would end our daily parade at this gate-arch, lining us up for inspection before the arch and dismissing us with lectures and punishments.

Not so this Saturday!

Straight on out through the arch strutted the little rooster, dragging the whole parade after him. Out we marched into the blazing desert—the flags, the bugles, the drums, the sweating column, parading across the sand as if the town was too confined and the colonel needed all that vast emptiness to maneuver us in. The column lagged a little and one of the buglers slid off-key. The colonel bawled an order to smarten us up.

"Close up, men!" the tired officers relayed the order. "Close up!"

I could feel the line jolting down its length behind me like a string of hunted freight cars. On we marched through thick dust and blinding sunshine. The town began to dwindle out behind.

Company right oblique! Column at fours! Left shoulder arms! Forward march!

Name of a name! we were heading straight into the desert.

THEN it came to me what the colonel was up to. Of course. He had to march us out to that archaeologist's excavation to show him that a French *commandant* had boots as splendid as those of an Italian ditch digger. But that sand-grubber did not seem impressed.

About two miles from the town there he was at his hole in the dunes, a thin and scholarly-looking bird with a sun helmet and near sighted spectacles, standing in the door of a tent with a book under his arm and a couple of lazy Arabs shoveling around.

I recognized him by his fine black boots which were exactly matched by those on Papa Rolant. He merely waved at us as we marched by. Passing the excavation, Papa Rolant strutted like a drum-major, looking neither right nor left. On went the parade. No order steered us back toward the town. The colonel was enjoying his new boots so much he was going to parade them all afternoon on the sand.

Now the thing grew ridiculous.

What good is a parade where there is no one to watch it? Deeper and deeper we marched into that ocean of sand—right oblique!—left oblique!—double file!—*pas gymnastique* and dead march!—executing all manner of intricate parade-drills and getting farther into the desert at every mile.

Was the colonel trying to punish us with this grueling drill? Forced marches were one thing, but parade maneuvers in full dress and regimentals in the desert were something else again. The buglers were winded. The drummers were panting. The Legionnaires, loaded with baggage and full equipment, sweaty, gasping from the heat, looked ready to drop in their aching boots.

By mid-afternoon the colonel himself looked exhausted. El Hamma had long since disappeared in the dust behind us. The sun was murder. Sweat trickled down the colonel's apple cheeks and soaked his tunic across his fat shoulder blades. But although his lungs were puffing his spirit was spry. As I, leading his horse, humped along at Papa Rolant's heels, I had an idea he was trying to show us how a French officer could outmarch his men. The contest was unfair. In the lead he was not eating any dust. He carried only his sword and his medals. We Legionnaires were clumping in nail-studded hoppers, not in natty and princely boots.

The colonel would not let up. When he wheeled around to flourish his sword and bark an order, the column had to step along. His eye was sharp for any flaw. After a halt he would step off again, lifting his plump knees with unexpected vigor.

To my surprise I saw the afternoon was waning and we were still marching south. Were we going to parade all day? What of garrison duty, the evening patrol, mess? Just before sundown he barked the order that lined us up for review inspection. Away out there in the desert he inspected us. Then, break ranks! Time out for a swig of wine, some hardtack and chocolate. Then to our consternation, parade call again! Bugles, drums and all the rest of it. In the twilight we continued to march south.

Well, we did not get back to El Hamma that night. Not with Puss-in-Boots for parade-master! We maneuvered on south in the desert until darkness; just when the column was ready to go down like a line of tenpins, came the order to pitch camp. Orders from the colonel were orders, but that black and unknown desert seemed hardly the place to bivouac like that, alive as it was with roving bands of nomads.

I saw officers were uneasy as they gathered around the colonel's tent, but no one dared to question the colonel's judgment. Papa Rolant was a famous tactician, an expert on military strategy. That night he was also jovial. He chuckled a lot to himself as if he had some secret joke, and his eyes were merry and sly. He sat at his campfire beaming down at his boots. No staff officer would have dared interrupt his good humor.

THAT march had just about finished the men. They and their feet were tired and sore as boils. "The devil!" Jensen groaned to me in passing. "Never have I made such a march. My left foot is dead. My right foot is dying. All because that poodle wants to promenade a pair of new pumpers!" Yankee Bill the Elephant growled, "I have just enough strength left to kick out his brains with these clogs, and for a cigarette I would do it."

A Belgian snarled, "You would think he was a *cocotte* in high heels, the way he swanks. What I would not give to be in his shoes."

And the American laughed, "Not I, Dog-Face. If this keeps up, I don't think Papa will be wearing them long."

There was a mutinous atmosphere in camp that night, but the colonel was as gay as Old King Cole. He called me into his tent to shine his boots, and I found him waiting with his feet propped up on a camp chair. "Ha, orderly!" He astonished me by a comradely nudge. "Shine them up for me, my boy. Are they not beauties? Ah, you do not know the satisfaction of a fine pair of boots, so easy and luxuriant. I tell you, Corday, I never have known such pleasure. I feel as if I had been walking on air."

I wondered if he was drunk. There was wine at his elbow, and before I left he was asleep. His boots were on and his expression was blissful. Conceive a colonel addressing an orderly like that.

Then conceive this! An hour before day-break, and the bugles were squawking again. Again the men were on their feet. Again parade call! *Oui,* camp was broken at the double quick, and again the column was tramping across the sand—colors flying—bugles and drums—full dress parade!

We Legionnaires were not walking on air. Do you think the colonel cared? He did not. He was out there once more at the head of the column, swanking like a Julius Caesar and striking still farther into the desert.

We were in more than dangerous territory that morning. There were Touaregs reported in that part of the wilderness—the most deadly fighters in Africa. It was no place to announce our arrival with blaring bugles and bright flags. On we went, marching and counter-marching, wheeling and pivoting and parading all over the sand, and working deeper into Nowhere under the murderous sun.

That noon the officers began to look at each other. I had glimpses of them frowning at Papa Rolant's back. During a halt they grouped around the colonel, their expressions reflecting anxiety. I heard Papa Rolant's voice explode in temper, "If I am not tired, why should the men be tired? What I can do, my soldiers can do. March on!"

That second day's march was an ugly business, take my word for it; I know my comrades would have revolted that night if the colonel had not reached the end of his parading. Listen! Tents pitched and bivouac-fires lit, the colonel ordered assembly. He strutted out of his tent and confronted the wilting line-up of Legionnaires. His eyes, in the firelight, twinkled.

"Soldiers of the Legion! I wish to congratulate you for the heroic way with which you have thus far carried out this campaign!"

What was that? We were on a campaign? What campaign?

"I have just received orders from the Paris War Office that the campaign is to continue!"

Just received orders! But our detachment had no wireless!

"We are to march at dawn to the relief of the garrison at Timbuctoo!"

The whole line staggered. Timbuctoo! Across the whole Sahara!

"There is to be no more dallying with these dancing girls we have encountered along the line of march. Naturally," the colonel laid his finger at the side of his nose and grinned at his startled officers, "men will be men."

"Dancing girls?" That was Captain LaSalle, his mouth gaping. "Did you say dancing girls, *mon commandant?*"

"Do not pretend you did not see them, Captain. Lovely little vixens they were too. The three blondes who beckoned to me last night as we went through China were the nicest. Too bad we are on this campaign with such pretty ladies about. That Japanese geisha girl was most charming!"

NAME of Jehovah! what was the colonel talking about? Certainly this was most irregular. You can see those Legion dogs drawn up in line, their lips ajar, their ears sticking out in amazement. You can see the under-officers staring in stark bewilderment at the colonel, then eyeing each other. Picture us there in the middle of that desert, the tents, the shadows, the firelight, our colonel standing there in a rosy glow with the night behind him. *Non,* but I wish you could have seen his smile.

His eyes were bright as nails, but his smile had become dreamy. He regarded his officers with the cheery amusement of a father pleased with stalwart sons.

"Ah, yes. Where was I? Japan. And midnight in India—!"

One of the officers said huskily, "Do not you think you should go into your tent now, Colonel Rolant?"

"What? Are you suggesting orders to your colonel? I am in command here!"

In quick anger the little man's face purpled and swelled. Beads of sweat glittered suddenly on his forehead. He brushed them away with his sleeve, frowning down at his boots. "Perhaps you are right, Lieutenant. The dancing girls last night, they tired me out. I must preserve my strength for this campaign. Tomorrow we march to Timbuctoo. Please post a guard before my tent. I expect to go to Bagdad tonight; there are some lovely dancers awaiting me there."

The captain also had sweat-beads on his forehead. "But you cannot go to Bagdad tonight, *mon commandant.* You are here in Tunis."

The colonel smiled softly. "Obey orders, Captain. Do not argue with a superior. Bagdad is not far when I can go twenty-one kilometers with every step I take in these boots."

Bones of the Little Corsican! You could have heard your hair grow after the colonel said that and strutted back into his tent, forgetting to dismiss the company. It was scary at night out there in that desert. More than scary. The captain's eyes were like candles as he ordered the assembly dismissed. The lieutenants looked sick and pale. A sergeant shrugged and tapped his forehead. It was the *cafard!* The terrible *cafard!*

"Can you equal that?" Jensen snarled to me. "This marching in the sun has driven the little fathead mad. The heat has sent him looney!"

"Off his conk!" Yankee Bill echoed angrily. "Went crazy over those new boots of his. Plain nuts! Did you hear him? Thinks he's been waltzing with dancing girls. Taking steps twenty-one kilometers long!"

If there was an ironic justice in it, it was not amusing. No joke at all to be there in the middle of the desert with a colonel gone stark out of his head. What could the under-officers do? There is nothing in the Legion rule book that tells a captain what to do when the colonel apparently goes crazy. Timbuctoo! Dancing girls! Boots that went twenty-one kilometers a step! I could see the worry on the captain's face when he told me to stand guard that night at the door of Papa Rolant's tent.

Much good that precaution turned out!

I could hear the colonel within snoring gently as a babe, but along after midnight a sandstorm blew up, and I could not hear anything. It was a thick, blinding night. Yankee Bill relieved the watch, and I took over again at dawn. I looked into the colonel's tent to see if he was still sleeping. The tent was empty. The back flaps were open to the rising sun.

We found one track, the track of his right boot there in the sand beyond the opened tent-flaps. It was headed northeast in the direction of Bagdad. Maybe the sandstorm had obliterated the other tracks. Maybe not. At any rate, we came up with the colonel at noon. Papa Rolant was lying dead in the sand. His face was jolly, but black. His left boot was twisted under him, the ankle broken as if he had landed on that foot after a tremendous leap. He was about twenty-one kilometers from the place where we had camped.

CHAPTER III.

NIGHT WING.

THE CAPTAIN had the boots. He was a tough officer, this Captain LaSalle. A gaunt, black-haired Gascon. Not in the least sentimental. He had buried the colonel there in the sand with full military honors, but, after all, why bury a pair of beautiful new boots that had cost their owner five hundred francs? Especially when they were a fairly comfortable fit on the march-blistered feet of Captain

LaSalle. They were his by right of being second in command. A proper symbolism that he should now step into the colonel's boots.

There was none of your Napoleonic complex about Captain LaSalle. He wanted to get out of that dangerous area of desert and back to El Hamma as quickly as possible. Our machine guns, food stores and water supply were in El Hamma. Heaven knew what might have happened during our absence while the colonel paraded us around the desert in crazy maneuvers. Accordingly, all pomp was dispensed with. Flags were furled and lowered. Bugles and drums were packed up. Scouts were deployed. Having stepped into the colonel's boots, both literally and figuratively, the captain ordered us home on the *pas gymnastique.*

Once more the Legionnaires found themselves tortured in their hobnailed rock-crushers. Strung out under the broiling sun, the column puffed and panted along like a weary freight-train. At the Legion quick-step one canters fifty minutes and rests ten. It is a punishing pace, not intended for dress uniforms with full marching equipment. Sweat poured down the jaws of the gasping men, soaking their garments, blistering their ill-shod feet.

At first the men did not care.

They were anxious to get back to base. They wanted to get out of the desert, and more particularly they wanted to get away from the grave where they had buried Papa Rolant. The colonel's death had sobered their tempers a trifle. There is something weird about madness, something a little unnerving to sane men. It makes one aware that the mind is a delicate instrument, somewhat beyond one's control. Your own little flywheel may slip without your knowing it. It had not been nice to hear the colonel prattling about dancing girls and Timbuctoo—an old officer of supposed military genius. Our trust in authority was shaken a little; and if a learned colonel can go batty, what of one's self?

"You know what I feel like?" Yankee Bill the Elephant whispered to me during a ten-minute halt. "I feel like I been on a train run by a loony engineer. Here we were full speed ahead off the main line out here, switching around and running through red lights, half the time off the track with the colonel gone nuts in the cab and none of us knowing there was a madman at the throttle. God knows what we might have run into."

"It is not the first time I have seen a soldier go *cafard,*" I said. "It is this cursed infernal heat, this African sun. That black look on Papa

Rolant's dead face—as if a blood vessel had burst."

"That was something more than apoplexy," Jensen panted in. "Myself, I do not like it."

"What do you not like, Monkey-face?"

The little Dane rolled his eyes. "I do not like the way Papa Rolant said he could walk twenty-one kilometers at a step. Well? He was on his way to Bagdad, was he not? One boot-print behind his tent. And when we found him, twenty-one kilos exactly. I myself counted the paces from camp."

HA! We did not like that either. We did not like the little Dane reminding us of it. It was one of those peculiar coincidences that had better not be examined too closely away out in a lonely ocean of sand. The sun that afternoon was too hot for heavy thinking, and the sooner we got away from the colonel's lonely grave the better for our peace of mind.

So we did not object to marching for El Hamma at the *pas gymnastique.* Only as the afternoon wore on, our hobnailed clogs began to pinch. Quick-step in that dust and heat was cruel. We were going straight north; El Hamma ought to presently be in sight.

Captain LaSalle could ease the pace, one would think. This was harder on your hoofs than parade drill. Of course, it was not hard on the captain's bunions. He was wearing those magnificently comfortable boots he had snaffled from the dead colonel. The dirty corpse-robber, little he cared if the men were suffering. Besides, he was riding the colonel's horse. All these Legion officers were brutes!

Little by little the feeling against the captain changed that afternoon. We began to hate him almost as much as we had hated the colonel. This forced march was cooking us, and we hated him because our feet were exhausted and his were not, because our legs were breaking and his were on a horse, because of all of us he had the only comfortable pair of boots.

With night coming on and El Hamma nowhere in sight, the men were looking tigerish again.

The captain, himself, had begun to look peculiar. He must have misjudged his pocket map and gone off his bearings a little, and he started to take it out on the column, cursing us for lagging, lashing at us as if we were slaves.

At nightfall he ordered a "Column right!" and sent us at a tangent to the east. A little while later he did an about-face, and we were trotting west again. Just as the moon came up he called in the scouts, and we knew that we were lost.

That night he tramped up and down among the campfires, swearing and fuming and kicking at the men with those expensive boots as if he thought he was the King of the Beasts ruling a jungle. Ah, he was working himself into a fine rage.

Nothing in camp suited him. The tents were unmilitary. The rifles incorrectly stacked. This was wrong. That was wrong. "It is the colonel's fault!" we heard him squalling at his lieutenants. "When he started off for Bagdad he took his compass with him and left me in the soup. His compass was gone when we found him. The only one we had!"

That was something for the outfit to hear. And this was something else! Suddenly Captain LaSalle called for his horse. Out of camp he rode at a gallop, disappearing in the night. The poor lieutenants eyed each other. They waited a while, then ordered taps because there seemed like nothing else to do. An hour later the sleeping men were awakened by a shot. Then another! Rushing out over a dune, we found Captain LaSalle with a bullet in his back, his horse dead beside him. Captain LaSalle was dying.

"I saw them!" he panted, loud enough for all to hear. "I dismounted and was walking. Suddenly I was there. I saw them."

"Who?" Lieutenant Blanc cried. "Who did you see, *mon capitaine?*"

"The dancing girls. Doing the Dance of the Seven Veils." Great globes of sweat stood on the captain's forehead. His eyes were black and shiny, like dots of enamel. "I was in India. They were beautiful—!"

With that, the captain closed his eyes and died. A night wind was scurrying the sand in ghostly whirls through the moon-light, and we found no footprints. We could not tell if it was a soldier with a grudge or some roaming Arab marksman who had crept up in the night and shot him. That did not bother us half so much as the fact that the captain, too, had gone mad!

CHAPTER IV.

THE CHINESE BLADE.

LIEUTENANT BLANC had the boots. He was a greedy little man whose mentality went no farther than the rule-book and keeping a full stomach. He was dull, mean and piggish, the typical product of years in a military routine of colonial outposts and border garrisons. He would do his job stubbornly, driving the men; and he had the body of Captain LaSalle underground before you could say an Ave Maria.

Scouts were sent out, and the guard was doubled around the camp. Then he walked to his tent with those boots he had taken from the dead man; and set them upright in the tent door to air them out, saying, "Whew!" Lieutenant Blanc had no imagination.

But we Legionnaires had imaginations.

There was little slumbering in camp the rest of that night, for all our tired feet; we were bivouacked too close to the captain's grave—the colonel's madness and death was still fresh in memory, and the captain dying a lunatic was too much of a bad thing.

Scouts came in to report no trace of Arab or any other tracks. But it was not the unsolved murder which unsettled our thoughts; tough officers had been shot before.

"Can you beat it?" Yankee Bill rolled over in his blankets to whisper to me. "Two officers go nuts within twenty-four hours. This *cafard* stuff gets on my nerves. It's like the sun is a hot cigar and your head pops like a toy balloon." He glared nervously at the night; face uneasy.

"There was an officer once went mad in Oran—" I began.

"But did you ever see two men go mad the same way?" Jensen, on my other side, interrupted. "Both with the same crazy illusions? What? Well, the dear captain, too, went traveling. India! Dancing girls!"

"Doubtless it was the colonel's death which affected LaSalle's mind. That and the heat. You might say the colonel had given him ideas. Those puffs of whirling sand made him think he was seeing dancing girls."

"But, Corday, have you thought about the twenty-one kilometers? The colonel said he had been in China. LaSalle said India."

"Shut that off, Jensen!" the American Legionnaire snarled. "The colonel went off his trolley—a man off his trolley is liable to think anything. The captain went goofy, too, and someone shot him for it. Try to make anything more of it than that and you'll have us all seeing dancing girls!"

Lieutenant Blanc was not worrying about any dancing girls; he was worrying about Touaregs and Arabs. Up at the crack of dawn, he had the column underway, determined to get the men to El Hamma that day. He was not making the same mistake as Colonel Rolant and Captain LaSalle.

He hung his coat over the top of his blunt head as a sunshade, and he stomped along in those big black boots, careful to keep on the shady side of the dunes. He did not march us quick-step, and he carried his revolver in his hand, on the lookout for trouble. Unfortunately he did not look for it in the right place.

We did not come to El Hamma. Two crazy-headed officers had led us on a fox-and-goose off the map, and, at best, trying to locate a town in the desert is like trying to locate a lost ship in mid Atlantic.

We did not know where the town was, and we did not know where we were.

Along about midday Lieutenant Blanc was calling frequent halts, taking a position off by himself on some dune, and staring around like Columbus looking for land. With that coat draped over his head he was sweating like a work-horse, and he called for and drank a lot of water. Then he would scowl at the horizon in a queer way. You could see he was boxing the compass.

Well, I do not know at exactly what time the belt slipped off Lieutenant Blanc's fly-wheel; as Yankee Bill said afterward, he didn't look as if he had enough brains to go crazy.

He drank too much water certainly—especially when our canteens were running low—but he seemed all right that evening when he ordered us to pitch camp. Nobody thought it queer when he retired into his tent without eating; all of us were too worn out to chew our hardtack.

Then all at once, he rushed out at us, his eyes like black flames, cheeks livid, lips dripping foam.

Straight at his junior officer he rushed, catching Lieutenant Delacroix unawares and by the throat. He was choking the junior to death before we realized what was happening. Raving like an animal.

"Keep away from my women, you scoundrel! Try to doublecross me while I am just now in Madagascar, will you? Those dancing girls are mine! Mine! I will share them with no snooty cadet from Saint Cyr!"

Delacroix was down and Blanc was kicking him to pieces with those fine black boots when Sergeant Gonse drew a pistol and shot the mad lieutenant through the head.

JUNIOR-LIEUTENANT DELACROIX had the boots. Poor Delacroix. He was young and unseasoned—it was his first year in the Legion—and besides those boots he had an imagination. I will bet you he wished he had neither. His three superior officers had died in those boots—the Colonel of a brainstorm; the captain insane and murdered; Lieutenant Blanc shot like a mad dog. I will bet you young Delacroix never wanted to put them on.

But he had been limping from a hole worn through his own boot; these hand-me-downs of the colonel's were certainly of fine workmanship and quality; in a way, too; they were symbolic of authority. Discard them, and the men would think he was afraid to step into the boots of command. He must not let these Legion scoundrels think he was afraid. He called for me to shine them up, and he wore them that night as we marched out to that third lonely grave in the desert.

"Men!" he addressed the company, trying to look like a veteran commander—but the boots did not fit him very well, and he only looked like a frightened cadet—"as your *commandant* I warn you I intend to keep discipline. There will be no more forced marching; we will proceed at early morning and after midday; we will get to El Hamma. I am not forgetting Captain LaSalle was murdered, and when we reach our outpost I shall order a strict investigation."

He set his jaw in an attempt to look stern and confident. "Meantime, there will be no more risk of *cafard,* not if every man does his duty. I would put a stop to the rumors whispered among you. There is a lot of nonsense going around, superstitious talk. Insanity is not contagious. Your officers were overworked, merely. Their hallucinations signify nothing, and there is nothing in this nonsense about their having been in India, China or Madagascar; all of us have such daydreams. If I am not afraid, what have you to fear? I thank Sergeant Gonse for saving my life. Company dismissed!"

That was a brave speech from a nervous young shavetail out there in the middle of the African night.

"The little Blue is all right," Yankee Bill applauded as we huddled around our camp fire. "Trying to pretend he doesn't wish he was safely back home at training school instead of out here in this desert of Nowhere with a company on his hands."

"That is nothing to what he has on his feet," Jensen murmured.

"Now look here, you piece of Danish pastry!" Yankee Bill caught and wrung his little comrade's wrist. "Quit rocking the boat! It's bad enough being camped out here with that grave out there in the dark and maybe an Arab attack any minute, without you pulling a face like a ghost story. The kid lieutenant was right. Put a stop to it."

The Dane smiled queerly. "Colonel Rolant. Captain LaSalle. That stupid Blanc. Does it not strike you, big Elephant, as funny?"

"Funny like a bughouse!" the American snarled. "Cut it off!"

Instead, the little Dane turned to me. "Corday," he murmured, "you were there at the blind cobbler's when the colonel was fitted for those boots. You have tended them, polished them. What are they like?"

My faith! his expression sent mice-creeps through my hair. The night was too black around us for this sort of talk. The moon had gone down, and out in the desert there was not a sound. I snarled, "They are like any pair of boots, you fool. I saw the cobbler making them, copying them from a pair that cursed Italian digger at El Hamma had bought from some caravan sheik. The colonel wanted the same kind for his own sacred corns. They are excellent boots of fine leather, no more. I tell you, I would like to wear them myself."

The Dane gave me a look. "You have a sergeant's rating, Corday. The way things are going—you may get a chance to wear them."

NAME of Saint Francis! it gave my nerves a twinge. The other squads grouped around their camp fires were muttering the same speculations; I knew the nerves of every Legionnaire in camp that night were twinging like zithers.

Beyond the fringe of the firelights the sentries were tramping over-loudly, like boys whistling on their way past a cemetery; and the desert that night was one vast graveyard, what with the colonel and the captain and Lieutenant Blanc out there under the sand.

Taps sounded like a funeral call. The men did not want to sleep in their dog-tents, yet nobody dared sleep outside by the dying fires. I felt sorry for the young lieutenant alone in his officer's tent. I shared a tent with Yankee Bill and little Jensen, and even so I kept waking up out of cold-sweat nightmares, fancying I heard prowlers.

I do not know what time it was when I heard the scream. It screeched through the night like the passing of your Lost Soul, and it flung the camp out of its blankets to a man.

In the dark there was wildest confusion. We piled from our tents in a terrified stampede, bumping into running guards, knocking each other down in a race for the gun-stacks. Non-coms squalled. Torches flared. Legionnaires milled in panic, waiting for a word of command. It became evident that Lieutenant Delacroix was not there.

Someone pointed to his tent, and we went for it in a rush. It was surrounded by a yelling swarm, afraid to enter. Tracks, if there had been any, would have been smudged out by that seething jam.

Then thirty men crushed into the tent, and we found Lieutenant Delacroix.

In the camp chair which he had inherited from Colonel Rolant, he was slumped down. His eyes stared sightlessly at the ridge-pole. His mouth was open and full of blood. He was half undressed, his tunic unbuttoned, belt open. One boot was half off, and both boots were dusty—as if, Jensen pointed out, he had just returned and was retiring after a long journey. So it seemed.

For when we turned him over we found a knife in his back. No Legion knife, or Arab blade. But an Oriental knife—a wavy-edged dagger—the hilt inscribed with Chinese writing!

CHAPTER V.

THE COBBLER WAS BLIND.

SERGEANT GONSE had the boots. He did not wear them. He was a shrewd red-whiskered Picard, Sergeant Gonse, and the boots had come down to him, along with the command, from poor dead Lieutenant Delacroix; but as he rushed our column across the desert through the dawn, he carried his new footgear slung on his shoulder. Himself, he wore Legion clodhoppers, and he was hobbling on blisters as big as anybody's, but he refused to put on those fine black boots.

He declared he was keeping them only to pawn in the bazaar at El Hamma. He said they did not fit. Ha-ha.

That was a day we marched like fools.

We got into a stretch of wilderness nobody had ever seen before, a desert of red sandstone hills and burning rocks and sharp stones like flint on the feet. We trooped around in that for a number of miles, and we were not the smart parade which had marched out of El Hamma four days before.

Sack of paper! The color bearers dragged their flags in the dust. The bugles were full of sand. Some of the drummers had dropped their clumsy instruments by the wayside.

The men were slop-shouldered, drooping, uniforms disheveled, plastered with sweat and dirt, limping and stumbling and out of step, quarreling together like a pack of mangy wolves. Canteens were drying, lips were cracking, nerves tightening like fiddle-strings.

The company knew it was lost; if a colonel, a captain and two lieutenants had not been able to find the way back to El Hamma, how could a top-sergeant? Blood-rimmed eyes glared suspicion and hatred at Sergeant Gonse—would he go crazy, too?—or had those other officers *been* crazy?—that Chinese dagger in Delacroix's spine—in the middle of an African desert—was the whole company going crazy, or what?

Now insanity can be infectious, not so? Look how one maniac has maddened Europe today, as one bad apple spoils the barrel. Well, our company of lost Legionnaires was not a very big barrel, and there had been four bad apples. Something had to happen pretty quick, or the entire outfit would resemble the glee club of an insane asylum. It happened. *Tiens!*

At dusk the column staggered out of that red patch of desert, topped a high, sun-baked ridge—there, miles to the north, for all the world a mirage in the twilight, huddled the walls of El Hamma. That was not all we saw. On a dune not far below the ridge there appeared with startling suddenness a band of wild Touareg tribesmen.

Guns cracked, and bullets purred over our caps. As if produced by magic, Arabs charged from a dune at the left. On all sides of that ridge the sands sprouted black and bronze fiends. That battle was as instantaneous as spontaneous combustion. Gunfire flashing. Horsemen charging in a flutter of robes through dust. The *spank-spank-spank* of Lebels. Oaths. Shrieks of the wounded. *Zip* and *plink* of flying lead.

We were ambushed, surprised, surrounded; El Hamma, an anthill on the horizon, was cut off.

But there is nothing like a battle to cure a stale army; the whistle of Arab bullets can clear a Legionnaire's head of mopes as a slap from a doctor can cure a hysterical woman of tantrums. Unhappily, Arab bullets can also perforate a Legionnaire's head.

Five of our men were fatalities before Sergeant Gonse could get us into a battle position. Defensively speaking, our position was good—we were on high ground where the enemy must charge upslope across open sand—but those desert fiends did not give us much chance for defensive speaking.

They had been waiting for the parade to come back, resting on their rifles, and if it was hard for them to take the ridge, it was as hard for us to get off it.

By Saint Anthony's fire! I never thought we could withstand that first charge. Formed in hollow triangle, we dug in behind a barricade of knapsacks, baggage, whatever we could flatten behind. Here they came! That was a hot scrap then, *mon ami.* Those Arab horsemen went over us—right over us like a wave!—and there were more of my comrades scattered dead around me afterward than I like to remember. We drove off that charge with God's help alone, bayoneting horses and riders as they jumped us, piling up the dead for a higher barricade.

A second wave charged, and we met it with a stunning fusillade. A third we drove back. A fourth. Those horsemen were not so reckless about attacking after that; our stacked cadavers made higher walls, not so easy to charge. But at the same time they made less men, and there were plenty of those Arabs and Touareg; too many!

OUR Lebel rifles scorched our hands after we repelled that last assault; I tell you, the fight had been terrific. We had slaughtered a couple of dozen Arabs and wounded a couple of dozen more, but a couple of dozen Arabs were cheap in that part of the country. After the smoke and dust cleared away we counted our dead at twenty, and Legionnaires were expensive. That was pretty stiff medicine to keep our outfit in sharp mental condition. *Parbleu!* I think it was an overdose.

Those desert fiends retreated. But not far. They sneaked off in the twilight and appeared to melt away, but we knew they were hiding behind the dunes, waiting for nightfall to blot out the scenery. Then they would attack from all sides and try to blot us out. They could wait. They had plenty of time.

Who was it said anticipation was worse than realization? If you want something nerve-racking, try sitting still in the desert with the night gathering around and the knowledge that out there in the darkness a horde of tigers are crouching to spring. We could not see them, but we could feel their presence.

A thin lemon-rind moon cruised in the sky, but its pale shine could not penetrate the blackness that lay like a sea of tar across the sands. That darkness was enemy camouflage. You could hear the zero hour approaching on tiptoe. Yet the only sound was the pounding of my own heart and the sobbing of a German Legionnaire who was dying with a bullet in his stomach—*"Mütterchen! Ach du lieber— Wasser, kleines Mütterchen—!"* It did not help that the moon-lit walls of El Hamma gleamed white and tiny on the far edge of the night, distant and unattainable as the Gates of Pearl.

After a half hour crouching behind a dead horse with my Lebel aimed across its reeky flank, my eye looking through the gun-sights at nothing, I could stand it no longer.

Groping my way over bodies alive and dead, I sought Sergeant Gonse. Presently I found him in the middle of our hollow triangle, surrounded by a little group of mutterers who did not know what to do about him. The men stood like shades—I recognized the mammoth silhouette of Yankee Bill the Elephant—and the sergeant was a shadow on the ground. Yankee Bill held a match in cupped palms for me to see. All I could see of Sergeant Gonse was the grinning red head on one end, and the shine of black boots on the other. There was not much in between. From knees to collar Sergeant Gonse had been riddled.

The American seemed surprised by my appearance. "We were wondering who would take command. Jensen and me couldn't find you. We thought you had been killed."

That gave me a shock. You bet it did. I had forgotten that as Papa Rolant's orderly I rated a top-sergeant's stripes. Holy Sebastopol! with Gonse dead, I was next in line for the company; and what a fine moment to win advancement.

"I was out there sniping behind a dead horse. I didn't know Gonse—"

"It was that last attack. He'd sprained his ankle that first charge in a hand-to-hand fight. He thought those boots would be a support. He changed into them, and stood up. Right in the face of a fusillade."

NOW that did not sound exactly propitious. Not a bit, in fact. I should say it did not do a thing toward giving those boots a good reputation. But it was no time for any kind of nonsense.

"Give me those boots," I said.

Yankee Bill showed me the whites of his eyes. "A lot of good men have died with those boots on, Corday."

"Then at least they have died with their feet in comfort," I snarled. "I would rather walk to Hell in those than in these hobnailed clogs which are murdering me. You will die with your own on, if you do not give me those boots. This whole sacred company will be wiped out."

They looked at me, those Legionnaires. Three days ago every mother's son of them would have marked the corpse, jealously, battled each other tooth and nail over the right to scavenge such footwear. Now they did not want to touch those boots; they thought me crazy for wanting them.

"Do not take them, Corday! Those pumpers are unlucky!"

"Not so unlucky as our being trapped on this ridge," I snarled. "Listen, you jackals. Our only chance is for a man to get through to El Hamma and bring help. There are two machine-gun squads left on garrison duty there; doubtless they believe by now that we have all been slaughtered. The Arabs cannot have taken the outpost or the town would be in flames. A runner must get through to them. I am going to be the runner."

"Alone?" Yankee Bill gasped. "I will go with you."

"Every man will be needed here," I snapped. "One runner is necessary. As I am now in command, I pick myself."

"It's suicide, Corday. At least twenty miles. You'll never make it."

"Not in these clogs," I thrust out my heavy hobnailed rock-crusher. "*Non,* they are crippling me. But in those fine boots I will try—!"

SO I had the boots. That is how I got them. How I, a penny-a-day Legionnaire, came to own a pair of handmade pumpers as fine a grade of leather and workmanship as any in a millionaire sportsman's club—light boots—staunch boots—snug, yet comfortable—stout, yet easy on the instep—serviceable, yet smart—truly a perfect pair.

Ah, that leather had the texture of the best Morocco. The soles, an inch thick, weighed light as birch wood. I carried them over to my dead horse and secretly examined them.

Their history may have been evil, but their last was well-shaped and the insole of felt as inviting as a carpet slipper. My feet ached in relief as I let them out of their hobnailed prisons.

Cautiously I tried on the boots. They were a little damp and sticky, but they might have been made for me to order. I experimented a step or two. Of course that colonel had been mad. Never had a soldier's feet enjoyed such luxurious comfort. By my oath! I would give these chic hoofers a run for their money.

"Corday—!"

The whisper came at me from behind, and I spun around.

Jensen's eyes, peering at me, were spectral. "Corday! Name of God! Yankee Bill told me, but I did not believe. You really mean to wear them?"

"Have I not got them on? Get back to your post, comedian!"

His anxiety for me was unsettling. He caught my sleeve. "Think, my friend! Think what happened to those officers! Rolant—LaSalle—Blanc—Delacroix—now Gonse. Always it happened when they wore those boots."

"Do you see any connection between men going *cafard* from the sun, a man's brains, and shoeleather?" The Dane's popping eyes and jittering infuriated me. "Keep on guard for the Arabs. Be off!"

"Wait," he begged. "Delacroix—! That Chinese dagger—!"

"What of it? A curio some veteran of us brought from Tonkin."

"Papa Rolant said he had been to China!"

"So! And LaSalle to India? But he was killed with a European bullet."

"Blanc spoke of Madagascar. Doubtless if Gonse could have told us he would have said he was starting for—"

"For the moon!" I choked the Dane off, catching him by the throat and shaking him till his teeth clacked. "Idiot, are you trying to tell me you believed those madmen—they actually went to those places— ?"

"Are there any dancing girls in this Tunisian desert? Did you see any out there in that waste?" Jensen rolled his eyes. "No, but those officers—those who lived to tell it!—saw them. Oriental dancing girls! And you heard what Papa Rolant said about those boots. And he was on his way to Bagdad—!"

"On his way to a madhouse, you mean."

"But he was twenty-one kilometers from that place where we camped. A single foot-print outside his tent. Then we found him exactly—"

"How do you know it was exactly? Did you measure it with a tape? That sandstorm had swept away his other tracks. He had brain fever, and ran off in the night. His heart must have collapsed."

"Or did it burst, Corday? Burst from the speed he was traveling. And that tough Captain LaSalle, did he look the type to go insane? A man the most hard-headed! But he, too, wanders off in the night and tells us he has seen India. Then Lieutenant Blanc with a skull of solid ivory, raving of Madagascar. Well, any numbskull might go berserk from the shock of suddenly finding himself at the other end of a continent.

"Young Delacroix, however, was no numbskull; but look at what happened to him. We saw him retire in his tent—even as Blanc had retired—then what? Five hours later we find him. He has not been to bed; he is just undressing. His boots are thick with dust—they had been shiny when we saw him turn in, remember—and there is a Chinese dagger in his back. Who among us would have wanted to stab that helpless cadet? No, Corday. It is those boots."

I DID not like that up there on that ridge in the darkness with Death in ambush all around us, the night like a loaded rifle waiting to go off and kill us all. I could have knocked that Dane over the head with my pistol-butt. "You jackass," I snarled, "are you trying to tell me there is some sort of sorcery in these kickers? Some magic that whisks the wearer to far-off places at lightning speed?"

He grasped my arm, and his voice came low through the tight-strung dark. "Listen, Corday. When I was a little boy my grandfather used to take me on his knee and tell me a story. He was a sea captain and had sailed to distant shores. This story, it concerned a wonderful pair of boots that had been made in Denmark for an ancient king. That king was lame, you comprehend; for years he had been confined to his castle. Always he had wanted to travel.

"One day there came to his door an old white-bearded cobbler, a man from the East who had crossed the world, mending boots. The castle guards arrested him and were going to behead him as a spy, but hearing the old wanderer's cries, the Danish king took pity.

"'Hear this!' he told the cobbler. 'You, a miserable shoemaker, have walked around the world, while I, a king, am unable to take a step, for the very touch of the earth causes my feet to cry out in pain. Always I am stepping on sharp stones or pebbles. But if this earth were covered over I could walk anywhere. If you can cover the whole earth with leather I will grant you your life!'"

Jensen paused for breath. Me, I was in a sweat to get away. Vibrations of emergency were tightening in the blackness; around me dead men were stiffening while the living crouched tense for the shock of assault; there was a smell of burnt powder and blood and doom, and it hardly seemed the time to be listening to a Danish bed-time tale.

But the Dane's clutch held me. Something in his low voice fastened me by the ears.

He went on fiercely, "That cobbler took a look at the Danish king's feet, and smiled. The king was wearing rope sandals. The man went into his cell, and in a week appeared before the king with a pair of magnificent boots which he had fashioned. The king tried them on. Ah, they were wonderful.

"'But have you covered the earth?' he asked the cobbler.

"'Sire,' answered the cobbler, 'in those fine boots you can walk anywhere. To him who wears boots, it is as if the whole world is covered with leather.'"

"Jensen," I snarled, "you are seven kinds of a fool!"

"Wait!" he gasped. "That is not all of the story. The king was so pleased that he let the shoemaker go. But that shoemaker was no ordinary shoemaker. He was from the East. Old men from the East can do marvelous things, and in return for the king's kindness, that cobbler put a sorcery in those boots.

"'You have not many years left to travel,' he told the king. 'To see all the world you must walk fast and far. I have made you a pair of boots that go seven leagues at a stride. But only at night, for the pace would be too swift in the heat of day.' Well, that king took a step, and to his astonishment found himself in Germany. And that is where the Seven League Boots came from, Corday. You have heard of the Seven League Boots—?"

Again I had the Dane by the throat. "You waste my time with this fairy tale—this Danish version of Mother Goose—?"

"My grandfather told it to me," he panted. "He said it was true. In a week that king had circumnavigated the globe, and he died from the excitement—!"

"I will circumnavigate you!" I gritted at him. "You dunce—!"

"The boots were captured by Chinese bandits," he gurgled on, ignoring the pinch on his windpipe, "who wanted them for their marvelous power. Then the Russians had them. They fell in the hands of the Britons where Mother Goose heard the story. It is said Magellan wore them—gave them to Marco Polo! Finally the Arabs got them, Corday. The Arabs—!"

"What a fairy tale! What a fable!" I was remembering how I had once fallen for a woman's recital of *Aladdin's Wonderful Lamp,* and I shook him as you would shake an old coat full of lice. "We are about to die, and you spin me a yarn. Magic boots, indeed! Fool! What has this fairy story to do with boots I saw handmade last week in a blind cobbler's shop?"

Jensen gave a last gasp. "They are not the same boots!"

I dropped my hands, staring.

"That cobbler in El Hamma is blind!"

"Well, what in the devil has that—?"

"You saw him copying a pair. The pair owned by that Italian professor who digs for ancient history in the sand. The pair which that Italian claimed to have purchased from an Arab caravan sheik in the desert. Or did he dig them up, Corday? Look at them. Do they look like Arab boots?"

Mère de Dieu! he was pointing at my feet. I whispered. "Are you trying to tell me—?"

"That cobbler is blind. He made those boots for the colonel to match the Italian's. I am trying to tell you, the blind cobbler got them mixed and gave the colonel the wrong pair of boots, the Italian's boots. I am trying to tell you, when the colonel took a step in those boots at night he found they went twenty-one kilometers. So with the others who wore them afterward. To the Orient. India. Madagascar. China. It would not be impossible—a fast trip—running—when every step carried one seven leagues. Corday! Twenty-one kilometers is seven leagues. The pace is too fast, a speed that burns out one's brain. And you are standing in the Seven League Boots—!"

I wanted to kick him. Boot him seven leagues straight up in the air. There I was poised for a death-race across a desert infested with invisible murderers, and this little clown telling me I wore boots that went so fast they would blow out my lights.

I batted him off with an elbow. "To your post, *coquin!* Your grandfather and the Seven League Boots be damned! Pray to God I can travel seven paces in these pumps; and dig yourself under the sand, hoping you will be alive in the morning when I get back. Off with you, and warn the men not to shoot me by mistake. I am no officer for them to murder. I am going now. *Va-t'-en!*"

He scrambled away, and I could hear him warning the sharpshooters. I called a low-voiced farewell, spat four times for luck, crawled over the dead horse, picked a hole in the darkness blacker than the night, and started out for El Hamma. I did not know it, but I was beginning the strangest journey I ever made in my life.

CHAPTER VI.

THE MAD JOURNEY.

I WASN'T taking any seven-league strides when I started out, either. You know I wasn't. Belly to the ground, I went crawling down the ridge like a lizard, inching my way down the slope of sand and pausing every few minutes to rear my head and hold my breath and listen. I was not going to do any sprinting until I got through those Arab lines, which meant I was probably not going to do any sprinting.

I could not see the Arab lines; I did not know where they were. In the thick dark ahead of me I could see nothing—only a sea of blackness stretching miles to the limits of the night where the tiny moon-washed walls of the town were clustered like a pale mirage. The intervening desert was black, I tell you. So black I felt as if I had been absorbed. Five yards down the ridge I looked back, and my companion Legionnaires had been absorbed, too. And silent? That darkness was like cotton stuffed in the ears. The moans of that German boy with a lead pill in his stomach only emphasized the surrounding hush. The pressure of that silence made me sweat.

Oui, the perspiration ran on my forehead as I crawled through that deaf-and-blind darkness. It was just like crawling toward a jungle alive with savage beasts. Any minute they might catch my scent. I had responsibility on my shoulders too, heavier than any knapsack. I had to crawl carefully, very slowly and carefully, and that weight of responsibility and the strain of it made every pore in my body a leaky faucet.

Believe me, I was sweating like a Turkish bath when I crossed the valley under the ridge and started up the dune, knowing those Arab butchers were on the other side. Or maybe they were Touareg, black desert fiends drugged with hashish and hate of the French. The thought turned my Turkish bath into a cold shower.

I am not lying when I say I was soaked in a dew of fear as I crawled on hands and knees up over that dune.

I knew those devils were around me then. Their nearness sent electric currents through the little telegraph wires under my skin. Fear stalled me, and for at least ten minutes I lay flat in the sand, afraid to go on and shaking like a wet leaf. But time was sifting away, *mon ami*—sand running through the hourglass—the lives of fifty men were at stake, you comprehend—my comrades, Yankee Bill and Jensen—trapped up there on that ridge they might outlast a midnight attack, another, perhaps a third, but help had to reach them—they could not last long after sunrise.

I pulled my belt tighter and crawled on. Nearby an invisible horse whickered. Gripping my pistol, I flattened. Was that formless shade ahead of me a Touareg? I was sure I could hear breathing. Teeth clenched, I crawled at the shade and through it. My imagination!

But certainly that was a movement off at the left. Again I flattened, not daring to breathe. The strain and cold sweat was making me a little sick.

No, that movement, too, was my imagination. But then I ran into something that was not imaginary. Crawling over a hummock of sand, I put my hand down squarely on a nose, mouth and beard. Wow! that hummock of sand rose up like an earthquake and turned into a screeching black man. Everywhere around me the dark sprang to life with a violence.

Nerves snapped in my head, and I fired in panic, and the night exploded with a bang!

IT was foolish of me to let off my gun like that. Mighty foolish. It was just what I had planned not to do. I should have bashed that sentinel's head in before he could give another squawk; that pistol shot roused the entire ambush. Firing blindly, I rushed through a mob of grabbing hands, dodged a spurt of gun-flame and raced in headlong flight toward that far off mirage of the town.

A river of bullets whistled after me, but those desert demons could not see me any better than I could see them, and I guess my presence in their midst had taken them by surprise. I heard shouting, howls to Allah, horses rearing, rifle shots. I did not loiter. I did not do any careful crawling. Take my word, I set a bee-line for that town on the rim of the night, and I tore through the black as fast as my legs would carry me.

That was not very fast, considering that mob at my heels. By the sound, every fiend in North Africa was coming after me. *Mère de Dieu!* do you know what I was wishing then? My thoughts went to the story that fool Dane had told me, and I was wishing for a fact that I had on Seven League Boots.

What a laugh that was! Those pumpers I was wearing, they were better than hobnailed clogs, but they were not a bit faster than my knees, and with twenty miles to go that would not be fast enough. Besides, they were sweating my feet.

Still, they were curiously light for such thick soles; after my first mad dash, when I had settled into a stride of running, I could not seem to feel them at all. I was keeping a lead on those fiends behind me, *oui.* Horsemen had scattered, and I could hear them off at my flanks, spreading out in an attempt to circle and head me off, but I was still alive, amazingly alive.

I do not know at what moment I began to sense in myself an odd vitality—I had run a couple of miles, I was sure—instead of tiring, I seemed to have found a second wind. My head felt dizzily clear, if you can understand me—light and a little balloonish—that sensation you have in a high altitude.

At the same time, I experienced a queerish nausea, a nausea that was not unpleasant, something like too much champagne. That taste in my stomach I could not identify, or the pleasant numbing in the top of my head. I was dripping wet, yet I had no feeling of fatigue. Strange, I had no sense, either, of passing time. Now I must have been legging it at top speed for a half an hour, but it seemed like only a few seconds.

I wanted to laugh as I ran. Really, this race to El Hamma with that demon-pack at my heels was rather delightful. Some of my senses had blurred and others had quickened; I felt as charged with energy as an electric battery. For two cents I would have turned around and fought that whole desert mob. What were a few hundred Arabs to one good Frenchman!

I sprang along over the sand and it seemed to have turned to rubber. I sailed over a dune. My feet were not touching the ground at all. Name of Jehovah! what had come over me?

Turn me into a pepper mill! I had taken a stride and swooped right off into space. I tell you, I went like a gull on wings.

The odd part of it was, the back of my consciousness knew I had never left the ground at all, I was running like hell across the sand; and my physical self had become elastic, beyond the laws of gravity, I could feel myself flying. That gave me a sensation. You can wager it did! I liked that flighty feeling, and I let go again.

That time I went farther. *Sacré!* That was great. How did I do it? I had never been able to fly before. With the knowledge of this rare accomplishment, a tremendous self-assurance came over me, a sense of superior cunning. I would show these Arabs a thing or two now. Ah, I was a fox. I started cutting crafty tangents, dodging at smart angles to throw them off, then zooming on the straightaway again. No Arab rats were going to catch me. I could outsmart any Touareg horsemen. I was Thibaut Corday, one of the greatest soldiers of France, fighter extraordinary, capable of any feat—look!—in these boots I could fly!

In these boots—! That was when I looked down, my friend, and saw the desert far below me. My knees were pumping like a runner's, but I was not down to earth; *non,* I was winging high in the air. I knew it then, when I found myself running in the clouds. I wanted to laugh. I wanted to cheer in exultation.

"Holy Saint Cristopher!" I could hear myself crying out to myself. "The little Dane was right! You are in them! The Seven League Boots!"

A REMARKABLE feeling of power coursed through me. Nothing could hold me down. What exhilaration! A mountain of sand rose in front of me and I went over it in three strides. No danger of Arabs now; single-handed I could conquer the whole Arab world. "Why," I thought to myself, "I could jump over Arabia. A few leaps in these boots would take me to Asia—India—!"

Now I am coming to a part of this story difficult to describe.

Sensations are hard things to find words for, and my brain was in a whirl of sensations. As I thought of India, I seemed to be projected through space at rocket-speed. Wind whistled in my ears, dust and darkness streaked past me, the moon sailed off at an unexpected arc—*voilà!*—before my eyes was the Taj Mahal, exactly as I remembered the picture from my schoolbook geography; then palm trees, elephants, fantastic rajahs, snake-charmers—suddenly I was in a harem full of dancing girls, nautch dancers from Calcutta, Delhi, Bombay.

Scenery formed and faded like views flashed dimly on a screen, but the dancing girls were clear; they writhed and spun around me, laughing at me, singing strange songs, gesturing at me to catch them.

All this time I was running through the air in my magic boots, and all this time, far in the distance ahead of me, beyond that scene of India, was the mirage of El Hamma's white walls gleaming in the moon-wash.

Can you make anything of that? Then what can you make of this? "There is plenty of time," I said to myself. "I would like to see China!" Almost at once I was there.

Shanghai, exactly as I had last seen it from a troopship deck. Office buildings and pagodas. Alleys lit by paper lanterns. Screechy music. Mandarins in slippers eating rice with chopsticks. Again dancing girls—slant-eyed maidens in pantaloons weaving at me, beckoning, inviting. Ah, they were beautiful. I would have stopped. I would have made love to one under a saladang tree, but far in the distance there was that cursed view of El Hamma, and if I wanted to see those other wonderful places I must hurry on.

So I jumped Afghanistan for Persia to see the dancers of Teheran draped like goddesses about the Peacock Throne. Ground fled away and I was in Nagasaki encircled by dark-eyed geishas in bright kimonas who held out their toy-like hands to me and begged me to stay. The little japanese maids sent after me a tinkling laugh, but I was going too fast to see much of their country; I wanted to return to the strange leopard-skinned ladies I had glimpsed beating tom-toms on a dark Madagascar beach, and the lotus-perfumed beauties I had passed in crossing Cambodia.

Enfin, you can see I made quite a tour of the world in those Seven League boots. Talk about that Danish king or Magellan! There were girls in every port, charmers of every race and hue and of marvelous beauty, who tried to wrap me in their arms, pleading with me to linger. Somehow I had to go on, although I would have given my soul to dally. But always ahead I saw those moon-washed walls of El Hamma, drawing me on past those alluring ports of call, hurrying me up like Conscience.

I took those few last miles into El Hamma planing from dune to dune like a flying fish hitting the crests of waves. Believe me, in my Seven League Boots I was covering ground. What enraged me was that the town kept drifting ahead of me, so that no matter how fast I ran it remained beyond reach on the skyline.

But I got there.

CHAPTER VII.

WHAT BOOTS A MAN...?

THE SOLDIERS who saw me from the outpost wall said I came out of the night at a bounding zigzag, like a jackrabbit with five hundred wolfhounds after me. They said Touareg horsemen were riding me down on either flank, and those horsemen would have cut me to pieces if a batch of Arabs had not piled over me and blocked the sword-swipes of the riders. They said I came out from under that pile-up of men, knives and horses as a diver rising out of surf; that I was laughing and shooting and throwing those Arabs around as if they were straw dummies. Then, they said, I came into that town like a one-man cyclone.

Me, I felt like a complete hurricane.

Those Legionnaires who saw me said I raced in through the gate-arch; came up the bazaar on a slow spin like a dervish, howling unearthly yells and firing at everything in sight. Arabs dropped on me from balconies. Black men charged me from dark doors.

All those wild men from the desert came rioting after me; dust and gun-smoke fogged the moonlight; the shrieks, screams, explosions, hoof-clatter and clang of hurled blades was like the din of Hell.

They saw me climb up walls and jump down from roofs. Ten times I disappeared in the heat of bedlam. Racing from barracks to rescue me, they saw me standing in an alley-mouth, calmly loading my pistol and hooting with laughter while bullets tore through my hair and every hellion in town whirled around me. They said my tunic was in ribbons, my britches in shreds, I was dirt and blood from head to foot, my face was a scarlet mask. But my eyes were like opals, and I leaped and dodged and charged at my attackers as if my life were charmed. They said it was a miracle I was alive.

But they did not see what I saw.

I saw I was in Hell, all right, but in my Hell there were more than Arabs. All those dancing girls from far places, they had come there with me. Around me they danced, leaping and twisting, clinging to my arms, running cool fingers through my hair, twining soft arms about my neck, imploring me with kisses to save them.

Like rainbows they flashed, girls in veils and girls without veils, anklets twinkling, bells shining on their feet—geisha girls, nautch dancers, the leopard women of Madagascar, the lovely maids from Persia, China, Tonkin. Bracelets jangled. Tom-toms roared. Cymbals crashed.

Savage hordes of natives charged at me to take my girls away, villainous devils who grabbed out and rushed, trying to catch my women. Do you think I was afraid of those curs when the most beautiful ladies I had ever seen were clinging to me for protection? Do you think I was afraid in my Seven League Boots? I did not climb the walls in that town; I walked over them. I did not jump down from roofs; I stepped down. What were a hundred Arabs to me—what were a thousand?

Those Legionnaires rushing to my rescue, they saw no mere man in rags and dirt battling a native mob. They saw a giant, a knight in invincible armor, a great conqueror surrounded by the world's loveliest harem, beating off with ease and supreme confidence all the devils in Hell. What a fight you can put up when ever step you take covers seven leagues.

The Devil, himself, came at me. I saw his face. On a black horse he came through the sulphur smoke, leaping from saddle on top of me. My side-jump had carried me to Italy. Satan was swearing in Italian. He had a thin, ascetic face and a bald head, and he was lashing criss-cross strokes at me with a whistling sabre. *"Corpo da Bacco!"* Veiled women clung to me, screaming in a thousand plaintive tongues. I hurled myself at this enemy. I never felt the slash that cut me to the shoulder-bone. He went down, and I was stamping on his face—

Tom-toms sounded like the thudding of machine-guns. Cymbals were rifles smashing. Dancers and veils dissolved in bronze swirling fog. Red lights banged on all sides; there was a smell of burnt powder, hot metal, salty sweat; suddenly in the smoke before me appeared Yankee Bill, Jensen, a squad of Legionnaires. Those fools, their shouts and bayonets had scared my dancers. A delightful creature in gauzy raiment beckoned from a roof-top, turned and sped like a rainbow for the moon.

Soaring in my boots, I went after her; together we fled across the sky. But my boots were heavy with caked, bloody mud—I was slowing down—the moon went out—her veils tore through my clutch, and I lost her.

Then I was falling—falling through endless night.

BARE feet. I could see them, toes upturned, sticking up beyond the horizon of the blanket. That bunion looked familiar. So did a corn. Could those miserable appendages be mine? I wiggled the toes. They were mine.

"The boots!" I whispered. "Where are my Seven League Boots?"

The face wearing a doctor's Van Dyke looked down and grinned. "Boots, indeed! From the way you have been talking I would have expected dancing slippers. For three days now you have been waltzing. What a dance! And with such women! Tut, tut! You have shocked the good nuns of this hospital, I can tell you; they have been saying hurry-call prayers for your soul. They are not used to the confessions of such a roué, such an adventurer, such a lady-killer."

I gasped out, "The dancing girls—!"

"You brought them to the hospital with you. What a subconscious! Was it imagination or memory? You have been in our Asian colonies? I envy you. I knew that stuff inspired a man. But you, *mon brave!* I have heard of nothing like it since I read the impressions of De Quincy."

"My Seven League Boots!" I panted.

He chuckled, shaping his beard with pointed fingers. "So that is what they were? Seven Leaguers! Well, I can believe it from what they tell me of the race you ran. Eighteen miles across the desert in five hours; dodging all over the map under cover of night, and outstripping a hundred Arabs and Touareg. How you outsmarted them, decoying them after you like that, so your comrades could escape that ambush trap. Do you know you saved your company? Your comrades reached El Hamma only a half hour behind you. It was wonderful strategy. The general will be here soon. All the way from Kairouan to give you the *Croix de Guerre.*"

I struggled to rise. "I do not want a medal! I want my Seven League Boots!"

"No, no!" the doctor lowered me back. "Your shoulder, *mon gars!* The stitches! But wait!" He tinkled a bell near my cot and a nun came in. After whispered words the good sister went out, to presently return with a parcel wrapped in paper. A very spruce lieutenant, one I had never seen before, was with her. He saluted the doctor and unwrapped the parcel.

"My boots!" I wailed. "Torn to pieces! Some villain has slashed them like that! The Seven League Boots that belonged to a Danish king and—"

Overwhelmed by the tragedy, I could not go on. As the lieutenant held up those ruined wonders, I could only weep. Ah, those marvelous boots. The calves had been cut to strips. The heels were split open. The magic soles had been ripped loose from the welt and hung down with nails showing like jagged teeth. The felt insole flapped out like a tongue, and the vandal who had worked this infamy had gouged out the bottoms and arches.

"Show him," the doctor said to the lieutenant.

Fumbling in a tunic pocket, the lieutenant produced a small packet of tissue papers. I could see scrawled lines and fine writing.

"Show him the rest."

The lieutenant held up a brown, flat gum-like slab of something about a half inch thick and six inches long—it was shaped as a bootsole, but it looked like an unwholesome, moist plug of chewing tobacco.

"Corday," the doctor shook his head, "those weren't any Seven League Boots belonging to any Danish king. They belonged to that Italian who was around here passing himself off as an archaeologist."

"I know," I cried. "And he bought them from a sheik in the desert—or he dug them up in the sand—!"

"Too bad for him he didn't," the lieutenant said grimly. "No, *mon brave,* he had them made to order—to very special order by that cur of a blind cobbler in the Lane of the Three Thirsty Camels. Then every night when he returned from his diggings he gave them to the cobbler to polish up; what choice boots that they must be shiny for his morning ride into the desert!"

"That cobbler made a pair to match for Colonel Rolant!" I moaned. "He got them mixed up! Switched! He gave the colonel the Italian's pair."

"OUI, and he gave the Italian the new ones he had made for the colonel. But attend! The match is close but not exact. The boots made for the colonel, they have solid leather soles and heels. These of the Italian? Well, every day when he rode into the desert he carried imbedded under that insole these nice brown slabs to pass out to nomad chiefs. Only he was more than a dope-runner, this *agent provocateur.*

"Here are maps of our whole Tunisian border, the deposition of our troops, a plan of our El Hamma outpost and the instructions for a secret uprising—on tissue paper concealed in the hollow heels. You can see how badly he wanted those boots of his; why he trailed your detachment and finally ordered a bold attack. Those spy-maps meant his life, if discovered. The drugs to bribe the desert tribes—that blind cobbler had bushels hidden under his shop."

I pulled my bare feet under cover in horror. "You mean there were drugs hidden in the soles of those boots?"

"Under the felt insole," the doctor pointed at the brown, gum-like slab that resembled chewing tobacco. "Concentrated opium and hashish with some native hell-oil mixed in. Just the fumes are enough to knock you silly. Believe me, those boots were ripe, Corday. I do not wonder the colonel felt it when his feet began to perspire. That felt insole soaked up the stuff. That spy never walked far in them. *Sacré!* Imagine marching!"

Eyes raised, the doctor called upon heaven to imagine it. "Out in Tonkin," he told the lieutenant, "I have seen native soldiers smuggle a pill of opium under armpit and go sky high. Conceive of absorbing a drug through the bottoms of your blistered feet! Especially hashish! No wonder those officers saw strange countries and dancing girls. Hashish is the most violent of narcotics; always it conjures up visions; the user loses all sense of time and space, temporarily goes mad, and is liable to run amuck. It is the drug of the assassins; only a little will drive one wild. And here was Corday steeping his toes in it; taking a foot-bath in the stuff. *Ventre bleu!*" he shuddered at me. "Never in my life have I seen such a colossal, world-beating jag!"

I did not want to hear any more, and I turned over on my pillow. I am afraid I did not appreciate the humor when the general walked in to give me a decoration and a speech in which he called me a hero and applauded the way I had brought to a victorious termination Colonel Rolant's brilliant campaign.

OLD Thibaut Corday swung his feet off the chair and tenderly lowered them to the floor as his story came to a halt.

The young British consular agent, who had dropped into the café for tea, decided to cancel the jam muffins.

Algiers hurried by in the afternoon sunshine on Boulevard Sadi Carnot, and the old Legion veteran's eyes were fixed bleakly on the procession of sandals, slippers and boots which made a passing show on the pavement beyond the *brasserie* entrance.

"And that," he snorted finally, "is what our French generals considered a brilliant campaign. A colonel loses himself, his mind and his men in a desert—every officer of the company and twenty soldiers are killed—it was the dope that went to Rolant's head to begin with—but it is brilliant!" His shoulders made that shrug only possible to Frenchmen.

"But what would you, of the military? The Arabs, you comprehend, they could not make head or tail of our parading out into the desert like that. They thought we must have been an entire army. Those crazy maneuvers scared them. Where a logical campaign would have failed, that insane parade for Timbuctoo frightened an overwhelming enemy force and broke up a cunningly planned rebellion."

Old Thibaut Corday sat back and made a wide gesture. Then he was silent, staring off into a great distance, as if his eyes were seeking the past which he had just recounted.

The young British agent exclaimed, "But those officers that were murdered, Corday! Captain LaSalle, and that chap killed by a Chinese knife?"

"The Italian snake! He had to have those boots of his, *non?* Think of his surprise when he saw the colonel strut by in a similar pair, only to discover he was wearing the colonel's and the Legion *commandant* had his. So he set out after us.

"By the time he caught up with the column, Papa Rolant was in his grave, the boots were on Captain LaSalle. When LaSalle wandered off that night, the spy shot him, but we got there before he could retrieve his footwear. The next night he waited his chance, sneaked into camp and caught Delacroix in his tent.

"Doubtless the youngster, uneasy, had been walking around, sleepless, and was just retiring when he got that knife in the back. Again we were there double quick, and the Italian had to run for it without the boots. In the dark we never saw him. The knife was probably his—a gift from Chinese dope-smugglers. I do not know.

"There in El Hamma I killed him. He was out there in that ambush with those devils, understand, and the whole pack chased me when they saw I was in those boots."

"What of the old blind cobbler?"

Corday shrugged.

"Murdered for his mistake. But since, I have often wondered. Could the pattern of those boots have reached Europe? What are these dictators wearing? Did you ever see one in shoes? Regard their gestures, delusions of grandeur, narcotic eyes! Listen to them talk of how they are going to go across the world. They are steeping their blisters in hashish! All of them think they are strutting in Seven League Boots!"

Old Thibaut Corday spat fiercely. "Give me the *brodequins* of common men. I was glad to get back into my clodhoppers, I can tell you. In these I am squarely down to earth. No more of your fine boots for me; they make me sick. Which reminds me," he glared off, "I was sent home from El Hamma on sick leave. What do you think? My little niece in school had learned to speak English. What a prodigious accomplishment! Proudly my sister produced the tiny scholar. Recite for Uncle Thibaut. Me, I could not stand it. I had to get up and leave. Can you hear that child reciting Kipling? That poem! *'Boots! Boots! Boots—!'*"

PULPMASTER:

THE THEODORE ROSCOE STORY

AUDREY PARENTE

FOREWORD BY THEODORE ROSCOE

THE ALLURE OF FRENCH FOREIGN LEGIONNAIRE THIBAUT CORDAY'S ADVENTURES FLOWED FROM THE PEN OF THEODORE ROSCOE. EXOTIC TALES FROM A DUSKY OUTPOST UNFOLDED IN GLOSSY-COVERED 10-CENT MAGAZINES, BEFORE TELEVISION. HUNDREDS OF ROSCOE'S YARNS, PUBLISHED ON CHEAP PULP PAPER UNRAVELED MYSTERIES, IMMORTALIZED HOMETOWN HEROES AND STIRRED THE IMAGINATION OF A GENERATION. IN REAL LIFE, ROSCOE STOWED ABOARD TRAMP STEAMERS AND MINGLED WITH LOCALS IN FAR AWAY CORNERS. HIS INTRIGUING STYLE LATER ECHOED IN NON-FICTION WORKS, WHEN HE WAS AMONG THE FIRST TO VIEW DECLASSIFIED LINCOLN ASSASSINATION DOCUMENTS AND WHEN HE DOCUMENTED HISTORIC AMERICAN MILITARY OPERATIONS. JOURNALIST AUDREY PARENTE BECAME STEEPED IN AMERICAN PULP HISTORY WHEN SHE LIVED BLOCKS AWAY FROM ROSCOE IN ORMOND BEACH, FLORIDA, WHERE SHE CHRONICLED HIS LIFE FOR THIS BOOK.

FOREIGN LEGION
THEODORE
ROSCOE

FOREIGN LEGION
THEODORE
ROSCOE

FOREIGN LEGION
THEODORE
ROSCOE

FOREIGN LEGION
THEODORE
ROSCOE

Made in the USA
Middletown, DE
22 March 2019